The Bookmark

A Novel

ANNE SUPSIC

SISTER HOUSE PRESS

Cover and Interior Design by David Prendergast
Editing by Andrea Robinson

ISBN 979-8-9859733-1-0 (paperback)
ISBN 979-8-9859733-0-3 (e-book)

FIRST EDITION 2022

Sister House Press

annesupsic.com

To my dad
who invented bedtime stories for me
when I was a little girl,
and to Frank who has always helped me
make my dreams come true.

CHAPTER 1

September 21, 1777

While I was trying to rally the troops, the gentlemen of England did me the honor of shooting me, which hurt my leg a little.

—*Letters of Lafayette*

Liesl was seated by the hearth, stirring soup in a kettle, when her father burst into the kitchen with a proud announcement.

"A wounded soldier staying here in our home?" Liesl echoed her father's words and nearly dropped her wooden spoon into the pungent, garlicky broth as she turned toward him in disbelief.

"Not a common soldier," her father said, "the Marquis de Lafayette from France."

As if a title made a difference. Any intruder would be an imposition, but she had to wonder if a common soldier might not be preferable to an ostentatious Frenchman.

The open fire in the hearth had already warmed her, but now she felt a fiercer heat spreading across her chest. She forced herself to maintain an even tone. "I thought we were determined not to become involved in the revolution."

Her father bristled with annoyance. "As you know, General George Washington asked for our help some months ago, and the Elders agreed to turn the Single Brothers' House into a hospital. When Doctor Glatt sought private lodgings for the marquis, I could hardly refuse him. Especially since you are one of his medical assistants."

Her father never acknowledged her medical skill, and Liesl resented his attempt to use it as justification for allowing a stranger into their home. She looked to her stepmother for support; however, Mother Boeckel stared at the floor as if the wooden planks might offer some guidance.

"But, Father, we are pacifists. This war has nothing to do with us."

A flush crept up her father's neck. "You have no right to question the Elders, or me! You will care for this wounded man, and you will do so without complaint."

Before Liesl could respond, Mother Boeckel spoke up at last. "Liesl, we are almost out of sugar. I need you to go to the market."

When Liesl remained rooted in place, her stepmother snatched the wooden spoon from her hand and added, with uncharacteristic sharpness, "*Now*, Liesl."

Minutes later, Liesl was striding down Bethlehem's main

street, her right arm brandishing a round oak basket as she fumed over her father's pronouncement. How could he violate the privacy of their home? And why couldn't this marquis recuperate in the hospital? She had no desire to care for a man who thought himself so superior he could not endure a convalescence surrounded by his own soldiers.

Of course, she and her stepmother had no say in Father's decision, even though they would bear the burden of the patient's care. She wondered if Mother Boeckel truly needed sugar, or if this was just another one of her attempts to avert discord. Unlike her stepmother, Liesl struggled to control her temper and nothing angered her more than being treated unfairly. She had learned long ago that acquiescence was her lot in life, but how could she hold her tongue when her father was being so unreasonable? Especially when his decision would make her life more difficult.

As she passed a row of stone buildings colored in browns and grays, Liesl slowed her steps and glanced at the redbrick lintels arched above each window like curious eyebrows. As if those windows were watching her every move. And perhaps they were—she was well aware that some members of the community believed she merited extra scrutiny.

Only a week ago, her father, who was the overseer for the community farm, had requested additional help and been advised by the Elders to use Liesl. Surely, Father merited a more suitable assistant, which made her wonder if Brother Timothy still doubted her. Perhaps he and the other Elders preferred to keep her hidden away at the farm.

She took no pleasure in farm work and believed her talent for medicine would be wasted on such menial chores; however, her father had ignored her opinion as usual. Even though she dreaded caring for this French nobleman, at least his presence would grant her a temporary reprieve from milking cows and collecting chicken eggs.

It was an unusually warm September day, and perspiration beaded her upper lip as she continued along the once peaceful street. Ever since the Battle at Brandywine Creek, the thoroughfare streamed with carts filled with soldiers headed for the makeshift hospital. Wagon wheels rumbled over the rutted roadway, and the moans of the injured escalated with every jolt and lurch. Even the air smelled tainted, the normal freshness fouled with the tang of unwashed bodies. As she approached the Sun Inn, two soldiers on sweat-drenched horses raced down the street, barely avoiding the carts of the wounded and engulfing her in a swirl of dust. She covered her mouth, but the powdery dirt prickled her nose, making her sneeze.

Finally, she reached a side lane, where she could turn her back on the reminders of war. After passing an empty apple orchard with row after orderly row of fruit-laden trees, she stood before her destination. Squire Horsfield's impressive home, with its wide front door flanked by gleaming white pilasters, had accommodated a changing array of visitors over the years, and John Valentine Haidt, the famous artist, maintained a studio in the building as well. When she was a child, his paintings had terrified her, especially the gruesome scenes of a dying Saviour with blood oozing from his wounded side. She believed without question that the blood of the Saviour would wash away her sins; however, saying it was one thing, seeing it quite another.

Liesl moved past the main house and entered the adjoining structure that served as the town market. As always, the number of goods crammed into every available space overwhelmed her. Small baskets and brooms hung from the ceiling, while storage containers made from tobacco leaves squatted on the floor, their scent repelling insects from mounds of the season's earliest green apples. Sickles, hoes, and pickaxes, newly created by the blacksmith, leaned against one another waiting to be put to use. And a well-polished counter stood in front of a wall of shelves holding reddish-brown pottery made with clay from the Menakasie Creek, candle molds, and an assortment of jams, including Liesl's childhood favorite, fig.

Sister Dorothea Lauer, the plump proprietress, peered at Liesl over a pair of bridge spectacles perched precariously on her narrow nose. "Sister Elisabeth, how may I help you this fine day?"

Despite Liesl's frequent visits, Sister Dorothea insisted on calling her by her given name, as if even the most meager financial transaction warranted a certain level of formality.

"I am in need of sugar for Mother Boeckel," Liesl said.

"Ah, yes. Your stepmother bakes a sugar cake to rival my own. Have I told you how much Benjamin Franklin enjoyed my cakes?"

Liesl nodded for this was a story she had heard many times. Before Liesl's birth, Benjamin Franklin had spent a month at the home of the hospitable Squire Horsfield. Sister Dorothea and some of the older Sisters still tittered about the paunchy and balding supposed charmer, but Liesl could never fathom being attracted to such a man. She preferred a man who impressed with actions rather than just pretty words.

"He said he normally favored a snack of apples or cranberries, but he could never turn down a slice of my sugar cake!" Sister Dorothea smiled at the memory and darted behind the counter to retrieve a cone of white sugar wrapped in sky-blue paper and sealed with a glob of red wax.

Truth be told, Sister Dorothea was no baker. Liesl hated to be uncharitable, but Sister Dorothea's sugar cakes tended to be dry and tasteless, whereas Mother Boeckel's cakes were renowned for their moist texture and sugary smoothness.

"Will you be needing some flour for that sugar cake as well?" Sister Dorothea trilled.

"No, thank you. But I would like to see your sewing needles. I am looking for something very thin."

Liesl watched with amusement as the prospect of such

a lucrative sale suffused the face of the proprietress with a glow like a beeswax candle at Christmastime.

Sister Dorothea led her to a display of sewing needles fashioned by the local blacksmith, but Liesl shook her head, barely looking at the rough-hewn collection.

"I need the finest, thinnest one you have," Liesl said. She was creating an intricately embroidered bookmark, and the delicate work required the narrowest of needles.

After a quick survey of the empty shop, Sister Dorothea whispered, "The best sewing needles by far are those from England. I have some, but you must tell no one I sold you a British needle."

"Have we reached such a point that even to buy or sell British goods is considered an act of treachery?" Liesl said, unable to hide her exasperation. She had no patience for political matters, especially now that they were interfering with her life.

"Lower your voice, girl! In these times, it is wise to exercise caution."

Sister Dorothea disappeared into the back room of the store and returned with a small envelope. Liesl inspected the front of the packet, pleased to see the name of Henry Milward & Sons of Redditch, England, for she knew that was where the finest sewing needles were made. She also knew her father would not look kindly on such an extravagant purchase, but when Sister Dorothea removed one of the needles, Liesl gasped at the tiny hand-punched eye, so small she could barely see it. Perhaps helping her father with the Frenchman deserved some compensation.

"Yes, this will do quite well," she said.

As Liesl left Horsfield House, she had a clear view across the cemetery to the graceful slate roof of the Gemeinhaus, the first major building constructed when the Moravians arrived in 1741. She admired those early settlers, drawn here by the challenge of bringing the word of the Lord to the spiritually needy. Or perhaps by a personal desire to start a new life, to leave the Old World behind. They created a community built around their faith, a closed society of devout worshippers who had managed to keep the outside world at bay.

Until now.

The war had shattered the tranquility of her small community, exposing it to a world of tension, sickness, and violent death. With men who drank to excess, took the word of the Lord in vain, and disported themselves with women whose screeching laughter disturbed the quiet nights. Liesl had no interest in the so-called revolution and nothing but disdain for the strangers who had descended on her town. Her only wish was that every one of them, including a certain French marquis, would soon return to wherever they called home.

"How much farther?" Lafayette shouted at the driver. He pounded his fist on the side of the carriage but still received no response. Perhaps the man was unable to hear him above the clatter of the wheels, or more likely, he simply chose not to answer.

"Colonists!" Lafayette muttered as he tried without success to find a comfortable position for his wounded leg in the cramped space.

He was miserable and not merely because of the musket ball that had struck him below the knee, although the events at Brandywine Creek still haunted him. That day, he had charged into his first battle astride his white horse, suppressing an inappropriate grin as the ground rumbled beneath him and cannonballs created great furrows in the earth. Racing toward his destiny, he had been certain a glorious future awaited him.

But fate had a different plan. Although the men rallied around him, it had been too late. The British troops were relentless, and he had been forced to give the order to retreat.

If only Washington had allowed him to leave his observation post earlier! Perhaps he could have turned back the enemy and come away victorious instead of finding himself with a boot full of blood from a leg injury that had left him languishing for days in a bleak, overcrowded Philadelphia hospital.

Now, at Washington's insistence, Lafayette was on his way to Bethlehem for a complete convalescence. He had admired Washington from the first time he beheld the man entering a smoke-filled tavern with a bearing more regal than any European monarch, but this latest order vexed

Lafayette. He had not traveled across the ocean, defying his father-in-law and his king, to lie about recovering from a superficial injury!

His carriage slowed and turned onto the street of a small town. The innkeeper at last night's tavern had described Bethlehem as a grim place run by religious lunatics, but Lafayette sensed only tranquility as he gazed out at immaculate multistory houses tucked between a curving creek and well-tended cornfields and apple orchards. A group of young schoolgirls followed their teacher in a perfect line, like ducklings on a first outing. Each child wore the same basic outfit: a dark skirt with a dark vest, a white blouse, and a simple white cap. The girls looked like miniature nuns, reminding him of the religious orders near his childhood home in the Auvergne. "I dub thee *L'ordre Sacré des Petits*," he murmured to himself. On closer examination, he noted red ribbons tied beneath each little cap and crisscrossing each tiny vest.

His carriage finally arrived at the Sun Inn, a two-story stone establishment that would not have been out of place in France. Lafayette noted with approval the inn's mansard roof, a common enough design in Paris but not one he had expected to see in the backwoods of Pennsylvania.

Inside the inn, a short balding man introduced himself as Doctor Glatt. He announced that he had studied medicine at the University of Würzburg and spoke with the guttural sounds of his native tongue.

"You are a lucky young man," Doctor Glatt said. "The

musket ball passed straight through the leg without shattering any bone. You have damage to nerves and muscle tissue, but your field doctor properly cleaned the wound to prevent infection. Many would have simply amputated."

Lafayette supposed he should be grateful, but his thoughts returned to the searing humiliation of being carried on a litter into a room reeking of onions and cabbages where he was laid out on a table still covered with crumbs from a recent meal. As if he were the main course at one of Louis XVI's banquets! All accompanied by the mocking voices of soldiers, joking that they hoped no one would eat him for dinner.

"When can I return to battle?"

"In a month, perhaps a bit more."

"That is unacceptable!" Lafayette roared in his most imperious voice, the one he employed whenever someone tried to thwart his plans. "I must return to the field."

Doctor Glatt gave him a steely look. "As I said, a wound like this requires at least a month to heal. Anything short of that and you risk losing the leg. Or your life."

Lafayette's anger drained away. From the first moment he heard rumors of revolution smoldering in the American colonies, his sole desire had been to join the fight for liberty. He had no intention of forfeiting this opportunity to change the world. He would endure a month of convalescence, but that did not mean he had to like it.

"And where will I spend my incarceration?"

"You will stay here at the inn tonight, and then I have

arranged for you to recuperate in the home of Frederick Boeckel where his daughter Liesl, one of my medical assistants, will attend to you. Rest assured you will receive the best of care. General Washington was quite clear we were to treat you with the utmost deference."

"A medical *assistant?*" Lafayette said, raising his voice. Utmost deference indeed. He would be lucky to survive.

Doctor Glatt hesitated before continuing. "While Liesl may not be the most docile of our Sisters, she is quite capable. She will change your bandages daily and keep me informed of your progress."

CHAPTER 2

The Bookmark

September 2005

"*Bienvenue à Bethlehem!*" said a familiar voice.

Abbey Prescott turned from the back of her Range Rover, and for a second, she thought she'd traveled back in time, even though she knew that was ridiculous. Beneath the halo of a streetlight stood a girl wearing a romantic peasant dress strewn with miniature pink and red flowers, looking exactly like her best friend's teenaged self.

But then, her faith in the order of the universe restored itself as a very much grown-up Kera Bruno brandished a bottle and two wine glasses. "Still a red wine drinker, *ma chérie?*"

"*Mais oui*," Abbey said. "It's so good to see you, but how did you know I moved in?"

"You know what Bethlehem's like. I got the word from old Mrs. Dotter. You can't fart in this town without her knowing about it."

Kera could always make her smile. Growing up, Abbey

had spent one month of every summer here in Bethlehem, and she and Kera had been inseparable—to the point that her father had started calling them Susan and Sharon after the twins in the original *Parent Trap* movie, which Abbey thought was weird but always made Kera laugh. That was her father. He could charm women of all ages, men too. Everybody except her.

"Go on in," Abbey said. "I'll be there in a minute."

"Don't be long." Kera waved the wine in the air. "I've been eyeing this bottle all afternoon."

Abbey hadn't seen Kera since Nana's funeral in that tiny windowless room with its pale gray walls and low-grade carpeting—creepy institutional decor that reminded her of the Department of Motor Vehicles, or even worse, a hospital waiting room. Kera had sat beside her through the whole ordeal, patting her hand and passing her tissues, the two of them seated alone in the row designated for family.

Kera was the sister she never had, but right now, Abbey was in no hurry to deal with her friend's inevitable questions. Instead, she took a moment to check out her new neighborhood.

In a window across the way, a woman sat at a kitchen table with a little boy, the two of them bent over a book, maybe trying to solve a sticky math problem. Other windows flickered with the distinctive blue glow of electronic devices. Homebodies of suburbia, not exactly a hopping scene.

Nothing like her Philly condo just a couple of blocks

from the buzz of South Street. On a Friday night like this, that street would be swarming with people drawn from all over the city: artists, attorneys, students, even bankers. And of course, the unavoidable tourists lined up outside Jim's, salivating for their first Philly cheesesteak like a pack of slobbering Basset Hounds. Right now, she could be sitting at Bob & Barbara's, sipping a Sassy Sweet Tea and swaying to the mix of sax and electric organ they called their "liquor drinkin'" music.

On this street, the only sound was a slight rustling as a gentle wind kissed the leaves on the maple tree in Nana's front yard.

No. In *her* front yard.

Nana had left her the house along with a small stock portfolio and a generous annuity, giving her a way out—just when she needed it most.

"New beginning. New beginning," she chanted her latest mantra, hoping she wasn't making her biggest mistake yet. Although that seemed unlikely. The mistakes she'd made with Michael had set an extremely high standard.

She stared at the Victorian house in front of her, rubbing her arms against the chilly evening air. How many summers had she stood before this house, swinging her suitcase from side to side, waiting for her parents to get out of the car so she could finally run up those steps into Nana's arms?

Her father always referred to their summer separation as "Abbey's annual vacation," even though she knew he couldn't wait to get rid of her so he and her mother could take off on one of his international business trips. It hadn't bothered Abbey much—she'd always loved staying in this house.

As a little girl, she'd taken one look at the lattice-patterned pediment above the butter-yellow porch and announced, "This must be the Waffle House." The creamy yellow rooftop turret and matching dormer were still visible, although the turret's stained glass had faded with the setting sun. Intricate wrought iron fencing enclosed the tiny front yard, and light filtered through the ornate design, forming lacy patterns on the pavement. Just looking at it warmed her like a cozy quilt draped around her shoulders. She still couldn't believe the Waffle House was hers.

The moving van had delivered all the large items a few hours earlier, including her Eames lounge chair and a floor lamp designed by Philippe Starck. She'd sold most of her furniture, but she wasn't about to part with those two splurges. Their sleek and unfussy modern style appealed to her sense of order, something sadly lacking in her life at the moment.

All she had to do now was carry in one last box. One too valuable to trust to the movers.

With a grunt, she lifted it out of the Rover and flicked a button on the remote to close the tailgate's split doors. God, she loved this car. Even if it was a guilt gift, her father's pathetic attempt to make amends for not attending Nana's funeral.

She pushed her way through the wrought iron gate, avoided snagging her silky Donna Karan sweater on a fleur-de-lis finial, and mounted the porch steps. Balancing the box on one knee, she opened the custom screen door specifically designed to fit Victorian curves.

In the kitchen, the sweet scent of sugar cookies still hung in the air. She took a deep breath as she boosted the box onto the granite kitchen counter and slowly exhaled, a handy trick learned in yoga class. Resting her head on top of the carton, her long sandy-blond hair partially obscured the hastily scrawled "Coffee Stuff."

"I'm in the parlor," Kera called.

Kera had ensconced herself in one of two Queen Anne chairs she'd positioned around a large box that served as a makeshift coffee table. The old-fashioned room Nana always called the Beckel Parlor suited Kera perfectly.

"Nice improvisation," Abbey said as Kera handed her a welcome glass of cabernet sauvignon.

"I've never been in this room before," Kera said. "Always just walked by."

"Nana never used it much, as you can tell," Abbey said, pointing to the Victorian chandelier overhead, its etched glass bowls hanging like strange dusty fruit from elaborate leafy gold chains.

Kera spotted a shoebox in the corner marked "Bookmarks."

"Don't tell me this is your famous bookmark collection?"

"*C'est ça, ma petite souris.*"

Kera hated being called a little mouse, but Abbey had teased her with this odd term of endearment for years. French had always been their lingua franca, and while other kids dreamed of going to Disney World, the two girls set their sights on Paris. Their favorite fantasy had involved *un petit appartement* with an Eiffel Tower view and a strict diet of hot chocolate and croissants.

Abbey opened the shoe box, revealing a colorful mound of rectangles that looked like glass fragments tumbled out of a kaleidoscope. Each one unleashing a vivid shard of memory.

Her bookmark obsession had started one glorious summer during a sweet-sixteen trip to Europe with her mom. Like a hunter on the trail of an endangered species, she'd stalked vendors in every city, prowling the shelves of pricy museum gift shops and the junky displays of tacky souvenir stands.

A bookmark of Nefertiti sat on top, her elegant profile as regal as ever.

"I first saw this face at the Egyptian Museum in Berlin," Abbey said, holding it up for Kera to see. "Mom dragged me there after the Berlin Wall and the Checkpoint Charlie museum, which I loved. All those stories about ingenious escape methods, like the one about two couples who crammed themselves and their four children into a homemade hot air balloon and floated over the wall to freedom. Anyway, rooms full of Egyptian artifacts seemed incredibly dull after that, but then I saw her."

The dark room had held just one illuminated sculpture posed on a simple black pedestal. Unlike the other idealized figures, this was a real woman with a slight trace of bags under her eyes, and an expression so lively and intelligent, Abbey found it hard to believe Nefertiti had been dead for over three thousand years.

"At that moment, I vowed I would see Egypt someday."

"You always wanted to be a world traveler. I'd be happy just to see France."

Abbey's hand shook when she saw the next bookmark, a glowing photo of Bangkok's Grand Palace, with the word "someday" written across the back in Michael's distinctive scrawl. Just one more reminder of his lies.

She quickly shifted it to the bottom of the pile and pulled out one she knew Kera would like, a watercolor of the Eiffel Tower straddling the Seine.

"Ooh la la," Kera said. "You know, I may never forgive you for seeing it without me."

"You'll get there."

Abbey admired the graceful curves of the familiar lacy metal. Thanks to her Francophile mother, Abbey could name this structure long before she knew anything about the Washington Monument or the Statue of Liberty. Looking at it now, she could almost feel the dampness of the Seine creeping up the backs of her legs, and the buttery sweetness of a French croissant melting in her mouth. Simpler times.

She shoved the box of bookmarks back into the corner, and Kera filled her in on all the local gossip: who was getting married, having babies, leaving their spouses. Abbey couldn't help wondering when Michael would realize she wasn't coming back. She'd give a lot to see the look on his face.

As the wine inched its way down to the bottom of the bottle, the tension in her neck and shoulders eased. No matter how long the separation, she and Kera always picked up as if they'd just seen each other the day before.

Abbey poured the last of the cabernet sauvignon as Kera's eyes bored into her. Kera had shown remarkable restraint so far, but curiosity had to be killing her. After all, Kera knew her inside out . . . except for why she'd moved back to Bethlehem.

"How are this year's batch of third graders doing?" Abbey asked, trying to forestall the inevitable. Kera loved to talk about her "kids."

"Settling in finally. The first couple of weeks are always tough, reviewing everything they forgot over the summer, breaking bad habits." She grinned. "But I'm madly in love with them already."

"Speaking of madly in love, when do I get to meet Nolan?" Kera had been dating an engineering professor at Lehigh University for over a year, a record for her.

"Soon," Kera promised. "But now I have a few questions for you."

Kera took a long, satisfying sip of wine while Abbey got ready to play defense.

"Why are you here?" she asked with the penetrating

look Abbey knew so well. If not for her love of teaching, Kera would have made a kick-ass prosecutor.

"Nana left me the house."

Kera leaned in closer. "I know. But you left a good job, your home, your friends. Why would you do that?"

Abbey stared into the sediment at the bottom of her glass as if trying to read her fortune in the dregs. Finally, she lifted her glass high into the air. "To old friends!"

"*À votre santé!*" Kera shook her head in defeat. "Whenever you want to tell me more, I'm here."

Abbey grabbed the wine bottle for recycling and rinsed out the glasses at the kitchen sink. When she returned to the parlor, Kera was standing in front of Nana's old piano, holding a picture frame.

"What's this?" Kera asked, handing it to her. "It was laying on top of the piano."

Abbey stared at a shadow box about the size of the square dinner plates at Jasmine Thai, her favorite Philly restaurant. *Former* favorite to be more accurate. She blocked out thoughts of her last visit there and concentrated on the exquisitely handstitched rectangle pinned against the velvety black of the deep-set box.

"It looks like a bookmark," she said.

Nana would certainly treasure such a thing, but why frame it? Abbey turned it over and gulped as she read the note attached to the back. *To my dearest granddaughter, Abigail Christiana.*

"I think you better sit down," Kera said, leading Abbey back to one of the Queen Anne chairs.

Despite Abbey's pleading, Nana had always used her full name, telling her a name was a powerful thing whose meanings needed to be respected. Abigail Christiana. The good: creative with a desire to travel. And the not-so-good: a dreamy nature prone to disastrous love affairs. She had laughed off the love-affair part, certain she would never be fool enough to fall in love with a man who would break her heart. *Guess I learned my lesson on that one.*

Abbey read the familiar handwriting, hearing Nana's voice with every word:

Abigail Christiana, I know you love to read as much as I do, and I am sure this will make a worthy addition to your bookmark collection.

This bookmark is believed to have been made by a Moravian Sister named Liesl Boeckel, who lived in Bethlehem in the 1700s.

I always hoped to find out more about her. Perhaps you could do some research.

Know that I want only the best for you and will love you always.

Nana

Abbey held the frame to her chest, silently thanking her grandmother for the precious gift. Then, she read the note out loud for Kera, unable to control the trembling in her voice.

"What a wonderful gift!" Kera said, squeezing Abbey's arm.

As the two friends parted on the front porch with their usual double-cheek kisses (just like the French, *bien sûr*), Kera gave Abbey one last, enquiring look, her unanswered questions suspended like a boulder between them. Abbey *would* tell Kera everything, but she needed to do some damage control first, get a handle on the pain—and the guilt.

"Want to go for a jog tomorrow morning?" Abbey asked in an attempt to ease the awkwardness.

"Sure. What time?"

"Meet me out front about nine."

Feeling woozy from the wine, Abbey trudged up the stairs to her bedroom with the red maple right outside her double window, ready to transform into crimson beauty any day, and the cheerful pale yellow walls with white furniture, a color scheme she'd chosen back when she was an optimist.

She stripped down to her underwear and crawled beneath the softness of the blue toile comforter. As she closed her eyes, she offered up a silent prayer that Bethlehem and this house still possessed their magical healing powers.

CHAPTER 3

September 22, 1777

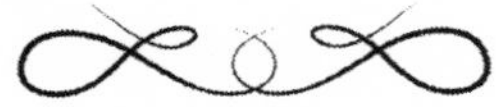

I have a new patient, the Marquis de Lafayette, who is staying in our home. I believe he will be most difficult and call upon the Saviour to grant me patience, a quality for which I am not well known.

—Diary of Sister Liesl Boeckel

"Gently!" Lafayette admonished the two soldiers, former farmhands from the look of their powerful arms and stocky physiques, who had arrived at daybreak to carry him to the Boeckel home.

He wrapped one arm around each pair of powerful shoulders as they lifted him just barely off the ground and made their way out into the street. The men stank of manure, and Lafayette immediately wished he could retrieve a handkerchief to place over his nose. He had already spent a sleepless night at the inn, sharing a bed with a burly fellow who reeked of garlic and snored like a gale at sea. And now, he had to endure this stench!

Mercifully, the humiliation of being transported like a sack of potatoes was brief. They soon reached the Boeckel home, and a woman, whom Lafayette assumed to be the wife of his benefactor Frederick, met them at the door. She wore a grown-up version of the clothing Lafayette had observed the little girls wearing the day before. However, her ribbons were light blue rather than shiny red, and her plain, pale face and dull brown eyes lacked the vivacity of youth. The woman looked bewildered, as if she could not fathom how she had ended up in this place, facing this foreigner.

"I am Barbara Boeckel," she said at last. "Welcome to our home."

"*Merci*, madam," Lafayette said, wondering when he would be rid of his smelly companions. "I am grateful to you and your husband for your hospitality."

The woman's face flushed with embarrassment as she explained her husband was busy with community affairs and would be unable to greet Lafayette until the following morning. She then instructed the bearers to deliver Lafayette to the second-floor sitting room and left him quite abruptly, distracted by the cries of a young child.

The two soldiers carried Lafayette up to the second floor, dumped him unceremoniously into the one good chair in the room, and clumped back down the stairs.

"*Bâtards!*" Lafayette shouted after them.

Left alone, he studied his latest place of confinement. The room was spacious but plain, with white walls and a simple white fireplace flanked by two black buckets. A small table stood beside his comfortable upholstered chair, and a narrow wooden bed was positioned nearby. A large squat table sat in the center of the room, surrounded by three wooden chairs with heart-shaped openings carved into their backs. Not the type of lodgings he would have deemed satisfactory if he were in France, but at least he had the room to himself. He shifted in his seat, unaccustomed to the silence. Where was that girl who was supposed to care of him?

Liesl pared one last carrot for their midday stew and dropped it into the kettle hanging in the hearth. She watched the bubbling mixture as she waited for her stepmother so they could face the Frenchman together. Mother Boeckel had looked quite flustered after her first encounter with the man, and Liesl was in no hurry. The back door creaked, and whirling around, she was startled to see her father.

"What brings you here at this hour?" she asked. Her father always stayed at the farm until the sun went down, returning home only when the dark made outside work impossible.

"I must speak with you about a matter of some urgency," he said.

Liesl's surprise turned to alarm. Her father seldom

sought her out, and lately when he did, it was always for another reprimand.

"Has our guest arrived?" he asked.

"Yes," Liesl said, and then paused in deference to the noisy thumping overhead. "Mother Boeckel greeted him but a few minutes ago, and I believe he has now been taken upstairs to his room."

"His arrival has been quite remarked upon," her father said, looking uncomfortable.

Liesl was losing patience. "A French general is certain to draw attention wherever he goes."

"Yes, but since you will be responsible for Lafayette's care, I must ensure that you will behave with every propriety," he said.

"As I always do," Liesl replied.

"Lafayette is not one of your typical patients. Since you are still a Single Sister, he may try to charm you, but you must guard against becoming too familiar with this man."

Liesl sighed. It seemed this urgent matter had more to do with her marital status than her patient. Surely, Father did not want to argue about that again.

"My sole interest is his health, and I do know how to behave properly. What has caused this sudden concern?"

Her father grimaced. "Some have questioned the appropriateness of a young Frenchman lodging in our home."

"I see."

"Your every action must be above reproach," he said in

his sternest tone. "We must safeguard your character and reputation."

"Perhaps that is something you might have considered before you invited him here," Liesl said, feeling the heat of anger flooding her chest. "My reputation is only a concern because you have placed me in this vulnerable position."

"Enough!" he shouted. "I will not tolerate your disrespect. It is this very insolence that has made members of our community question your character."

Before Liesl could respond, Mother Boeckel came running into the kitchen. She moved between the two of them and gripped Father's arm as she said, "Please calm yourself. Sound carries quite well in this house, you know."

Father Boeckel brushed away her hand and scowled at Liesl. "I interrupted my day to instruct you as to how you must conduct yourself. Now that you know, I have pressing duties awaiting me at the farm."

Lafayette feared his hosts had forgotten him, but his growing annoyance was replaced by curiosity when angry voices drifted upward from the room below. What sort of people were these Moravians? Had they no sense of decorum? In France, disputes were normally settled with calm debate, and under no circumstances, would a guest be subjected to this kind of commotion. Perhaps that innkeeper had been right.

The words were muffled, but Lafayette could distinguish two voices, one agitated but melodic and another booming louder with every exclamation. Suddenly, a third person joined the fray, the voices went silent, and then he heard footsteps on the stairs.

Barbara Boeckel, looking more distressed than ever, entered the room with a young Moravian woman she introduced as Liesl. The younger woman carried a round oak basket by two small handles, reminding him of a medieval novitiate collecting alms. Although she wore the same simple clothing as Barbara Boeckel, the severe style looked almost graceful on her lithe form. A snug-fitting white cap hid every strand of her hair, but nothing could diminish the comeliness of her face. And her ribbons were the pink of French cabbage roses, a color that accentuated the slight blush on her cheeks.

Having made the required introductions, Barbara Boeckel hovered uncertainly by the doorway for a moment before leaving, explaining that her young son needed her attention.

"*Bonjour, Monsieur Le General. Comment allez-vous?*" Liesl asked in perfect French.

Lafayette was unable to hide his astonishment. "How is it that a young girl in a colonial frontier town speaks French?"

"I am twenty-two years old sir, hardly a girl. And I speak four languages: German, English, French, and Iroquois."

"Iroquois, *ce n'est pas vrai!*" Lafayette cried with disbelief and delight.

Liesl stood as tall as her small stature allowed. “I do not know how French girls are educated, but Moravians believe girls should be educated in exactly the same manner as boys. I learned all the essential subjects: mathematics, science, geography, history, and foreign languages. Education is not just for boys, monsieur.”

Strange dark blue eyes, like two shards of lapis lazuli, stared back at him with ill-concealed defiance. That generous mouth was made for laughing, not for the prim pursing he observed now. A mouth made for kissing. A revelation that made him smile for the first time in days.

“Does the general find me amusing?”

Her voice, which was unusually deep for a young woman, had a husky quality he found quite alluring. No doubt, he could happily listen to her speak for hours.

“Amusing?” he said. “No not particularly. Rather too serious, since you asked. But pleasing, yes, quite pleasing.”

A deeper pink suffused her cheeks, a shade like the Rhône wines his grandmother favored.

Liesl assumed a more professional tone. “Doctor Glatt described your injury and instructed me on the care of your dressings. I will change the bandages daily and apply a poultice to promote healing.”

“You will be my nurse,” Lafayette said.

“I am a medical assistant, not a nurse, but I will care for your wound.”

“Whatever your title, I will look forward to your ministrations,” Lafayette said, his earlier concerns forgotten.

"As bored as I am bound to be, I suspect your visits will be the highlight of my stay."

Liesl continued. "Doctor Glatt will see you once a week; however, I will discuss your progress with him every day."

"Will you be applying leeches?"

"Certainly not!" Liesl shuddered.

"I am glad to avoid it, although it is a practice much used in Paris."

"Our enlightened doctors avoid such excessive therapies, believing instead in the use of herbs to allow the body to heal itself. Mother Boeckel and I will also see to your meals, providing you with a healthful diet to assist in that healing."

"Ah yes, Mother Boeckel. Your mother appears to be less than pleased with my arrival."

"She is my stepmother."

"That explains it."

"Explains what?"

"Why you and she share no family resemblance."

Liesl's mouth tightened with disapproval.

"I heard loud voices a few moments ago," he said. "Is something amiss in the household?"

"Not in the least," Liesl replied. "I am sorry if we disturbed you, but a more courteous guest would have made no mention of it."

Lafayette wanted to argue that a more courteous host would never have behaved in such a manner to begin with, but now Liesl's expression had turned into a glare, and he thought it wise to redirect the conversation. "May I ask you a somewhat personal question?"

"Since you show no compunction about discussing personal affairs, I doubt that I can stop you. However, I shall determine whether I choose to answer."

"*Je comprends*. Is your loyalty to the revolution or to the British Crown?"

Although Liesl looked surprised, she responded with unassailable conviction. "My loyalty is only to God."

"Be that as it may, we live on Earth, and in the end, we must all choose a side. When I was in France, I believed every man and woman in the American colonies to be a lover of liberty, united for the common cause of independence. Imagine my astonishment when I arrived here and witnessed loyalty to the British, openly professed."

"Things are never as simple as they first appear," Liesl confided. "We have been treated quite well by the British; however, at George Washington's request, we agreed to care for wounded revolutionary soldiers. Which is why you are here."

"You support the revolution, then?"

"We believe all disputes must be resolved by peaceful means. Men should fight with prayer, not carnal weapons."

"A noble belief but a naive one. This quarrel will be decided as all quarrels among nations have been resolved since ancient times."

"By violence and death," Liesl snapped, and her strange dark eyes grew darker still. Like the sea squall his ship, *La*

Victoire, had barely avoided on his voyage across the Atlantic.

"By brave soldiers willing to risk their very lives for *un idéal supérieur*, for a better life for all," he said.

"Well, our lives are not improved at present. The peace of our orderly town has fallen victim to noise and tumult. Even our church services are disrupted."

"Are all Moravian women as outspoken as you are?" Lafayette asked.

He had not intended it as a criticism, but a flash of wariness crossed Liesl's face, and then her passionate expression dulled, replaced by an unreadable demeanor. An act of self-preservation that reminded him of the red poppies growing wild in the fields of his youth, whose sparkling petals closed up each night to protect themselves from the dew.

Liesl set her basket on the small table next to Lafayette and began removing the linen dressings from his leg. "Let us leave the travails of the world outside this sickroom and concern ourselves only with your health and well-being."

"Very well, mademoiselle. I shall do as you wish," Lafayette said with rare acquiescence. Perhaps staying with this peculiar family would not be so disagreeable after all. If he must suffer this forced removal from battle, at least he would have a captivating girl to distract him.

Later that evening, Liesl lay in the narrow bed of her tiny third-floor room, a cramped space that would have been insufferable if not for the single window. On this clear night, soft rays of moonlight drifted across her face as she considered her newest patient.

Lafayette looked exactly as she had expected. An overblown peacock of a man dressed in a pretentious royal-blue waistcoat trimmed in red and topped with silly tasseled gold epaulets. A vest of golden brocade adorned his chest, and an absurd, slightly askew, white wig crowned his head. The wig gave him the look of an older man, but Lafayette was younger than she expected. In fact, she guessed his age was close to her own. Which only made his disdainful treatment of her all the more aggravating.

Ensconced in their best chair as if it were his right, he had already adopted the attitude of the lord of the manor, master of all he surveyed. She pictured his haughty face and kicked at the quilt she had drawn over herself as anger surged through her. Anger at Lafayette for his condescending behavior, at her father for placing her in this untenable position, but also at herself. Unused to having a guest in the house, she had never considered that Lafayette might overhear the argument with her father. She was only grateful Lafayette had not discerned the subject of their disagreement. At least, she had been spared the embarrassment of that.

She was used to criticism, but the thought of having to face Lafayette with his presumptuous ways every single day was unbearable. And such impertinence! Treating her as if she were an uneducated peasant and inspecting her as if she were chattel. He had scrutinized her in such a probing way she blushed to think of it, even alone here in her own bed.

She calmed herself by picturing another man, her gentle Matthew, who had always treated her with the utmost respect and made her feel his equal. The memory soothed but carried with it the searing pain of loss. How different her life might have been. She would have been content—and no one would have any reason to question her character.

She wished she had not responded to Lafayette's questions, but people seldom asked her opinion on anything. The invigorating joy of sharing her thoughts, a long-forgotten pleasure, had made her careless, but she would be more guarded in the future. She had no intention of divulging anything of a personal nature to this arrogant Frenchman.

She rolled over onto her side, the ropes groaning beneath her, a sorry sound that matched her mood. How would she ever abide this popinjay? Merely picturing his white-wigged head with those ridiculous corkscrew curls set her insides churning.

Taking a deep breath, she allowed the gentle moonbeams to comfort her. Highborn or not, he was her patient and a guest in her home. He held no dominion over her. The answer was simple enough. Starting in the morning, she would treat him like any other patient, concentrating on his care and nothing more.

CHAPTER 4

The Ghost Walk

September 2005

"Good morning, Abster."

The sheets were silky, and the man beside her nibbled her ear before moving down her back, kissing her sleep-warmed skin as he went.

"It's not even light out yet," she said.

"What can I say?" he murmured between kisses. "I'm so crazy about you, I can't sleep."

His familiar scent engulfed her, a dusky fragrance like the woods right after a rain. He took his time, his stubbly chin tickling her and making her gasp. Abbey's breath came faster and faster as he began a return journey up her spine. She moaned and rolled over.

A sudden brightness splintered the illusion, and sunlight poured through her front window reminding her where she was and why. Her pulse slowed as she pushed the passionate images aside. That was a closed chapter in a book she would never finish.

She pulled on her black running tights and topped them off with a pink Eiffel Tower T-shirt. Tucking her thick, slightly tangled hair into a high ponytail, she trotted down the stairs to the kitchen. Nana always kept an assortment of coffee cups hanging beneath the cupboard, and Abbey pulled out an artsy cup with a picture of Bernini's statue of Apollo and Daphne. Bernini had captured the very moment when Daphne's delicate fingers sprouted leaves as she turned into a tree to escape Apollo's amorous advances. A pretty extreme way to avoid a man. Too bad she couldn't have used that trick with Michael.

She opened the Coffee Stuff box and liberated the Keurig, unleashing one more unwanted memory. A Christmas gift from Michael, it was her favorite kitchen appliance, which was the only reason she hadn't heaved it into the trash with the other stuff he'd given her. The only good thing to come out of that disaster.

Soon the tantalizing aroma of Original Donut Shop filled the air, taking her mind off her sordid past. The barren kitchen offered little in the way of breakfast food, but some rummaging yielded a jar of outdated fig jam and an unopened box of crackers.

Before leaving the house, Abbey retrieved a hot-pink Mace container from her designer handbag and clipped it onto her pants. Hard to imagine needing it in Bethlehem, but a self-defense course had ingrained the habit. Defense is the best offense as her instructor used to say.

Kera stood outside, stretching her hamstrings and looking better than ever. Only one explanation for that.

"Did you see Nolan last night after you left here?" Abbey asked, immediately regretting her bluntness.

"How did you know?" Kera said with a pretty blush.

"Just a guess."

"Are you seeing anyone?" Kera asked.

Before Abbey could answer, a friendly Beagle made a well-timed entrance, running between them and giving Kera an imploring look. She bent down to nuzzle his neck while Abbey stepped back. She'd never had a dog —or any pet for that matter—and sensing her inexperience, dogs always ignored her. A harried-looking woman, possibly the homework mom Abbey had spied the previous night, thanked Kera and scooped up her wayward canine. Abbey should have introduced herself, but she couldn't face any more questions.

"Ready?" she asked Kera.

"Let's do it."

The neighborhood looked unchanged as they ran past a mix of dignified colonials and exuberant Victorians. They entered the historic district, passing the stately Horsfield House, site of the first store in Bethlehem, and then the towering trees of the old Moravian cemetery, their two ponytails swinging in rhythm with their feet. In a couple hours, gawking groups of tourists would descend on the historic sites, but for now, they owned the pavement.

"What's the Nain-Schober House?" Abbey asked as

they passed a small building with a gleaming red roof and a historical marker.

"They just finished restoring it," Kera said, morphing into teacher mode. "It's actually quite special—a rare Indian home built when the Moravians offered Native Americans refuge here after the French and Indian War."

It was hard to spend any time in Bethlehem without hearing about the Moravians. When Abbey was young, Nana had filled her head with stories about them and how they had founded the city on the edge of what was then the colonial frontier.

A Zen ringtone sounded, and Kera stopped to pull out her cellphone. "Sorry, I better take this. It's my sister-in-law."

Abbey waited impatiently, ignoring the one-sided conversation. Below her, the Central Moravian Church green offered a clear view of the reconstructed colonial blacksmith shop and a glimpse of Hotel Bethlehem. Its brownish bricks always reminded Abbey of the walnuts her father cracked open for her every Christmas. But time plays with memories, and the building itself appeared to have shrunk. With only nine stories, it didn't even qualify as a high-rise.

Downtown Bethlehem was nothing like Center City, where her old jogging route had taken her from Society Hill to Rittenhouse Square with its view of the stunning high-rise Liberty Place spiking the skyline of staid brick and concrete like an alien invader. A renegade construction of silvery blue glass, Liberty Place broke the unwritten rule that no building in Center City Philadelphia could rise above the William Penn statue on top of City Hall. She'd always admired its sheer audacity, even though she wasn't much of a rule breaker herself. At least not until recently.

Kera finally hung up and sighed. "I was taking my niece on a Ghost Walk tonight, but now she's got bronchitis and can't go."

"That's too bad," Abbey said, ready to get back to her run.

"Maybe . . ."

"Don't even go there. You know I hate that kind of thing."

"But it would be fun. Give you a good reintroduction to Bethlehem."

"Why don't you take Nolan?"

"He has to work. Please go with me. I've already got the tickets, and I was really looking forward to it."

"Oh, alright," Abbey said. Might as well. It's not as if she had anything else going on.

At the end of Heckewelder Place, they made a left onto Church Street and entered the oldest part of town. Abbey always loved the old stone buildings mottled like tortoise shells and supported by buttresses that looked downright medieval. The oldest of them all, the Moravian Gemeinhaus, rose from the edge of the pavement like the ultimate grand dame.

Nana had brought Abbey to the Gemeinhaus Museum when she was twelve years old, and an elderly tour guide had led them through room after boring room, droning on about German architecture and eighteenth-century religious practices. Until this moment, Abbey had forgotten all about it.

"Can we take a break?" Kera asked. "I'm not the fitness freak you are."

Abbey stopped in front of an incomplete quadrangle formed by the Gemeinhaus on one side, the Single Sisters' House opposite, and the belfry-topped building known as the Bell House connecting the two.

"Thanks," Kera said, bending over to catch her breath. "Isn't jogging supposed to be at a gentle pace? Jogging with you is like doing back-to-back fifty-meter sprints."

"Sorry, I guess I'm used to jogging by myself."

"I bet you miss Philly. Any news from the big city?"

"No, not yet," Abbey said, even though she knew she wouldn't be hearing from anyone.

She'd sold her condo and exercised her own personal scorched-earth policy, leaving her project management job and friends behind. She didn't care much about the job, but she hated to leave her friends, especially Sherry. On their last night together, Abbey met Sherry at a seedy bar crammed with the after-work singles crowd. Abbey had been stood up once again, and a rush of retaliation fever drove her to gulp down two of the dangerous-sounding smokin' blackberry sage margaritas in record time. The drinks, combined with an empty, stressed-out stomach, made Abbey so sick, she'd had to cut their evening short.

Sherry's last words to her had been: "You know you deserve better, right?"

Wasn't that the truth.

Abbey shaded her eyes with her hand and squinted at the belfry's turquoise blue dome and cream-colored cupola, topped with a metal weather vane in the shape of a lamb carrying a cross.

"Nothing ever changes here," Abbey said. "Not even the weather vane."

"That's the Moravian Seal up there with the Lamb of God signaling the direction of the wind while victoriously triumphing over sin and death," Kera said.

"You've turned into quite the historian—I'm impressed."

"Don't be. I bring my kids here every spring for a tour."

"I always wondered about the Single Sisters," Abbey said. "I used to think it sounded like fun, living with other women in a house of their own. But now, it sounds too much like a nunnery."

"*Au contraire*," Kera said. "The Moravian Sisters never lived like nuns, and they certainly weren't cloistered away. In fact, they had more freedom than most other women in the New World."

"But why did so many of them choose not to marry?" Abbey asked. Even after all she'd been through with Michael, she hated to think of a life alone.

"I don't know," Kera said. "But maybe your Liesl lived here. Nana said she was a Single Sister, right? You really need to visit the museum."

Abbey's response was to start jogging in place. *Ghost tours, museums. Wow, my social life is really picking up.*

Abbey shifted from one foot to the other in front of the Moravian Book Shop, shivering as she waited for Kera. She wished she'd worn her boots and woolen socks, but at least she'd had the good sense to pull on her heavy Aran sweater.

Autumn weather in Pennsylvania swung wildly from sunny days hot enough for the beach to chilly nights snuggled under a down comforter. Nana always said fall was as contrary as an old Pennsylvania Dutchman, usually giving Abbey's grandfather a pointed look. Her grandfather would argue that Pennsylvania Dutch was a misnomer anyway, since he wasn't Dutch at all. It was only a corruption of *Deutsch* that left German immigrants with the misleading nickname. Nana would laugh and say it must be the identity crisis that made them so ornery.

The memory made Abbey chuckle out loud, causing a mother clutching her little boy's hand to give Abbey a wide berth. *Great, now I'm turning into one of those crazy old ladies who scare little children.*

She attempted to look like a serious person by studying the familiar gold lettering on the elegant bookshop sign. She'd always liked the way the middle letters of the word "Book" were intertwined like an infinity symbol. Founded in 1745, locals touted the bookshop as the oldest in the country. Maybe that infinity symbol was a subtle reminder they intended to retain the title. How could anyone not love a city with a bookstore like that?

Each summer, Nana would let her choose one special book to celebrate her visit, and Abbey spent happy hours in the children's section of the bookstore, debating the pros and cons of each contender. One year she picked *The Secret Garden*, another year *Little Women*. She'd saved every one of them, and even now, opening one was like embracing a long-lost friend.

She checked her watch. Speaking of lost friends, where was Kera?

Just when she thought she'd lucked out and could go home, Kera arrived in a last-minute flurry, enveloped in a gray cape with a touch of fringe around the bottom. "*Désolé, ma chère!* Thanks so much for coming with me. Especially since I know this isn't your thing."

"Not a problem. Just don't go all Ghostbusters on me."

Kera leaned forward and whispered into Abbey's ear, "Who you gonna call?"

They were still laughing when Sarah the ghost-walk guide arrived, dressed for the part in a black cape and black jeans emblazoned with white skeleton bones. She carried an old lantern shaped like a mace and handed each guest a makeshift light of their own, a candle protected by the cut-out shell of a plastic soda bottle.

Sarah immediately offered a disclaimer. "I will do my best, but please understand the ghosts of Bethlehem are a fickle bunch, so paranormal sightings are never guaranteed."

Abbey sighed and surveyed the motley group ranging in age from about twelve to a sixtyish gray-haired couple. The older man's expression suggested he shared her lack of enthusiasm for the supernatural. He shrugged and gave her a comical wink.

At least he was a good sport. Even if Michael had agreed to do something like this, which was doubtful, he'd be making snide remarks and wanting to ditch the tour early. Perhaps that was the answer. Instead of a domineering man consumed with lust and ambition, maybe what she needed was an older man, one whose rough edges had been softened by time.

Sarah led the small group of ghost hunters down Main Street past the church green and gathered them on the corner across from the historic Single Brothers' House where she began her spiel.

"During the Revolutionary War, the Moravians turned the Single Brothers' House into a hospital and treated many soldiers here, particularly following the Battle of Brandywine. However, higher-ranking officers recuperated at the Sun Inn, and one very special patient, the Marquis de Lafayette, received personal attention in a private home."

Abbey's mind wandered as Sarah launched into a discussion of soldier ghosts. Why had nobody ever told her about Lafayette staying in Bethlehem? Her mother was a huge Lafayette fan, and Abbey had first learned about him during their European adventure. After climbing

Notre-Dame and gaping at the Eiffel Tower lit up like the world's biggest Fourth of July sparkler, Abbey had been crushed when her mother insisted they waste precious Paris time visiting the grave site of the Marquis de Lafayette. Abbey figured nothing could be more boring than hanging out with dead people, but no amount of scowling and moping would deter Regina Prescott.

After a stuffy subway ride into a nondescript neighborhood, they finally stood before the surprisingly unassuming spot where Lafayette and his wife, Adrienne, were buried side by side under simple slabs of stone with no ornamentation other than an American flag. Her mom explained that despite being only nineteen when he crossed the Atlantic to fight in the American Revolution, Lafayette became a hero on the battlefield and convinced Louis XVI to provide troops and funds. She insisted many historians believed the American Revolution would never have been won without him.

She also described how the flag was replaced each year on the Fourth of July. A tradition that began during WWI when an American colonel named Stanton placed the first American flag there and uttered the famous phrase "Lafayette, we are here."

Her mom had stood silently for a few moments, and then whispered, "Lafayette, *je suis ici.* I am here." And the power of history washed over Abbey for the first time.

That European trip was a turning point. Abbey switched her language studies to French, ignoring her father's insistence that Spanish was the more practical choice. And history, which had bored her silly the year before, became her best subject. The trip had also marked the last happy times of her childhood.

"So when do we see a ghost?" Abbey whispered as she linked arms with Kera and reminded herself how lucky she was to have such a friend.

Mercifully, the walk ended two hours later, and Kera suggested they finish their night at McCarthy's pub located at the rear of the Donegal Square store.

Kera pointed at the historic plaque out front. "Look at this."

Here stood the George Frederick Beckel house, 1762–1872, famed as the place where General Lafayette convalesced from a leg wound suffered at the Battle of Brandywine, 1777. Beckel was then superintendent of the community farm here in Bethlehem.

Abbey stared at the plaque, her mind buzzing with possibilities. Could George Frederick Beckel be related to her grandmother? And what about the Lafayette connection? Before tonight, she hadn't known Lafayette ever visited Bethlehem much less stayed with someone who might be a relative.

As soon as they entered the Irish shop, Abbey was drawn to a display of claddagh rings. Her mother had explained the significance of the ring's placement when the two of them were in Dublin. An engaged woman wore the ring on her left hand with the heart facing outward until her wedding day when the heart was turned inward.

She'd always dreamed of wearing one, and even now, her stubborn heart whispered, "One day."

At the back of the store, Abbey and Kera entered a large but cozy space with tin ceiling tiles, wooden tables covered in green-and-white gingham, and a large Guinness sign hanging above a wooden bar that looked like it had been transported from the old country. They sat at a corner table and ordered Harp beers along with bowls of hearty potato leek soup to chase away the evening chill.

"What did you think of the ghost walk?" Kera asked.

"Not bad. Even I have to admit it was fairly entertaining."

"My favorite part was that incredible story about the ghost hunters who got a photo of the ghost of Hughetta Bender, the woman who founded the Sun Inn Preservation Society. She swore she would never stop fighting to save the inn, and I guess she's still at it."

"'Incredible' is the word all right." Abbey's voice oozed with sarcasm. "And I suppose you liked the bit about ghosts having a party in the dining room too?"

Before Kera could answer, their waitress arrived and placed two frosted mugs of beer in front of them. Kera lifted her glass. "To ghosts and ghouls and all things unexplainable."

Abbey shook her head but joined the toast. "May all good things come to light."

Another waitress stopped by their table and greeted Kera by name. "Where is that nice young man of yours tonight?"

"Working," Kera said, "but I'll let him know you were asking about him."

"He's a keeper that one." The waitress winked and moved on to another table.

"Is Nolan really working at this hour?" Abbey asked.

"Not much longer. He'll be coming over to my place later." Kera's high cheekbones turned a rosebud pink, a perfect complement to her flowery peasant top.

"Well, then, we better make sure you aren't late," Abbey said, and even she could hear the strain in her voice.

Kera paused, looking uncomfortable. "I promise to get the three of us together sometime soon. I really want you to like him."

"I want to meet him too. Don't mind me. I'm just jealous."

The food arrived, and the two friends concentrated on the steamy soup and luscious Irish soda bread.

"Great choice, Miss Kera," Abbey said, wiping up the last of her soup with a piece of bread. "Before we leave, I need your help. I want to turn my dining room into a place where I can work."

"Like an office?"

"Not exactly. Something warm and inviting, more like a library. I want someone to reopen the fireplace, refinish the floors, and repair the walls and ceiling. What I need is someone who really appreciates old houses."

"I know just the guy. His name is Pete Schaeffer. Really

nice. *And* really easy on the eyes, if you know what I mean."

Abbey gave Kera a dramatic eye roll. "Other than being nice and good-looking, does he have any real qualifications? You know, like experience fixing up old houses?"

"I was getting to that. As a matter of fact, he completed a restoration job for Historic Bethlehem last year. He knows what he's doing. I'll give you his number."

As they walked back through the Irish store, feeling warmed inside and out, the woman behind the counter beckoned them over. "Is that a real Aran sweater?" she asked Abbey.

"It is. My mother bought it for me when we were in Ireland."

"I thought so!" the woman said with a self-satisfied grin. "I'm from Ireland myself. You'll never find a warmer or better-made sweater. And they wear like iron. I heard you girls say you were on the ghost walk. Did you have a good time?"

"*I* really enjoyed it," Kera said. "However, my friend here is a spoilsport who doesn't believe in ghosts."

The woman laughed and then turned serious. "We have a ghost here in this building, you know. She hangs around the upper floors. I've never seen her, but the owner has. Swears it's the ghost of a young woman. I think her name is Lisa? Or, wait, Liesl. That's it! Liesl Bickle. Something like that. They say she pines away for her unrequited love."

"I don't believe it," Kera said once they were outside. "That ghost she was talking about has to be your Liesl, right?"

"For the last time, I do not believe in ghosts! But even I have to admit there are some strange connections here."

"Maybe Liesl's haunting you!" Kera said, and they both laughed.

After saying goodnight, Abbey hurried home and headed straight for the parlor, her mind spinning with thoughts of ghosts and lost loves. She needed to take a closer look at that bookmark.

Abbey retrieved the shadow box from the top of the piano and set it on the carton she and Kera had used as a coffee table. Taking a seat on one of the Queen Anne chairs, she carefully pried open the back panel of the frame, exposing the attached bookmark. Then she removed the pins holding the bookmark in place and gently lifted it from the soft dark panel.

The deep gold fabric on the back of the bookmark looked slightly scorched, but the fine stitching on the front was intact, revealing a swirling motif of vivacious flowers: drowsy red tulips, daisylike clusters of red and pink petals, and a stunning royal blue dahlia taking center stage amid a tangle of intertwining stems. The artistry was enviable, but the real power of the piece was its passionate display of nature. From somewhere in her schoolgirl past, Abbey recalled a quote from the poet William Blake:

To see a world in a grain of sand and a heaven in a wild flower,
Hold infinity in the palm of your hand and eternity in an hour.

What sort of eighteenth-century woman could have created this extraordinary embroidery? She rubbed her thumb across a strange roughness at the top of the bookmark and discovered an open seam. Looking closer, she could see something sticking out through the opening. Probably some backing to give the bookmark stiffness. But when she tugged on it, a long piece of narrowly folded, yellowed paper fell into her palm.

With shaking hands, Abbey spread the delicate sheet in front of her and stared in disbelief. The tiny old-fashioned handwriting was nearly impossible to read but appeared to be written in French, and in alternating hands. One script was boldly written with heavy pressure while the other was precise but dainty.

What could be the meaning of these messages? And why in the world were they hidden inside Liesl's bookmark?

CHAPTER 5

September 23, 1777

Every morning Father leads the family worship in endless discourse intended to bring our hearts closer to the Saviour. It saddens me to know I shall never achieve the level of piousness demanded by my father for I fear my heart is stubborn and yearns to find its own way.

—Diary of Sister Liesl Boeckel

The Boeckel household always rose with the dawn. The earliest rays of morning sunlight barely flickered in the windows as Liesl gathered with the rest of her family in the sitting room, all except for her three-year-old stepbrother, who was permitted to sleep until breakfast.

She and her stepmother sat at the round table on the chairs with the carved hearts while Lafayette rested on the only upholstered chair, his wounded leg outstretched and discreetly covered by a small blanket Liesl had made years before. Mother Boeckel had selected the coverlet quite specifically, hoping Lafayette would be pleased by the checkered squares of red, white, and blue.

Liesl struggled not to smile at Lafayette's disheveled appearance. The bottom button of his waistcoat had been left unfastened, and his wig sat on his head at an alarming angle. It seemed the general had grown unaccustomed to waking at such an early hour.

Her father stood in a commanding position by the fireplace. He was not a large man, but he exuded a self-satisfied confidence and moved with an agility that belied his sixty-one years. His most noteworthy feature was his silvery-gray hair, which he wore overlong like an aging Visigoth. Her father had not been born a Moravian, but he loved to tell Liesl of the first time he met their revered Count Zinzendorf and how Zinzendorf had guided him to join the family of God. And accept the burden of leading his own family in the ways of the Saviour.

Her father often said the day the community received word that Count Zinzendorf had died was one of the saddest in his life. Within two weeks, Zinzendorf's wife died as well, in an act of loyalty Liesl knew her father greatly admired. Liesl sometimes wondered if her father thought she should have pined away after her own marital disappointment, but Matthew would never have wanted that. He would have been horrified at the thought.

Count Zinzendorf believed every day should begin with family worship in the home, and her father followed this custom without fail. However, for the first time, Father had moved the gathering upstairs to the sitting room, thereby ensuring Lafayette's attendance in the hope of impressing upon his guest the piousness of the home in which he was recuperating. A wasted effort in her opinion, for she doubted Lafayette would appreciate the worship service any more than he appreciated being disturbed at such an early hour.

"We shall commence," Father Boeckel announced in a booming voice. "The Watchword for Tuesday, the twenty-third day of September in the Year of our Lord one thousand seven hundred and seventy-seven is taken from the book of Matthew, chapter twenty-five, verses thirty-five and thirty-six." With a pointed gaze at Lafayette, Father Boeckel recited, "'I was a stranger and you welcomed me, I was naked and you gave me clothing, I was sick and you took care of me.'"

He then launched into a lecture on the duties of discipleship. As he expounded on his favorite topic, Liesl saw him becoming more and more aware of the smug look on their guest's face, an expression that soon bordered on amusement. No doubt her father already regretted his decision to allow Lafayette into their home.

As soon as Father Boeckel finished intoning a lengthy prayer espousing the love of the Saviour and repeating once again the joys of discipleship, he abruptly left the room and returned carrying his prized copy of *The History of Greenland.*

"I am sorry, General," he said, "but I shall be unable to

spend much time in your presence apart from our morning worship, as my position as overseer of the community farm requires that I spend my days in the fields. I leave you in the good care of my wife and my daughter."

"Thank you, sir," Lafayette said, managing to sound more respectful than his expression suggested. "I am most grateful for your kindness and have no doubts that I shall receive only the best of care here in your home."

Father Boeckel held out the leather-bound tome. "I offer you this book, *The History of Greenland*, in the hope that it will help you to productively pass the hours of your convalescence. As a missionary in the service of humanity, our Brother David Cranz lived for a year on the island of Greenland. I believe you will find his observations of the heathen way of life in that frozen wasteland most illuminating, and I trust you will discover in his devout faith an inspiration to strengthen your own. For without faith, we are nothing." Those last words were spoken with particular emphasis as he gave Lafayette a hard stare, daring him to disagree.

"Thank you, sir. I am most honored," Lafayette said, and accepted the heavy book without further comment.

Lafayette was tired and bored. The early morning service had disrupted his sleep, and now nothing but empty hours stretched out in front of him. Mother Boeckel had brought him a bowl of porridge but then darted off like a scared rabbit. Reading about missionaries held little appeal, but apparently, Father Boeckel's hefty tome would be his sole entertainment.

He had barely started reading *The History of Greenland* when a clamor outside his window reached a crescendo. A crowd had gathered at an intersection just to the east of the Boeckel home. The inner circle of the crowd was made up of soldiers, easy to distinguish by their rough garb and wild gesticulations. Beyond them, a second ring of grave-looking Moravian men calmly observed the fracas. And at the very fringes, Lafayette could see several Moravian women, identifiable by their pure-white head coverings, dipping and bobbing like agitated swans.

As if the raucous interruption were not annoying enough, the family had left him completely alone. Where was that infernal girl who was supposed to change his dressings? Had everyone forgotten him so soon?

"Where have you been?" he demanded when Liesl and Mother Boeckel finally arrived.

Mother Boeckel seemed shocked by his agitation, but Liesl eyed him with a steady, unperturbed glance. "Sir, I do not owe you an accounting of my time. However, if you must know, I was out on the street. We have had a good deal of excitement this morning."

"*Je le sais!*" Lafayette shouted. "I may be injured, but I am not deaf."

While Mother Boeckel paled, Liesl looked as if she were suppressing a smile.

"A wagon bearing the Great Bell was passing through our town when one of the rear wheels broke," she said. "I have been told the bell weighs over two thousand pounds. No doubt the wheel broke as a result of the extreme weight and the braking with the chains."

"I know nothing of the Great Bell or of this braking with chains, mademoiselle," Lafayette said with exasperation.

"How surprising that a patriot like yourself would not have heard of the Great Bell of Philadelphia," Liesl said. He glared at her but before he could respond, she continued. "It has become a revered symbol of the revolution. I was close enough to read the inscription: 'Proclaim liberty throughout all the land unto all the inhabitants thereof.'"

"A noble sentiment indeed." His voice was quieter now, and he felt ashamed for his irrational anger. "The battle for Philadelphia must be imminent. Washington must have decided to remove the bell to prevent it from being captured. The British would want it for the symbolic value . . . or to melt it down for cannonballs."

Liesl shuddered. "I cannot imagine so handsome a creation being turned into instruments of death."

"Washington will never allow that to happen," Lafayette said with pride. "Where is the Great Bell now?"

"Eventually a new wheel was located, and the broken one replaced. The Great Bell is now on its way to a safe location."

As Liesl began removing the dressings from Lafayette's leg, young George Frederick howled from the floor below. Mother Boeckel immediately moved toward the door and excused herself with an expression of ill-concealed relief. Apparently, Mother Boeckel found him even more trying than her demanding son.

"And the braking of chains?" Lafayette asked Liesl.

"Farming wagons have no braking systems," Liesl explained. "At the top of a hill, a farmer will lock one of the rear wheels in place with chains to slow the movement of the wagon. The method usually works quite well. Unfortunately, in this situation the weight of the bell was too great, and the rear wheel broke."

"I had no idea you were so knowledgeable about farming wagons," Lafayette teased, his good humor fully restored.

"You forget, sir, that my father oversees all the farming for our town. I have often been called upon to help him."

"A nurse, a farmhand, and a speaker of Iroquois. Is there no end to your accomplishments?"

"As I have told you, I am not a nurse, and we Moravian women are not cosseted creatures like your French ladies. We are knowledgeable well beyond the arts of needlework and dancing."

"And what do you know of the art of dancing?"

"Apparently more than you know about farming," Liesl said as she turned her attention back to his bandages.

"I know more about agriculture than you might imagine.

I grew up living with my grandmother in a small farming village called Chavaniac. What a wonderful woman she was, kind and generous, venerated throughout the province."

"And I suppose she adored her darling grandson."

"Of course, how could she not?" he said, his voice softening with nostalgia. "She let me run wild like a gypsy child. I roamed the fields and forests with the peasant boys from the village, brandishing homemade wooden swords at imaginary British villains. When I was only ten years old, our village was beset by a monstrous beast that ravaged the livestock, and some said, slaughtered women and children. I grabbed the musket my father had hung on the wall and charged into the forest, determined to kill it. Unfortunately, a hunter found the creature first and shot what was only an exceptionally large wolf."

"Your grandmother must have been terrified you would be injured."

"No doubt she was, but I told her, 'I am the Lord of the village. It is up to me to defend it.' I am afraid I was rather full of myself, not to mention quite spoilt."

"That comes as no great surprise to me," Liesl said as she secured the last of his bandages. "Although I must admire you for the acknowledging of it."

"*Merci*, mademoiselle," Lafayette said, pleased to have curried her favor even regarding such a small thing.

He spent much of the day reading *The History of Greenland* and soon realized the Moravian missionaries were almost as fascinating as Greenland itself. He felt a surprising *esprit de corps* with these Moravians who were infused with a fervent zeal along with a burning faith in themselves and their mission.

He tried to picture what Liesl might be doing. Was she caring for other patients or helping her father at the farm? He found himself hoping to hear her light step upon the stairs, but his sole visitor was Mother Boeckel, who brought him a tray with a serving of hearty chicken pie along with several slices of thick brown bread and then rushed out as if he were contagious. It seemed Liesl would provide his only relief from solitude, and the afternoon passed slowly with no company other than his own.

Until that evening when Liesl reappeared.

"This is a welcome surprise," he said, looking up from *The History of Greenland.* "I expected Mother Boeckel."

"She asked me to retrieve your dinner tray since young George Frederick is being even more obstinate than usual," Liesl said as she removed the tray from the small table. "It seems the evening meal fuels him with an uncontrollable energy at the very moment Mother Boeckel wishes to put him to bed."

"I must thank the young man for I much prefer your company." Lafayette closed the large book. "I disagree with your father on many things, but he was right about this. The story of Greenland is quite remarkable, and I am most intrigued by the adventures of your Brother David Cranz; however, I am lonely for conversation. Will you stay for a moment?"

Liesl set the tray back down and gave him an inquiring look.

"How did your family come to live in Bethlehem?" he asked.

"My parents were born in Europe in a German-speaking area known as the Palatinate."

"That would explain your father's accent," Lafayette interrupted. "It is much like that of Doctor Glatt."

"Yes, they both came here from Germany, as did many Moravians. Within months of their marriage, my parents bid farewell to all they had ever known and boarded a ship called *The Harle* bound for the New World. My mother often spoke of that journey, of the poor souls who were tormented by all manner of illnesses including seasickness, dysentery, and scurvy. She said it was as if they had embarked on a journey into hell."

"It *is* a difficult voyage," Lafayette said, thinking of his own formidable experience crossing the Atlantic. "Did they come here to be missionaries like the Moravians in Greenland?"

"No, they were not Moravians then. They settled in the center of Pennsylvania, and one night, Father heard a sermon by Count Zinzendorf, our spiritual leader. Father told me that for the first time, he had a sense of his mission in life."

Lafayette smiled. "It is obvious that your father is a very devout and determined man."

"My mother hesitated to leave her Lutheran faith, but

Father convinced her to join him as a member of the Moravian Church, and they eventually moved to Bethlehem."

"What does it mean to be a Moravian?" Lafayette asked. It was a question he had struggled with all afternoon.

"That is not an easy question to answer," Liesl said, hesitating before continuing. "We are a community of faith with three guiding principles: In essentials, unity. We believe the Saviour, who died that we might live, is the essence of our unity. In non-essentials, liberty. We believe in not only tolerance but also in true acceptance, and we open our arms wide to embrace all of life. And, in all things, love. This, our greatest principle, teaches us that to love God is to love our neighbor."

Lafayette remained silent for several minutes. Liberty and unity were certainly principles he held dear, and who could argue with love? However, his passions had never been particularly spiritual, but focused more on the intellect of man and the power of reason. Lafayette believed that, rather than relying on a deity, men were responsible for shaping their own futures and all of humanity was obliged to work together to achieve a better world. Religion had never played a major role in his life, certainly not at the level of piety professed by this simple girl.

Lafayette ran his fingers along the spine of the borrowed book. "Cranz speaks of living under the choir system. Please tell me, what is that?"

"It is a concept those outside the church struggle to comprehend. Our choirs are groupings based on age, gender, and marital status. We have choirs for every stage of life. Choirs for children and choirs for Single Sisters, Single Brothers, Married Brothers, Married Sisters, and for Widows. At present, parents and children are permitted to live together as families, but not long ago, each individual lived with their appropriate choir, starting almost at birth."

"Did you live in a choir when you were young?" Lafayette asked.

"Of course. Soon after I was born, I was placed in the communal nursery and cared for by Single Sisters. When I grew older, I joined the Little Girls' Choir and lived with them. We did everything together: attending school, eating our meals, and worshipping side by side. In many ways my choir became my family."

"Did you not miss your parents?"

"I saw Mother almost every day, and you must understand, I knew no other life. I kept busy with my lessons, and I had many friends. It was a joyous time for me."

"But why would husbands and wives choose to live apart from each other? And from their children?" Lafayette asked.

"Count Zinzendorf taught us we would grow more steadfast in our faith if surrounded by those just like ourselves."

"I do not mean to be indelicate," he said slowly, "but if married men and women did not live together when did they find time to be alone?"

He had feared he would offend her with such an

improper question, but Liesl showed no reaction at all.

"Count Zinzendorf devised a practical arrangement," Liesl said, her voice as calm as if he had asked her about the weather. "A private room designated as the conjugal room, a place where married couples took turns spending the night together."

Lafayette could not contain his amusement. "I have never heard of such a thing. A conjugal room! As you say, you Moravians are indeed *très pratique*."

Liesl picked up his dinner tray, but Lafayette gestured for her to wait. "I have one more question. What is the purpose of the covering you wear upon your head?"

Liesl set the tray down for a second time, clearly struggling to control her impatience. "The cap is called a Haube. We wear it because we believe it is immodest for women to display their hair."

Lafayette looked at her closely. "What is that slight marking on yours?"

"You are most observant, monsieur. My initials are embroidered on one side so my Haube may be identified from others."

"Such delicate work," Lafayette murmured. "Do you know what John Adams had to say about Moravian women? He greatly admired your city, but he said, and I quote, 'The women resemble a garden of white cabbage heads.'"

"Hardly a flattering description," Liesl said, although she did not look affronted.

"Of course, my red hair is hidden beneath this wig," Lafayette said, playfully tapping his white curls. "In France, a woman's hair is her glory. Our queen Marie Antoinette wears hers in exceptionally magnificent styles, decorated in all manner of ribbons and feathers and often reaching a height of over thirty-six English inches."

Liesl shook her head. "I cannot imagine such ridiculousness. And how do the women dress in Paris?"

"French women are like brightly colored tropical birds flitting to and fro in silken gowns that whisper with a gentle swish as they pass by."

Liesl lowered her head as she fingered the coarse linsey-woolsey fabric of her dark blue skirt. How clumsy of him. He had not intended to make her feel inferior—that was something she could never be.

"Of course, true beauty has no need of extravagant dress," he said. "America has its share of beauties as well. I consider myself quite fortunate to spend time with one."

Liesl picked up his tray one final time and returned to her brusque professional demeanor. "You must rest. If God wills it so, I shall see you in the morning."

"*Bonne nuit, ma belle amie*," Lafayette called after her as she left the room.

CHAPTER 6

The Moravian Museum

September 2005

The first thing Abbey noticed when she entered the Moravian Museum was the smell, an oddly pleasant old-building mustiness laced with just a hint of cinnamon. That was followed by an impression of stark simplicity and of a silence lost to the modern world, as if the peacefulness of long ago had soaked into the white plaster walls and the wide wood plank floors.

The chaste white walls were empty except for a painting of a slightly absurd-looking Moravian Sister with a tight-fitting white cap on her head and a shiny pink ribbon nestled like a bow tie beneath her chin. And yet even those unfortunate clothing choices could not detract from her porcelain skin and compelling dark eyes. For a moment, Abbey felt the present slip away, the silence replaced by the whispers of Single Sisters, the gentle sway of their skirts, and the soft patter of their shoes across the hard wooden floor.

A grating New Jersey accent broke the spell as a woman with eyes rimmed in more eyeliner than Abbey wore in a month entered the museum with a teenaged girl trailing behind her. The woman lectured on and on about the importance of studying history, while the girl kept her eyes glued to her cellphone. The pair reminded Abbey of traveling with her mother. Only now, she sympathized with the mom and wished the girl knew how lucky she was.

A tour guide named Louisa swept into the room and welcomed them to the museum. Salt-and-pepper curls framed her smiling face, and the laugh lines at the corners of her eyes crinkled as she said, "Today, we'll time-travel back into the world of the early Moravians."

The teenaged girl grimaced. At least she was listening.

Louisa began the tour with what she called her Moravian history in a nutshell, a story Abbey only vaguely remembered. In the year 1415, in an area of Eastern Europe called Moravia, a Catholic priest named Jan Hus was convicted of heresy and burned at the stake for questioning some of the church's practices. His followers, who became known as Moravians, spread Jan's beliefs throughout Europe, although they wisely worshipped in secret to avoid a similar fiery fate. At least until the 1700's, when Count Nikolaus Ludwig von Zinzendorf of Germany became their revered leader.

"It was Zinzendorf who first suggested the Moravians become missionaries," Louisa said. "Soon small bands of the faithful traveled throughout Africa and other unlikely outposts like Iceland and Greenland. Eventually, their missionary zeal brought them to the American colonies. Once the thirteen original founders were settled here in Pennsylvania, they sent word to Zinzendorf and asked him to send more church members."

Louisa pointed to a model of a small wooden ship. "Soon Moravians from all over Europe were making the dangerous voyage across the Atlantic Ocean in ships like this one."

Abbey thought about her "gutsy" move back to Bethlehem. What kind of courage did it take to board a little wooden ship and sail to a new world? It must have been the modern-day equivalent of rocketing to the moon. Except unlike astronauts, these were ordinary men, women, and children who had no reasonable expectation of ever seeing their loved ones again. She tried to imagine their last hugs and desperate attempts to memorize tear-stained faces.

Louisa led them through the rest of the house, sharing stories of life in early Bethlehem and eventually ushering them into a small schoolroom.

"The Moravians valued education and promoted literacy," she said. "Everyone kept diaries. Individuals kept private diaries, the head of each choir maintained a choir diary, and there is even something known as the Bethlehem Diary, which continues to be updated every single day."

Abbey's heart raced. What if she could read Liesl's diary? It might explain a lot. Like why Liesl had hidden messages inside her bookmark.

Abbey only half listened as Louisa directed their attention to what she called one last treat—an amateurish painting of three figures seated around a wooden table.

"When Lafayette arrived in Bethlehem, George Washington sent instructions for Lafayette to be treated 'as if he were my son,'" Louisa said. "So rather than recuperate with the rest of the common soldiers, Lafayette was cared for in the private home of the Boeckel family."

Now Louisa had her full attention. Abbey's heart thumped as the guide gestured toward the painted figures.

"You can see the marquis, with his wounded leg discreetly covered by a quilt," Louisa said, "along with Mrs. Barbara Boeckel and her stepdaughter Liesl. Liesl had some medical training and would have cared for Lafayette's wound."

Abbey crouched down to read the small wall label. The date of the painting was 1934, more than 150 years after the event itself, and yet, the painting had to be based on some truth.

She took a closer look. Lafayette sat in a high-backed chair, wearing a fancy uniform in royal blue with red trim and gold epaulets. He sported a white wig with tight curls at the sides and held an open book in his lap. Mrs. Boeckel stood in the center, slightly hunched over as she served what looked like glasses of wine. And on the right, Liesl Boeckel leaned forward slightly in her chair, holding a wine glass almost as if she were about to raise a toast.

So, this was the mysterious Liesl Boeckel, the woman

responsible for creating a remarkable bookmark and possibly hiding secret messages inside it. Like the Moravian Sister in the painting at the museum's entrance, both women wore unattractive white caps plastered to their heads, and drab clothes enlivened only by the brightly colored ribbons tied under their chins. Abbey studied the expressions on the three faces. Lafayette's gaze, rather than looking out at the viewer, turned toward Liesl, while Mrs. Boeckel's eyes were downcast as if she were ashamed or refused to see what was right in front of her. Only Liesl stared directly out of the picture at Abbey. A beautiful, confident young woman who looked like she knew exactly what she wanted and wasn't about to let anybody stand in her way.

"I've told you the facts, but now I'll share the gossip," Louisa said. Her eyes sparkled as she purposely kept them in suspense. The teenaged girl even looked up from her cell. "The word around town was that Liesl fell madly in love with Lafayette, and he broke her heart."

When Abbey gasped, Louisa laughed and said, "You seem to have a special interest in Liesl and Lafayette."

Abbey snapped a quick cellphone picture and struggled to pull her eyes away from the painting. "I'm a little confused. The historical plaque on Main Street says Lafayette stayed in the home of George Frederick Beckel spelled B-E-C-K-E-L."

"That's right. Frederick was Liesl's father. As you probably know, spellings often change over the years."

Abbey tried to contain her excitement. "I'd really like to learn more about Liesl." *Especially since we might be related!*

"Well, I would start with the Moravian Archives, located near the college. They're the best resource for all things Moravian. Contact them, and they'll dig out everything they have on Liesl."

Abbey thanked her for the advice and started to follow the mother and daughter, now arm in arm, toward the exit.

"Would you be interested in seeing Liesl's grave?" Louisa asked.

Abbey waited as Louisa rummaged through an overstuffed file cabinet and finally pulled out a smudged Xerox copy. She drew a circle on it and handed the map to Abbey.

"This will lead you right there," she said.

The map looked more cryptic than clear, but Abbey thanked Louisa and stuffed it into her bag for another day. The cemetery could wait—she needed to get her hands on Liesl's diary.

"I'm looking for any information you have on Liesl Boeckel who cared for the Marquis de Lafayette during the Revolutionary War," Abbey repeated into her cell. She'd called the archives and been transferred to some old grouch who made her feel as if she were keeping him from something worthier of his time.

"Of course, I'd be happy to make an appointment," she said. "Thursday will be fine. I'll see you then."

Another task accomplished! She only hoped this archivist was more helpful in person than he was over the phone. Thursday was shaping up to be a big day: she'd already scheduled Pete Schaeffer for the morning, and now, she'd check out the archives in the afternoon. It felt good to be making progress on something other than unpacking boxes.

Feeling restless, she wondered up the stairs to the second floor, but bypassed her bedroom for the one in the back, the one where Nana's spirit still resonated. A three-piece bookcase ran almost the full length of one wall, its shelves overloaded with souvenirs: a Russian nesting doll alongside a sad-faced Venetian clown, a cannibal fork from Fiji propped next to a photo of her grandparents riding an elephant in India. Every inch of the remaining wall space served as a backdrop for Nana's vintage postcards, Impressionist prints, and posters including several from Musikfest, Bethlehem's summer music extravaganza.

As a young girl, Abbey had studied every single piece of this collection, begging Nana to repeat the background stories over and over. It fueled a wanderlust in Abbey, making her yearn for new places and new adventures. She wondered what had happened to that girl—the fearless one who wanted to hop on a plane and see the world.

If only she were more like Nana. The kind of person who dove into the deep end of the pool with no hesitation. Instead, Abbey was the one hovering on the edges, studying depth measurements, gauging the distance between the pool ladders, and evaluating the expressions on the faces of the swimmers.

Looking around the room, it was clear that Nana valued souvenirs more than bedroom furniture. A cozy chaise lounge with a pile of books stacked next to it sat in one corner, along with a low-lying table cradling a jumble of family photos. A simple chest, a nightstand, and a narrow single bed were squeezed into what little space remained.

Nana's bed looked too small for a child, much less an adult. On her seventh birthday, Abbey's parents had surprised her with a full-sized canopy bed, every little girl's dream. She'd been thrilled when the bed first arrived, but the splotchy red roses overhead looked like giant spiders when the lights went out. In order to fall asleep, Abbey had devised a bedtime ritual: she'd pull her knees up toward her chest until she was a small half-moon in the big bed and then pile all the excess bedding around her body to create an impregnable fortress. Comfortable at last, she'd picture the house she loved best. The one with the creamy yellow porch that glowed as if lit from deep within. The one place able to chase away the sadness and make her feel safe.

That house was hers now, and she had to believe life would be better here.

CHAPTER 7

September 24, 1777

I try to begin each day anew, to concentrate on the present, but my memories will not let me be, and I find I am haunted by the past.

—Diary of Sister Liesl Boeckel

As she tucked her hair inside her Haube and tied the pink ribbon beneath her chin, Liesl thought about Lafayette's comments. Cabbage heads indeed! Although in all honesty, she often wished to be free of the useless cap that made her scalp itch and her head ache. She never spoke of her dislike for it, but surely the Elders could concern themselves with more pressing affairs than how a woman fixed her hair.

The morning service was conducted in the sitting room once again, giving her the opportunity to observe Lafayette more closely. To his credit, he maintained a respectful expression even as her father expounded on the subject of heathens in our midst. When her father moved on to a familiar recitation of the qualities of discipleship, Liesl's mind drifted back to the night before.

After leaving Lafayette and his talk of French women, she had stood in front of the window in her tiny bedroom, observing her own reflection, her expression grave and still as a John Valentine Haidt portrait. Wearing nothing but her plain white shift, her pale skin glowed in the wavy glass, haloed by the golden haze of her unbound hair falling down upon her shoulders. She had not thought about her appearance in a long time, but at that moment she wondered. Was she beautiful, as Lafayette had said?

As if hearing her thoughts, her father ended his lecture with an admonition that true followers must avoid conceit and narcissism. Liesl lowered her eyes, chastising herself for the sin of pride and pledging to guard herself against Lafayette's worldly influences.

At midmorning, she and Mother Boeckel returned to the sitting room for the daily changing of Lafayette's dressings. Father insisted Mother Boeckel be present whenever Liesl attended to Lafayette; however, Liesl had barely begun removing the linens from his leg when a familiar screech sent Mother Boeckel bolting from the room.

"I must confess I am not sad to see her leave," Lafayette said with a smile and an air of familiarity Liesl found discomfiting.

She responded by pulling rather roughly on the dressings.

"Be gentle with me, mademoiselle! Do not forget I am

an injured patriot, wounded in battle for the cause of liberty."

"The circumstances of your injury interest me not," Liesl said. "You are lucky it is but an in-and-out flesh wound."

"Surely my dear nurse would not make light of my injury?"

Despite her explanations, he still insisted on referring to her as a nurse. His use of the term was inaccurate, but not displeasing, for it was a title she hoped to claim one day.

"The redness will diminish, and the pain will ease as well," she said. "In time, the wound will fill with new flesh and the margins will reunite."

She moved briskly to the basket she had placed on the side table and removed a small earthenware bowl made from the red clay of the Menakasie Creek. "Our bees have kindly contributed fresh honey, which will help to reduce the inflammation," she said, slathering the sticky concoction on his leg. "The honey will also constrain the wound from infection."

"I believe your touch alone is enough to heal me."

Liesl ignored his mindless chatter and observed him carefully. "Please move your head from side to side and then open and close your jaw."

Lafayette looked puzzled but complied nonetheless.

"Very good. Tetanus is a critical concern with an injury of this type; however, you show no signs of either a rigid neck or jaw, which are the primary symptoms." She smoothed the fresh linens. "Your wound is healing quite satisfactorily."

Lafayette raised his head proudly. With his long narrow nose tilted slightly upward, he was the very picture of a French aristocrat. "I do believe if a man wished to be wounded just for his own amusement, he should come and see my wound and have one just like it."

Liesl collected her medical basket. "If it is so minor a wound, I am sure I can find other patients more in need of my ministrations."

Lafayette attempted a contrite expression. "I can imagine no patient more deserving of your tender care than myself."

"And I can imagine no patient more presumptuous," Liesl said as she left the room.

In fact, Liesl did have another patient to see that day. Sister Susanna suffered from chronic asthma, and Liesl stopped by the Single Sisters' House once a week to monitor her condition. The chatty Sister prided herself on knowing everything that went on in the town, and at each visit, Liesl could count on hearing all the latest gossip. As if she cared about which Brother had fallen asleep during service or which Sister always dropped her stitches.

Despite Lafayette's annoying qualities, Liesl had to admit he was by far her most intriguing patient. She should write more about him in her diary. Someday when she composed her memoir, caring for Lafayette would no doubt be a highlight.

After the previous day's excitement with the Great Bell, the town was remarkably calm. She encountered no one until she reached a group of Brothers and Sisters gathered in front of the apothecary. As she paused to greet each one by name, the door to the apothecary opened, revealing a tall, lanky man standing by the compounding hearth.

Matthew! For an instant, an impossible hope flared within her, only to be immediately extinguished when she recognized the face of the master tanner. Would this pain never end? Somehow, she needed to accept that Matthew was gone, and that she would never again see him upon this earth.

She forced herself to continue on, leaving the past behind. But when she opened the gray door with the familiar herringbone pattern, it was as if she had never left the Single Sisters' House. The sweet sounds of singing from a nearby workroom filled the air, and her fingers longed for the softness of flax fibers and the pleasure of feeding them into a spinning wheel.

The sensation of reentering the past was reinforced by the shining face of the Sister coming toward her.

"Sister Adelina!" Liesl cried, her voice filled with joy. "When did you return from your missionary work in the Ohio Territories?"

"Last night," Sister Adelina said, encircling Liesl with her plump arms. "I am glad to see you looking well. But I had heard you were getting married."

"I turned down Brother Eugene," Liesl said.

Sister Adelina nodded as if she were not surprised.

"Father is still angry with me, for he wants nothing more than to marry me off as quickly as possible. Brother Eugene is a kind soul, but I could never love such a simple man." *Certainly not after Matthew.*

Sister Adelina patted her arm and wisely changed the subject. "As you know, our precious Labouress was called home not long ago, and I am afraid our dear friend Benigna does not fare well either. When I stayed a night in Lititz, I attempted to see her but was told she never leaves her room and will see no one other than the one Sister who cares for her."

Liesl shivered. "I am very sorry to hear that. I keep Benigna in my prayers always."

"Are you feeling faint?" Sister Adelina asked, her eyes narrowing with concern. "You have gone very pale."

"I am fine," Liesl reassured her. And yet she was shaken. Her past seemed intent on assaulting her at every turn this day.

Liesl promised to visit Sister Adelina soon and continued up to the third floor. When Liesl lived here, the floor had been a dormitory for the Older Girls' Choir, but now it was divided into tiny apartments.

Sister Susanna was feeling well and had plenty of news to share. Which Liesl found easy to ignore, as thoughts of her old nemesis, the Labouress, whirled through her mind. She remained in an unsettled mood for the rest of the day and looked forward to retiring early. However, when she returned from the evening service, she was greeted by a fraught Mother Boeckel.

"Liesl, there you are. Would you retrieve Lafayette's dinner tray?"

Liesl nodded but groaned inwardly. It seemed Mother Boeckel had permanently delegated this task to her. A circumstance that pleased Lafayette if not herself.

She plodded up the stairs and into the sitting room.

"My dear nurse, how happy I am to see you. You left me much too quickly this morning. Please have a seat so that we may chat for a bit."

Liesl perched herself on the edge of one of the small wooden chairs, hoping to make it clear she had no intention of sitting for long.

Lafayette must have noticed her distracted air, for he asked, "Was something wrong with one of your other patients?"

"No. I met an old friend, Sister Adelina, and seeing her brought back many memories."

"Please tell me about her," Lafayette said. "I wish to learn more about you Moravians."

"Sister Adelina is one of the kindest souls I have ever known. She is also an Indian."

"Indians live here in Bethlehem?" Lafayette asked.

"They did many years ago, but then they moved west. Except, of course, for Sister Adelina."

Liesl explained that Sister Adelina had been born into the Mohawk tribe, a member of the Wolf Clan. But when she was a little girl, her family had sought refuge in Bethlehem to escape the bloodshed of the French and Indian War.

"Although the war was primarily a struggle between France and Britain," she said, shifting back into her chair, "some of the Indian tribes, such as the Shawnee, sided with the French. British colonists often made no distinctions among the tribes and conducted random raids against all Indians, resulting in the deaths of innocent men, women, and children."

Adelina and her family had converted to the Moravian faith, and Adelina had joined the Little Girls' Choir headed by Sister Esther Bitterlic. All went well until the Pennsylvania government decreed the Moravian Indians must relocate to Philadelphia for their own safety because a group of violent settlers called the Paxton Boys were targeting Indians and had threatened to attack the town.

As the day of relocation drew near, Adelina became hysterical at the thought of leaving all she knew and loved. She ran to the Bell House where she had recently lived with the Little Girls' Choir, and Sister Esther found her there in the dormitory, curled up on her old bed sobbing. Sister Esther had taken Adelina into her arms and asked if she would like to remain in Bethlehem with her.

"But what about her parents?" Lafayette interrupted, leaning forward.

It gave Liesl a strange sense of power to see him so immersed in the story.

"According to Adelina, Sister Esther vowed to petition for her parents to stay as well, but that permission was never granted."

Adelina had witnessed the sad departure of her parents along with all the other Indian families. Her mother had promised the exodus would be for only a short while, but time dragged on through the winter and into the spring. Adelina received cheerful letters from her mother describing how fortunate they were to be in a secure place on Province Island in the middle of the Delaware River and how grateful they were that Adelina could continue her studies under the watchful eye of Sister Esther. But Adelina overheard other less encouraging reports discussed in hushed tones outside the chapel after service, and she became more and more concerned.

One day in May, Sister Esther took Adelina's hands in hers and read a letter containing the news that Adelina's parents had died of the pox within days of each other.

"Sister Adelina told me she never would have survived if not for the love of the Saviour and for Sister Esther, who comforted her throughout her suffering," Liesl said. "Later, the survivors of Province Island returned to Bethlehem but did not stay, deciding to move westward to open territories beyond the rule of government."

Liesl stood, indicating an end to her storytelling. "Adelina declined to join them on their trek, choosing instead to remain in Bethlehem and become a helpmate to Sister Esther."

"*Une histoire tragique*," Lafayette said. "I thank you for sharing it with me. Someday, we will live in a world where all people are free and equal with no distinction of blood or color."

Liesl thought how serious he could be at times and wondered what it must be like for him to be in a foreign country surrounded by strangers. Her world must seem small and sad compared to his, and yet, she could not imagine going through a day without seeing a familiar face. As much as she loathed to admit it, she was curious about him.

"Do you miss your home in France?" she asked.

"Of course," he said, and pretended to lift an imaginary glass to his lips. "I quite miss French wine."

Liesl left the room, chiding herself for thinking Lafayette could remain serious for more than a moment or two.

CHAPTER 8

The Handyman and the Archivist

September 2005

Pete pulled up in front of Abbey Prescott's house right on time, early actually. Just as he'd planned it. He prided himself on his professionalism, even if his clients thought of him as just a handyman.

He stepped out of his metallic blue Ford pickup and stood for a moment, studying the small house. Buildings were his passion, and he never entered one without appraising it first. Gothic monstrosities or sleek cubist constructions, it didn't matter, he could find something appealing in every one of them. He liked to think buildings were a lot like people—you could always find something positive if you looked closely enough, and right now, he was quite taken with this small Victorian. In spite of the usual froufrou flourishes, the house retained an appealing simplicity. He especially liked the lattice pattern in the pediment above the porch.

Based on their one phone conversation, Pete expected his new client to be a rather stern middle-aged lady, which meant the attractive young woman who met him at the door was a surprise but no disappointment. Dressed in an outfit more suitable for corporate litigation than a home-improvement estimate, her pointy-toed high heels looked excruciating, but he liked her unusual dark blue eyes and her camera-ready smile.

"I'm Abbey," she said, offering a firm, practiced handshake in true power broker style. However, she failed to hide a wince at his calloused palm. He guessed she was used to hands that never did anything more strenuous than holding a cellphone.

He followed her down the hall but paused in front of a perfectly proportioned room and let out a low whistle as he admired the wood-trimmed front bay window, the wide plank floor, and the Victorian chandelier. The room was empty except for two Queen Anne chairs placed around a packing box and an old upright piano, its ornate cabinet decorated to look like a Greek frieze. The walls and floor needed work, and the dusty chandelier practically begged for a good cleaning, yet the overall effect was enchanting.

"You don't often see rooms like this," Pete said, wishing he'd been hired to restore this gem. "The woodwork and the floor are in great shape, and that chandelier must be over a hundred years old."

"My grandmother always called this the Beckel Parlor," Abbey said.

Clearing her throat, she motioned for him to follow her into a room with ugly blue carpeting and two lonely pieces of furniture: an incongruously modern lounge chair and a weird floor lamp that looked like a tripod with a lampshade on top.

Pete wrinkled his nose in distaste. "Nice furniture."

Abbey launched into a lecture on the merits of modern design, but Pete barely listened as she rattled on about clean lines and organic curves.

When she was done, he asked, "What work did you want to have done in here?"

"Obviously, the room needs a total face-lift," she said. "I want the old fireplace opened up and repointed. The plaster needs to be repaired, and I want the floor restored."

Pete wasn't crazy about her schoolmarmish tone, but when she lifted up a corner of the disgusting carpet, he forgot all about it. The floor underneath was the same gorgeous wood he'd admired in the parlor.

"I'll start with the fireplace," he said. "Then I'll remove the damaged areas of plaster and meld a veneer over it."

She arched her perfectly curved eyebrows. "Is a veneer the best approach? I don't want anything that looks cheap."

Pete bristled, but his voice remained congenial. "Yes, that is definitely *the best* approach. I've used this technique many times. It's standard practice. I apply a bonding agent and some reinforcing mesh followed by a couple of coats of new plaster. When I'm done you'll have gleaming walls to rival the originals. If you have any doubts, I can give you more references."

He knew she'd already called several.

"Okay," she said. "You're the expert."

The remaining doubt in her voice made him wonder if this job would be worth the hassle. Clearly, she was not going to be an easy client, and yet . . . he wanted to get his hands on that floor. With any luck, she'd be off at some corporate office most of the time and leave him alone.

She led him into the kitchen, where they sat at a round pedestal table to sort out the details. With its cheery oak cabinets and generous granite island, the room had enough warmth to offset the chilliest disposition. Even Abbey warmed up a bit. She was more flexible than he expected, readily agreeing to a somewhat sporadic work schedule that allowed him to honor his other job commitments.

"One thing I insist on," Abbey said, "is a meeting once a week to review progress and plan the next week's work schedule."

He should have guessed she'd be a micromanager, but no sense in arguing about that now.

"Fine by me," he said, digging a pencil stub and a crumpled work order out of his back pocket. "Okay, that's Abby Prescott, A-B-B-Y—"

"No," she interrupted. "It's A-B-B-E-Y."

"That's Abbey as in Westminster?"

"Exactly," Abbey said her eyes shining. "Such a

beautiful church. I'll never forget seeing the memorials to Jane Austen and the Brontë sisters."

"Have you traveled a lot?" Pete asked.

"Not as much as I'd like to," she said, and just like that, she was all business again.

The odd name suited her. For a moment, she'd looked and sounded like a different person—like someone he might want to get to know. He had to admit this job intrigued him, and it wasn't just because of the floors.

As Abbey drove the short distance to the Moravian Archives, she tried to concentrate on her second, much more important, meeting of the day; however, she couldn't stop thinking about the handyman. Kera was right, he wasn't bad-looking. Not Abbey's type, of course, but she admired his solid muscular build, and his chocolate-brown eyes were warm and inviting. A jeans type of guy, verging on sloppy. Definitely not a snappy dresser. Oh Lord, he probably had tattoos on his biceps . . . although the biceps weren't bad. She liked a man with strong arms. Maybe a tattoo wouldn't be so awful.

Abbey had expected the weekly project meetings to be a sticking point, but Pete went along with the idea even though she could sense his hesitation. He would come to appreciate her involvement soon enough. She was a project manager after all.

Abbey entered the neighborhood near the archives, a residential area struggling to avoid being engulfed by the college, and parked behind a modern redbrick structure. Before walking inside, she stopped to assess her reflection in the car window. It had been a while since she'd worn a work outfit, and the heather-gray regent jacket and black pencil skirt fit her perfectly, but the black Prada pumps were killing her. Apparently her spoiled feet preferred wearing sneakers.

Abbey hobbled up to the front desk and greeted a stringy-haired receptionist who looked like she was playing hooky from middle school.

"You need to sign in," the girl said in a bored voice, barely glancing up as she shoved a register book and pen in Abbey's direction.

Abbey filled in the date, time of arrival, her name, and reason for visit, growing more annoyed with every stroke of the crappy Bic. By the time she wrote "Research on Liesl Boeckel" in the reason column, her handwriting was nearly indecipherable.

"All personal items have to be stored in a locker," the girl said.

"What?"

"In a locker," the girl repeated slowly as if Abbey were hearing-impaired and gestured at a row of metal compartments behind her. "All personal items have to be stored in one of our lockers."

What a bunch of rigmarole just to look at some old

documents. Abbey sighed and handed over her blue bag.

"Is this a real Brahmin?" the girl asked, finally showing some interest.

"Yep," Abbey said. "So take good care of it."

The child receptionist gripped the bag with both hands, as if she had just been entrusted with the crown jewels.

Armed with only her cellphone and a low-tech pen and paper notepad, Abbey waited impatiently for the archivist to appear. Their phone conversation had been so brief, she had no idea what information might even be available.

As a distraction from her throbbing toes, her thoughts drifted back to the handyman. When she corrected him on the spelling of her first name, she'd braced herself for the inevitable comment about the Beatles album. In high school, Derrick Trolinder had tormented her relentlessly, calling her "Abbey Road" along with lots of snide remarks such as "I'd like to go down Abbey Road." But Pete never blinked, and what really threw her was his Westminster Abbey comment. Not something you typically got from the hired help.

A tall auburn-haired guy with a disarming smile appeared by her side, and her image of a fusty curmudgeon underwent a major modification. That made two miscalculations in one day. All this time off must be destroying her brain cells—she really needed to get back into the workforce.

"Hi! I'm Adam Wright. You must be Abbey," he said, offering her a smooth hand in a confident handshake.

Abbey gave him her standard once-over, admiring the prominent cheekbones, expertly styled hair, and the fashionable pair of rimless rectangular eyeglasses. As well as the subtle stripes of his classic oxford shirt and the perfect crease of his khakis. She'd always been a sucker for a well-dressed man.

"We don't have a great deal of information about Liesl Boeckel," he said, "but I've found a couple of documents. What's your interest in her?"

"Historical research."

"We get a lot of that here," Adam said with another charming smile.

"Where are the documents?" Abbey asked. He was attractive, and under different circumstances she might have enjoyed chatting, but men were off her radar. Her only interest was Liesl.

Adam led her into a room bathed in the hush of libraries everywhere. A wall of arched, floor-to-ceiling windows provided cheerful natural light and a sharp contrast to the portraits lining the two side walls. She studied the somber faces of what she supposed were archivists through the ages. At least they'd gotten better-looking over time.

"You can work here," Adam said, indicating a simple wooden table with a single chair. When he picked up a manila folder neatly annotated with "Liesl Boeckel," Abbey had to restrain herself from snatching it out of his hands.

He tapped the folder with his finger almost as if he

were purposely tantalizing her. "All the documents are in here. If you need any help, just ask."

"Thanks," Abbey said as he finally handed it to her.

Adam hung around a bit longer, but Abbey ignored him, and he eventually moved to a desk on the other side of the room. She opened the folder, eager to dig into her research without someone hovering over her. Inside, she discovered a spiral-bound report with a worn blue cover sheet sporting a coat of arms and the words "Boeckel 1190." She couldn't believe her luck. A genealogical record of the Beckel (Boeckel) family in America compiled by Frederick Truman Beckel in 1968. Abbey sped through the document, which began with the first descendant, a Syrian astrologer named Ignatius Boeckel. The name Boeckel meant "stargazer" in German, a fascinating tidbit she wished she could share with Nana.

Eventually Abbey came to George Frederick Boeckel who arrived in Bethlehem, Pennsylvania, in 1747. She scanned the rambling treatise until she discovered that George Frederick Boeckel, known as Frederick, had one son from his second marriage, and five daughters and a son from his first. Could he be Liesl's father?

Abbey shifted her reading speed into high gear, devouring the words, while still taking care to handle the pages as gently as possible. And there it was, a simple statement: "An event in the life of George Frederick Boeckel of more than passing interest, was the visit to Bethlehem of the Illustrious French General, the Marquis de Lafayette."

Abbey could scarcely breathe as she read that Lafayette stayed in the Boeckel home from September 22, 1777, to October 18, 1777. And then this sentence: "There he [Lafayette] was attentively nursed by Boeckel's wife Barbara and daughter Liesl." Abbey had found Liesl at last!

Another small paragraph indicated Liesl never married but "dedicated her life to the care of the sick and became the town nurse." Abbey searched the subsequent pages for any other references to Liesl but found none.

Scanning the rest of the document, she traced the history of the Boeckel family—now spelled Beckel—into the 1900s. At the very back of the genealogy, she found a reference to her grandparents:

Anna Christiana Beckel, born January 9, 1918.
Married 1940 to
Joseph Stuart Anders, born January 31, 1913.

She almost squealed with delight. Her grandmother *was* part of this Beckel family. No wonder Abbey felt such a kinship with Liesl.

Every so often, Adam looked over as if gauging whether she needed his help, but she was doing just fine. The next document looked even more intriguing, a booklet with the title: *A Radio Talk on Lafayette's Visit to the Beckel Home during the Revolutionary War.* The talk had been presented by a Mrs. Frederick T. Beckel on February 28, 1955.

The talk began with a lengthy recap of Lafayette's early

life followed by an equally lengthy discussion of the history of the Moravians in Bethlehem and George Frederick Boeckel's emigration to America. Abbey suppressed a yawn. *This must have been one snoozer of a radio show.*

Finally, the talk covered Lafayette's convalescence in the Boeckel home and added this: "Tradition also has it that a romance grew up between the beautiful young Liesl and Lafayette, but all thoughts of romance were soon dispelled by the urgent need of his services by the hard-pressed Revolutionary Army. Liesl never married, and what emotions lay deep in her heart no one ever knew."

Obviously, this later generation of Beckels believed a romance existed between Liesl and Lafayette. She thought of the paper she'd found inside Liesl's bookmark. If there *had* been a romance, could those messages be some kind of love letters?

Abbey opened the folder one more time and pulled out a slightly yellowed scrap of paper. Her hand trembled as she struggled to read the handwriting. At the top of the page, she could clearly see a familiar name.

Elis. Boeckel

For nursing Joseph Yates	$ 6.
For Wash, Wood & Soap	1.33.5
	$ 7.33.5

Bethlehem 2 April
1810

Abbey carefully laid the piece of paper on the table, flabbergasted that such a thing was available and feeling guilty for not wearing gloves. Grabbing her cellphone, she took several pictures, unable to take her eyes off the simple note Liesl must have handled. Was it a receipt or a bill? In any case, this seemingly insignificant scrap of paper reconfirmed Liesl's role as a nurse.

"How's the research going?" Adam interrupted in a library-level whisper.

"It's going well, but I really hoped to find Liesl's diary."

"I can't help you there, but I have her memoir."

"Are you kidding?" Abbey cried in a voice loud enough to scandalize any proper librarian. "Liesl wrote a memoir?"

"Of course. Moravians were known for creating memoirs documenting their lives and particularly their personal relationships with their savior. Let me get it for you."

"Thanks," Abbey said with a tight smile. Why hadn't he placed the memoir in her folder to begin with?

After what seemed like an eternity, Adam returned with yet another manila folder and a peculiar expression. Abbey figured out why when she opened the folder and could not read a single word on the paper inside. Scowling, she wondered what the penalty would be for strangling an archivist.

"It's written in Old German," Adam explained. "Would you like me to translate it for you?"

CHAPTER 9

September 28, 1777

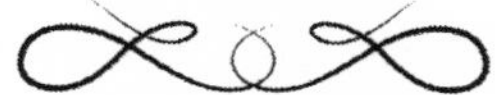

I must begin by telling you that I am perfectly well because I must end by telling you that we fought a difficult battle… and that we were not the strongest. I will have to stay in bed for a little while, which has left me in a bad mood.

—*Lafayette, letter to his wife, Adrienne*

All morning long, Conestoga wagons had rumbled down the street below Lafayette's window. He had first seen those distinctive wagons at Brandywine, where he had been duly impressed by their curved cargo holds designed to prevent contents from shifting. Even though these American colonists were mostly simple, unschooled farmers, they had an innate cleverness and an uncanny belief in their own abilities. Who else would dare to oppose one of the world's richest and most powerful nations?

Now, the town swarmed with soldiers frantically putting

up tents as they struggled to set up camp in the open ground along the Menakasie Creek. The rowdiest of the men were ripping apart the tidy Moravian fences to feed their campfires, transforming the peaceful little town from a paradise into a smoking vision of hell. Although he winced at the destruction, the scent of woodsmoke, the shouts of the men, and the nickering of the horses made him yearn for the battlefield and reminded him of all his dreams of glory still unrealized. His frustration spilled over when Liesl appeared at his door.

"When will I be allowed to return to battle?" Lafayette roared, slamming his fist on *The History of Greenland* and causing the small reading table to wobble. "I waste my time sitting here reading when I should be leading men into battle."

As Liesl knelt by his leg to unwind the white linen dressings, she spoke with exaggerated patience. "Doctor Glatt will visit again in a few days, but as he told you, a wound of this type will require at least one month to heal. It has been but one week." When Lafayette groaned with exasperation, Liesl added, "Father would not look kindly on your treatment of his valued book."

Lafayette hung his head. "*Pardonnez-moi*, my dear Liesl. I am behaving like a fool. It is the sounds of the army encampment. I traveled across the ocean to fight for liberty and freedom, not to sit and read. How disappointed General Washington must be with me."

Liesl raised her head, curiosity in her deep blue eyes. "What is he like?"

"I doubt my words can do him justice. His majestic figure and deportment make it impossible to mistake him for an ordinary man. When first I met him, he spoke to me with utmost kindness, acknowledging my personal sacrifices for the American cause. I thought I had never beheld so superb a personage. I have no doubt his name will be revered in every age by all true lovers of liberty and humanity."

"Your words are almost blasphemous, as if Washington were more God than man."

"I confess the sentiments of my heart are much stronger than so new an acquaintance should admit. However, Washington is the embodiment of all I believe in. All the wants and desires that brought me here."

"Why did you come here?"

"Because my greatest wish is for the happiness and liberty of this country."

"Count Zinzendorf once said, 'We have nothing to do, but to be happy.'"

"A man after mine own heart," Lafayette said, pressing a hand to his chest.

"My father would say Count Zinzendorf was referring to the happiness that follows a life devoted to duty."

"And what do you say?" Lafayette leaned forward, admiring her swan-like neck as she bent over his leg and noting the single strand of blond hair that had escaped from her snug Haube.

"I am no longer certain where duty ends and happiness

begins," Liesl said, and then went completely still, as if shocked by her own statement.

"Why is that?"

"My work is done here," Liesl said, ignoring his question. She secured his bandage and left the room.

Lafayette stared out the window, thinking about the concept of duty versus happiness, and for the first time, he wondered how his Adrienne was managing without him. He knew she wanted for nothing; her father would see to that. But could leaving his wife to come to America be considered a dereliction of duty? He refused to believe so, even though he knew his father-in-law would vehemently disagree. Lafayette had acted according to a higher good, and his choice would result in a better world for all. Surely, Adrienne understood that.

Lafayette worried that Liesl might avoid him after their awkward exchange, but later that afternoon, she and Mother Boeckel joined him as usual for what he called the Ritual of the Great Cake. Soon after his arrival, he had expressed sadness at no longer enjoying the French custom of eating a sweet in the afternoon. Upon hearing his sorry lament, Mother Boeckel immediately offered to bake one of her renowned sugar cakes, and now, the three of them gathered daily for a relaxing social time after young George Frederick succumbed to his afternoon nap.

Mother Boeckel proudly laid her sugar cake on the round table as Liesl set out plates, small wine goblets, and a finely etched decanter filled with a cherry-red concoction. In France, Lafayette would have taken hot tea; however, amiable guest that he was, he readily accepted Mother Boeckel's suggestion to serve her red currant wine instead.

As Mother Boeckel sliced the cake, Liesl raised an eyebrow at the generous portions. "I still maintain sugar cake is hardly a component of a healthy diet."

"I beg to differ," Lafayette said. "In France, an afternoon sweet is considered *de rigueur*. Even Marie Antoinette indulges in this practice daily."

Mother Boeckel's face reddened as she added, "And here in Bethlehem, the entire community praises my sugar cake."

Lafayette smiled as Liesl sighed in defeat, and then, he proposed a toast. "To Mother Boeckel and her Great Cake!"

Mother Boeckel beamed as the three raised their goblets. The wine offered no discernible aroma but tasted sweet and tangy. While it was no substitute for a Margaux, Lafayette's wine of choice, it was drinkable enough. Following the toast, Lafayette pointed his wine glass toward the sugar cake.

"Tell me, Mother Boeckel, how do you create this heavenly delight?" he said, even though he had asked the same question the day before.

"One might think you planned to take up baking when you return to France," Mother Boeckel chided, although she clearly appreciated his interest. "First, I make the dough and allow it to rise through the night. Then I poke holes in its surface and fill each one with a simple mixture of butter, brown sugar, and ground cinnamon."

"But Mother Boeckel, you crafty cook, you have left out the most important ingredient!" he said.

Mother Boeckel blushed. "The secret ingredient, as you well know, is the potato. I add mashed potato to the dough for it is the potato that makes the sugar cake light and fluffy."

Lafayette raised his goblet once more. "To the potato!"

At that moment, young George Frederick returned noisily to consciousness, and Mother Boeckel ran to his side.

"Your frame of mind is much improved since this morning," Liesl said.

"How could I not be filled with cheer in such fine company?"

He did feel strangely content with the heat of the sun pouring in the window behind him caressing his shoulders, and the red current wine warming his belly. Not to mention the girl seated across from him in the small wooden chair, erect as any queen, her pale fingers languidly encircling the wine glass as she slowly sipped the ruby liquid. In a sudden rush of passion, he wished he could bring her to him, set her on his knee, and taste the wine that lay upon her lips. His better self immediately admonished him. Had he forgotten who she was? A Moravian maid, as unattainable as any Roman goddess, like

Diana the huntress or Venus on a scallop shell, immutable and forever beyond his reach.

Sated with cake and wine, Liesl retrieved her half-finished bookmark from the sideboard and sat on a spindle chair near the kitchen hearth. Using her tambour drum, she had already created several flowers, including a vibrant blue dahlia. Now, she pulled out her brand-new British needle to create dainty vines around the flowers. As she worked, she thought about how different Lafayette's ambitions were from hers. Her life had been bound by duty for so long, any personal pursuit seemed like the imaginings of a child. While many would say Lafayette had spurned his duty to his family and his country by coming here, he believed in himself above all else. His absolute certainty made her wonder: Must her sole source of happiness be the satisfaction of duty properly performed?

When she held out her bookmark to survey her progress, she was surprised to see the vines had become intertwined in a way she had not originally planned. The blue dahlia was so tightly surrounded, it almost looked imprisoned.

That evening, as she trudged up the stairs to remove Lafayette's dinner tray, Liesl told herself she must stop having these conversations with him for they only led to thoughts best avoided. But when she reached the sitting room, Lafayette once again assumed she had nothing better to do than listen to his ruminations.

"Please let me share with you what I am learning about Greenland from this wondrous tome," he said, and then proceeded with an enthusiastic description of the travails suffered by the Moravians in Greenland. How they struggled to find sufficient food and initially survived mostly on seaweed. And how they expended great effort to construct accommodations for the growing number of missionaries, all while struggling to address the unusual linguistic challenges.

Lafayette prattled on about subpolar climates, traditional sleds pulled by dogs, and the terrible epidemic of smallpox, a disease that caused such excruciating pain, the afflicted often stabbed themselves or jumped into the sea.

While Liesl liked the sound of his French-accented English, her father had told the same tales many times, and she found herself moving restlessly about the room. Just as she was contemplating jumping into the sea herself, Lafayette finally noticed her growing boredom.

"I see your thoughts are elsewhere," he said with a touch of pique.

"I apologize, monsieur. Perhaps I should leave you now."

"I beg you to stay. I do so enjoy your company." Lafayette searched the room for a new diversion, and his eyes landed on a flute propped in the corner. "Is the flute yours?

"No, it belongs to Mother Boeckel."

"May I play it? It has been many years, but I believe I may still be able to coax some manner of notes from it."

Liesl hesitated but then sighed and handed him the flute. It was easier than devising an acceptable excuse. The truth would be too hard to tell, bringing with it memories of heartbreak and tears.

He raised the flute to his lips with practiced ease and played a spirited version of a movement from one of the Brandenburg Concertos. He actually played quite well, but Liesl could not dispel the melancholy of seeing the instrument in use once again.

"You look so unhappy. Do I play that poorly?" Lafayette asked as he set the instrument aside.

"No, no. I confess I am not very fond of the flute."

"What instrument do you play?"

"Sadly, I never mastered one; however, when I was a little girl I sang. One year, I led the congregation in the singing of the hymn 'Jesus Call Thou Me' on Christmas Eve. It was quite an honor."

"I would be most honored if you would sing for me."

Liesl remembered trembling with excitement when she was chosen to perform for the community. The weeks of practice flew by, until at last, she filed into the chapel with the other children and took her place on a wooden bench, facing the congregation. Candles flickered on every window sill, and the white walls glistened in the gentle light. The Christmas Pyramids stood in each corner, as if the floor had sprouted perfectly shaped trees. The pyramidal frames were like naked tepees whose wooden supports were covered with fresh greens and decorated with candles, fruits, and Bible passages written on small scraps of paper. All adding sparkling light and contrasting colors to the dark-green boughs. Despite her nervousness, Liesl had felt as if she were sitting in the center of a woodland clearing, surrounded by the deep calm of a forest.

Closing her eyes, Liesl could still smell the scent of pine mixed with the sweetness of beeswax candles and hear the swish of the newly starched white dresses worn by the Single Sisters who had fluttered like angels about the room.

"Father was so proud of me," Liesl whispered, hardly aware of Lafayette waiting in expectation. Then she sang in a sweet, clear and slightly husky voice:

Jesus, call thou me
from the world to thee;
speed me ever, stay me never;
Jesus, call thou me.

Not Jerusalem -
lowly Bethlehem
'twas that gave us Christ to save us;
not Jerusalem.

Favored Bethlehem!

honored is that name;
thence came Jesus to release us;
favored Bethlehem!

Wondrous Child divine!
warm this heart of mine;
keep it burning, for thee yearning,
wondrous Child divine!

Jesus, call thou me
from the world to thee;
speed me ever, stay me never;
Jesus, call thou me.

After a moment of silence, Lafayette found his voice. "That truly was divine," he said, making no attempt to hide his emotion.

He paused and then added, "I see that I must include singing on your lengthy list of accomplishments. I shall add it just below your knowledge of pumping water!"

Liesl turned from him and left the room without saying a word. For an instant, she had felt a true connection with Lafayette, something she rarely experienced with anyone. But then, he reverted to his usual cavalier self, and now she felt only embarrassed.

CHAPTER 10

The Project

September 2005

"It's going to be a bit noisy," Pete apologized, as he carried an assortment of buckets into her dining room.

Pete had arrived for his first day of work wearing a frayed flannel shirt and jeans so stained they reminded Abbey of a Jackson Pollock painting. But appearances to the contrary, he was a fastidious worker, and she was pleased to see him laying tarps all around the fireplace. He'd even placed long strips of cardboard along the hallway before rolling in an industrial grade Shop-Vac.

"It'll be dusty too. But I'll control that as best as I can," he said.

Then, he lugged in the biggest drill motor she'd ever seen, giving her a glimpse of bulging arm muscles beneath his ratty shirt. Always curious, Abbey followed him out to his pickup to see what else he'd brought with him. The day felt more like August than September, warm and humid with a blazing sun overhead. She stopped in front of something that looked like another throwback to summer: a bright-green rectangle about the size of a child's backyard swimming pool.

"And what is this?" she asked.

Pete looked sheepish. "It's a Bagster. A dumpster in a bag."

She laughed. "I've never seen anything like it."

"I know it looks corny, but it works great. It'll hold all the rubbish from the fireplace, and when I'm done, the Waste Management guys will come haul it away."

"Sounds good to me," she said, and gave him her first genuine smile.

As Pete had warned her, the job *was* noisy. The earsplitting squeal of the big drill made her teeth hurt, as she envisioned unspeakable dental procedures. But Pete used the Shop-Vac constantly to keep the dust down and was careful not to slam the front door as he made trip after trip out to the Bagster. By the end of the day, the old fireplace was visible and all the rubbish was hauled away just as he'd promised.

Abbey peered into the dark space Pete had uncovered, carefully avoiding brushing against him. "How does it look?"

"You're in luck. The original fireplace is intact, and in pretty good shape. It shouldn't need too much work."

"That's great news. You made real progress today. Thanks!"

"You're welcome," Pete said. "As soon as the fireplace is ready to use, I'll have the building inspector come by."

He certainly knew what he was doing, and she couldn't help being impressed.

"You're the boss," she said without a trace of sarcasm.

On Thursday, Pete showed up in an outfit with fewer stains but still something most men of her acquaintance would never wear, especially not in public. He got right to work, and she started her own project: cleaning out the kitchen. Nana always said music and cooking went together like chocolate chip cookies and milk, and her old stereo console still sat behind the kitchen table. Abbey carefully placed one of Nana's favorite records on the turntable and was surprised to hear Pete humming along with the music.

When she walked by the dining room, he called out, "You can't beat Bellini, and *Norma* is one of his best."

"You like classical music?"

"Don't sound so surprised. My grandfather was an orchestra conductor in his spare time. He played classical records constantly, but he was more of an orchestral guy, especially Beethoven. Never listened to opera."

"Both my grandmother and my mother were opera lovers, particularly Bellini."

"I discovered Bellini when I backpacked around Europe," Pete said. "I took a ferry from Naples to Sicily and ended up in Catania. I knew nothing about opera, but the woman who ran the hostel insisted I go to a concert at the Teatro Massimo Bellini to hear the music of their hometown hero. I saw *I Puritani*, and from then on, I was hooked. I even visited the building where Bellini was born."

Abbey leaned against the doorjamb. A classical music fan and a world traveler. Who was this handyman?

"My mom would have loved that. She always said she was drawn to Bellini because he accomplished so much in such a short time. He was only thirty-four when he died." Abbey could feel herself getting emotional, and her voice turned harsh as she struggled to stay in control. "But I suppose you already know all about Bellini."

Pete ignored her tone and inquired gently, "Do your parents live around here?"

"My dad lives in California with his new wife and twin boys." She paused, and looked down at the blue carpet. "Mom died when I was eighteen. When I listen to Bellini, I sense her spirit in the music."

"I'm sorry," Pete said.

The last thing she needed was sympathy from a stranger. She returned to the kitchen, turned off the old stereo, and slammed a couple of cabinet doors to make herself feel better. She wasn't even sure why she was angry—Pete was only being kind. Maybe she was mad at herself for revealing something so personal.

Or maybe she was mad at Michael for never even asking about her family.

With her kitchen finally in working order, Abbey was ready to give it a test run—even though the only kitchen appliances she ever used at her condo were the microwave and her coffee maker. Pete had half-heartedly agreed to join her for their first weekly meeting after he finished up in the dining room, and she planned to make it worth his while. Especially since she still felt guilty about her rude behavior earlier in the week.

She pulled Nana's Mixmaster out of a perfectly organized kitchen cabinet. Abbey had given away a pile of things, including some canning pots and boxes of jars to a very appreciative Mrs. Dotter. And Kera had scooped up an assortment of Tupperware containers destined for second careers storing crayons and other third-grade supplies. But the Mixmaster was one kitchen item Abbey would never part with.

The stainless steel mixer looked brand-new even though it had churned out hundreds of batches of cookies—not to mention cakes, muffins, and dark, gooey brownies. She and Nana had spent many happy hours in this kitchen, laughing and singing along with Nana's records as they whipped up decadent delights, including Abbey's favorite treat, Moravian sugar cookies.

Nana wrote her recipes on three-by-five cards, which she stored in two dark-green file boxes that looked like they may have seen military duty during one of the great wars. Abbey quickly thumbed through the recipes behind the "S" tab and pulled out a tattered yellow card awash in brownish stains.

Instead of Nana's stereo, Abbey turned to her Bose Wave, and soon the music of Roy Orbison soared through the room. The whirring of the mixer nearly drowned out poor Roy, but the familiar drone was comforting. She felt as if Nana were standing next to her, nodding with approval. Abbey loaded up two cookie trays, and within minutes of closing the oven door, the tempting smell of baked goods got Pete's attention.

He followed the scent into her kitchen, sniffing the air like a hound dog tracking a fox. "Are you baking?"

"Does that surprise you?"

"Maybe," Pete said, a slow grin spreading across his face.

"I'm making sugar cookies. Want some?"

"You bet! Let me clean up, and I'll be right back. I like the music too. Nothing like the Big O."

"The Big O? Never heard him called that before."

"I got the nickname from my dad. He even saw Roy in person once."

"Lucky man. My college roommate owned every one of Roy's CDs. Whenever one of us went through a breakup, we'd sing 'It's Over' until we were hoarse."

Pete's voice boomed from the powder room at the end of the hall, totally butchering his attempt to mimic Roy's operatic vocals. While she couldn't fault his taste in music, his singing voice sounded more like primal scream therapy. Still, the smell of the cookies and the familiar melody filled her with an unexpected contentment. The first time she and Nana baked these cookies together, Abbey had to stand on a chair. When they were done, Nana had lifted her up, kissed her, and swung her around. The oven timer buzzed, disrupting the memory, but the feeling of being airborne still remained.

She loaded two coffee cups and a plate of golden-topped cookies onto a tray.

"I'll carry that," Pete said, and followed her out into the garden.

The Indian-summer day was too tempting to stay indoors. Nana's garden was stippled with sunlight, and her Knock Out roses really delivered a punch as the afternoon rays amplified the rosy red of each small petal.

The wrought iron garden chairs on the patio were missing their cushions, but Pete didn't seem to mind as he sipped his coffee and munched on a sugar cookie. "These are incredibly good," he said, and added with a sly look, "Funny, I never would have pegged you as the domestic type."

"I am a woman of many talents."

"I don't doubt that for a minute."

They sat in companionable silence while Pete licked his index finger and used it to dab up every last crumb.

"What's with the Buddha?" he asked, pointing to a small statue seated on a pedestal surrounded by rosebushes.

"Nana was a big fan."

"Really?"

"Nana traveled the world and was always open to new ideas. She loved to quote the Buddha. Her favorite was 'No one saves us but ourselves. No one can and no one may. We ourselves must walk the path.'"

"She sounds like a neat lady."

"She was," Abbey said, feeling a rush of grief when she used the past tense. She stared at the Buddha, seeking some inner calm before gathering up the dishes and carrying the tray back into the kitchen. She returned with a pen and some papers.

"I've developed a work plan," Abbey announced, producing two copies of a sizable spreadsheet.

"Impressive, but I'm really more of a seat-of-the-pants kind of guy."

"It never hurts to have some structure."

"I lived a structured life once, and it didn't work for me," Pete said.

Abbey studied his suddenly serious face, waiting for an explanation, but when he offered nothing more, she forged on. "I have a lot of experience with this. I was a project manager. Managed multimillion-dollar projects."

"No kidding. I doubt we'll hit the million-dollar mark, but who knows? I could have some serious cost overruns."

Abbey couldn't hold back a smile. She was finding it impossible not to like Pete Schaeffer. Still, she had to stay focused. This was a negotiation after all, and she always liked to come out on top.

She reviewed her plan, noting the completed task of reopening the fireplace and a new task for obtaining approval from the building inspector. Next, she covered the remaining jobs, including repairing and plastering the walls and refinishing the flooring. Pete made no comment, which she assumed meant he was satisfied with her detailed descriptions of the steps required. A good thing since she'd spent the previous evening slogging through do-it-yourself home repair websites, making sure she got the processes and the lingo right.

They discussed her ideas for some additional work, and with Pete's approval, Abbey took notes for new tasks, including installing extra electrical outlets and finding an oak mantel to mount above the fireplace.

After reviewing the next week's schedule, she tried not to look smug. "That wasn't so awful, was it?"

"The cookies helped. I guess having a plan isn't a bad idea. Okay, Madame Project Manager, we'll try doing it your way."

Abbey smiled. She was used to that.

"I should get going," Pete said. "Wouldn't want to run up any overtime with the MPM."

She wrinkled her nose at the nickname, but she enjoyed talking with him. He was good company and actually listened to what she had to say. She'd been alone so much lately, she hated to see him leave.

"Let me tell you about my other project," she said.

Abbey described what she'd learned about Liesl and Lafayette on her visits to the Moravian Museum and the Moravian Archives. Pete listened intently, his expression unchanged except for a slight narrowing of his eyes when she mentioned Adam Wright. She wondered briefly if they knew each other, but before she could ask, Pete had a question of his own.

"This house belonged to the Beckel family, right? That would explain why your grandmother called the living room the Beckel Parlor. Which means you and Liesl are probably related!"

Abbey nodded and told him about discovering her grandparents in the Boeckel family genealogy. Pete seemed just as intrigued by Liesl as she was.

"But wait until you see this." Abbey flew up the stairs to retrieve the bookmark from its hiding place in her nightstand. She'd decided to keep it out of sight. Maybe that was a bit paranoid, but she wanted to keep her discovery a secret at least until she had a better idea of what was going on. And yet, she wanted to show it to Pete. She wasn't usually so impulsive, but somehow, she knew she could trust him.

She opened the drawer and pushed aside the plastic bag holding the cryptic piece of paper she'd found hidden inside the bookmark. She wasn't ready to share that with anyone. After her visit to the archives, she'd studied the writing more closely using a magnifying glass, but the words were still impossible to decipher. Each entry appeared to be signed, and the signatures may have started with the letter "L." But maybe that was just wishful thinking.

"This is a remarkable piece of work," Pete said, holding up the bookmark so the brilliantly colored flowers blazed in the bright sunlight. "Hard to believe it's more than two hundred years old. Your Liesl was quite an artist."

"I think so. I'm hoping her memoir will tell me more about her. Adam is supposed to have the translation finished next week."

Pete looked ready to share something significant but instead he said, "It's pretty cool that Liesl took care of the famous Lafayette. Do you really think he broke her heart?"

"Maybe. I just know I need to find out."

CHAPTER 11

September 29, 1777

My patient Lafayette is as difficult as I expected. He is petulant and demanding, and yet I am inexplicably drawn to him for he is unlike anyone I have ever known.

—Diary of Sister Liesl Boeckel

"Good morning, monsieur," Liesl said, as she entered Lafayette's sitting room alone, for Mother Boeckel no longer even attempted to fulfill her role as chaperone. Apparently, she had fallen victim to the Frenchman's charms and no longer deemed Lafayette a danger to her stepdaughter.

"Is it?" Lafayette asked. "I would not know for I am unable to sleep at night due to the deep throbbing in my leg. And I have nothing to occupy my mind during the day, so all I think about is my constant pain and the fact that I am incapable of accomplishing anything worthwhile!"

Liesl merely nodded, offering little in the way of

sympathy as she examined the offending limb. Men were always the worst patients. While women bore suffering in silence, men could not stop talking about every single ache and pain. Besides, she was still annoyed with the way the previous evening had ended.

"You seem unusually quiet, my dear nurse. Are you not feeling well?" Lafayette asked when he finally shifted his attention away from himself.

Liesl gathered up her basket and headed for the door. "I am fine."

"Before you leave me, may I ask a favor?"

"You may."

"Would you procure for me paper, pen, and ink? I would like very much to resume my daily correspondence."

"But of course," Liesl said. Perhaps his writings would distract him from thinking too much about his pain.

She wrote every day herself, updating her diary as she had been taught to do since she first learned to read and write. The diary normally contained nothing of great interest, but she had recently begun placing it beneath her mattress, preferring to keep it out of sight.

She had almost reached the doorway when the faint sound of music drew her to the window.

"What is it?" Lafayette asked.

"The trombone choir," she said. "Trombonists play from the belfry of the Bell House so their music can be heard throughout the town. They announce the arrival of sunrise on Christmas and Easter and provide other communications throughout the year."

Liesl concentrated on the somber tones. "A married woman has passed from this world to the next."

"How do you know that?"

"The trombone choir informs us of every death with three hymns," Liesl explained. "The first announces a death, the second identifies which choir has been affected, and the third, which we are hearing now, offers comfort to the community." She whispered the words of the last refrain, "Lord, when I am departing, depart thou not from me."

"Liesl, I am sorry for your loss."

She turned from the window. "I must leave, for I fear Sister Johanette Luise has died in childbirth and help will be needed to care for the infant. Her pregnancy was a difficult one from the beginning, and as of late, she seemed much distressed by the disruption caused by the arrival of the army. As you must realize, it is not only soldiers who suffer when the world is turned upside down by war."

The home of Sister Johanette Luise and her husband, Caleb, lay at the northern end of the main street, one of the newer, two-story homes on the outskirts of town. By the time Liesl entered the small front room, Doctor Glatt and one of the other medical assistants were lifting the lifeless body onto a wooden pallet. Liesl barely noticed the high-pitched cries of the squalling infant; instead she stood paralyzed at the sight of the pale face and frail body wrapped in bloody linens. Johanette Luise was only one year older than herself.

"Sister Liesl, the infant needs attending," Doctor Glatt said as he gestured toward a corner of the room where Brother Caleb sat slumped on a chair, holding his head in his hands. Inside a wooden cradle at his side, a flurry of little limbs thrashed the air.

"I have sent for some fresh cow's milk," Doctor Glatt said. "A boy will bring it soon."

"In the meantime, I shall feed the infant some sugar water," Liesl said, her medical training overriding her sadness.

"Excellent idea," Dr. Glatt said with a nod that conveyed his confidence in her.

Liesl wrapped a blanket around the baby boy as best she could and lifted the flailing creature to her chest. She had held babies before, of course, but never one this new or this frenzied. Without thinking, she began to sway back and forth, a soothing motion that at least slowed the unrelenting kicking.

"Brother Caleb," Liesl said, but the man never raised his head. "Brother Caleb," she repeated in a loud, authoritative tone. "Your son needs your help. Please bring me some clean water and some sugar. Can you do that?"

Brother Caleb shook his head as if awakening from a dream, or in this case, a nightmare. "Yes, of course. I will get it now."

"And a piece of clean cloth."

Liesl looked down at the tiny face and kissed the downy cheek. No child deserved to come into this world motherless.

Brother Caleb returned with a liquid-filled teacup, a sugar bowl made from baked clay, and a half-finished bit of blanket.

"Johanette Luise had not yet completed this for the little one," he said, wiping away tears with the back of his hand.

"It shall supply him with his first meal," Liesl said as she mixed some sugar into the water. She dipped a corner of the blanket into the cup and brushed the baby's lips with the wet cloth until the tiny mouth opened and began to suck. At last the little legs and arms went limp.

"How did you know exactly what to do?" Brother Caleb asked.

"I had an excellent teacher. A kind man who taught me of medical matters."

She couldn't stop the thought that followed: *Matthew and I might have had a child just like this one.* She clutched the baby even tighter, not sure at that moment who needed the other more.

The front door opened and suddenly the small room was filled with people. A boy stumbled in and splattered the stone floor with fresh milk as he rushed to lift a bucket onto the table. Sister Johanette Luise's mother arrived right behind him, and despite her distraught state, wasted no time taking charge. She ordered Caleb to clean up the spilled milk, thanked Liesl for her help, and wrested the infant from her arms, leaving Liesl feeling empty and bereft.

After finishing an ample serving of chicken pie, Lafayette stretched out his legs, even though the injured one ached whenever he moved it, and closed his eyes. He tried to picture Liesl dealing with the death of a young mother. How calm and capable she would be. She was truly remarkable, and the more he learned about her, the more impressed he became. If he concentrated, he could still hear her sweet clear voice singing "Jesus Call Thou Me." And he could feel again the wave of tenderness that had engulfed him and left him shaken.

At last, he heard gentle footsteps in the hallway and was soon rewarded with the sight of Liesl entering his room.

"I can see your news is not good," he said, noting her sagging shoulders.

"As I feared, Sister Johanette Luise died from complications during childbirth. Her mother has taken charge of the infant."

"My cousin Marie died in childbirth," Lafayette said. "When I lived with my grandmother, Marie and my Aunt Charlotte lived there as well. Marie had a face like an angel and the soul of an artist with an uncanny ability to capture the essence of a person on paper. She loved to sketch the peasants in the village. She made me laugh with her bold drawings of the *boulanger* who was as wide as he was tall and whose wispy hair was always streaked with flour. And the *boucher* with hands like mutton chops and a seldom-washed apron attesting to countless bloody hackings. I still have some of her drawings."

"She meant a great deal to you."

Lafayette bowed his head to hide the sadness he knew must be plain on his face. "I adored her. Her death was my greatest sorrow." After several moments, he raised his eyes to hers. "I am sorry for your loss and for the poor child. It is difficult to be without a mother. My mother died when I was twelve years old."

"And what of your father?"

"I never really knew him. He died when I was a baby. Killed by a British cannonball during the Seven Years' War at the Battle of Minden."

"Which means that when your mother died, you became an orphan," Liesl said.

"Yes." He paused, allowing the familiar surge of grief and anger to roll over him. His mother's death still shocked him, as if the universe had played an unfair trick. "I became the richest orphan in France. And you? When did your mother die?"

"I was seventeen. A grown girl."

"Still, it must have been hard for you."

"Only my mother truly understood me, and I miss her every day. I was with her in her final hours. She knew she was dying, and the closer her time came, the more she longed for it. At the end, she sang. I could barely hear her, but I recognized the words of her favorite hymn: 'Come, O Father's saving Son / who o'er sin the vict'ry won / Boundless shall your kingdom be / grant that we its glories see.'" Liesl took a deep breath. "And then she fell asleep for the last time."

"She had a peaceful death."

"Yes. I was glad for that."

"And then your father remarried."

"It was difficult for him to be alone, and he did not know what to do with me. Not that Mother Boeckel does either. She is a good woman, but she is overwhelmed by motherhood and has little time to concern herself with a grown stepdaughter. Which suits me quite well.

"In spite of all the changes, my new family members bring me great pleasure, and I particularly enjoy watching Father struggle with young George Frederick. While my sisters and I were always cowed by Father's raging temper, George Frederick simply laughs as if Father's shouting were part of a game."

"Perhaps your father has finally met his match," Lafayette said, thinking how fitting that would be. "I like Mother Boeckel very much, and I could not endure without her sugar cake. Which by the way, I did not enjoy nearly as much as usual without your presence."

"I am sure you managed quite well without me," Liesl said, and looked ready to leave, but then hesitated as if debating with herself. "I would like to hear more about your childhood."

Lafayette was happy to comply. "As I told you before, I spent my earliest years with my grandmother, running wild in the Auvergne. When I was eleven years old, Mother summoned me to Paris. I was sad to leave the countryside and had little curiosity about the city. Nevertheless, it had been decided I must carry on the family martial tradition."

He gave her a wry smile. "You must understand, I come from a long line of renowned military men. One of my ancestors acquired the true Crown of Thorns during the Sixth Crusade, and another, Gilbert de Lafayette III, served as a companion-at-arms with Joan of Arc during the Siege of Orléans. The men of my family have always been soldiers. In fact, so large a proportion of fathers and sons were killed on the field of battle, the misfortunes of my family became a kind of warning. *Un proverbe prudence* for those who would send their sons to war."

Lafayette paused as he considered a new topic. He always enjoyed talking about himself, and she was a good listener. "Do you know my full name?"

"I know you only as the Marquis de Lafayette."

"I will tell you my full name, but only if you promise not to laugh."

"I promise," Liesl said, her eyes dancing with anticipation.

"Marie-Joseph-Paul-Yves-Roch-Gilbert du Motier, Marquis de Lafayette, Baron de Vissac, Seigneur de St. Romain."

Liesl struggled to control herself, but in the end, she was unable to suppress a giggle. "I have never heard of such a name in all my life! And one of your names is Marie? Is that not a name for a girl?"

Lafayette pretended to be affronted. "I would be happy to tell you my whole life story, which I might add *you* requested, provided you contain your mirth."

"I apologize, monsieur. I shall try harder, but please understand you are like a rare, exotic bird that has gone off course and landed here among our common flock."

"An interesting comment. I only hope you will acknowledge I am well plumed!"

Liesl covered her face with both hands but not before Lafayette glimpsed a maidenly blush.

"I was always meant to be a soldier," Lafayette said. "I was baptized like a Spaniard, with the name of every conceivable saint who might offer me protection in battle. When I arrived in Paris, my great-grandfather enrolled me in a private school for young knights, and for the first time, I carried a scabbard and a sword. And wore a powdered wig. I could have done without the wig, but my education was a revelation. I studied great thinkers like Isaac Newton, John Locke, and Voltaire who declared that all men should have the right to a fair trial, freedom of speech, and freedom of religion. My mind reeled with new ideas, and I became an outspoken pupil. My teacher once described the virtues of an obedient horse as one that submitted at the sight of the whip. I disagreed, saying the perfect horse is one that, at the sight of the whip, has the sense to throw his rider to the ground."

"You have quite a different understanding of obedience than I do," Liesl said, looking quite prim.

"Perhaps. But despite the many differences in our backgrounds and opinions, you and I are much alike. And I cannot recall when I have enjoyed conversing as much as I do with you."

"No doubt that is only because of your limited circumstances," Liesl said, but her smile belied her words. "*Bonne nuit*, Marie-Joseph-Paul-Yves-Gilbert, Marquis de Lafayette."

"You missed a few, but close enough," Lafayette said with an approving look. "I am impressed with you, mademoiselle, as always."

CHAPTER 12

The Lover

September 2005

Abbey sipped her coffee and tapped her newly painted nails on the table of a booth at the Brew Works. When Adam called saying he'd completed the translation of Liesl's memoir, she'd been ecstatic. However, he refused to divulge any details over the phone and insisted on a lunchtime meeting. The coffee was part of her plan to derail any ideas Adam might have about a lengthy beer-drinking lunch. Even though she preferred wine, she could feel her resolve weakening as tray after tray of foam-topped glasses passed by. The yeasty smell in the air didn't help either.

Adam finally arrived, looking as groomed and pressed as the last time. He slid into the booth and greeted her with a big smile that dimmed when he noticed her cup of coffee. "No beer? You can't come to the Brew Works and drink coffee."

"I'm not much of a beer drinker," Abbey said.

They placed their orders, a tall cold one and a burger for Adam and a Cobb salad along with a coffee refill for her. After some inconsequential small talk, Abbey handed Adam a check, and asked him for the translated memoir. He seemed hesitant to part with it but finally handed over a typed sheet of paper.

Abbey eagerly scanned the translation, mumbling bits of it out loud as she searched for one name in particular. When she didn't find it, she waved the paper at Adam.

"Is this all of it?"

"I'm afraid so."

"But there's no mention of Lafayette." She reread the translated memoir once more, hoping she had missed something.

"Take a closer look at the first sentence."

Abbey read aloud, "On October 1, 1831, our Sister Elisabeth Boeckel blessedly departed; she did not leave behind anything in writing about her course of life through this time; therefore, only the following can be said."

Abbey tossed the translation back at Adam. "You told me Moravians always wrote their own memoirs!"

"And that is almost always the case. In fact, this is the first time I've ever seen one that wasn't written by the individual. Most Moravian memoirs include a postscript written by someone who attended the death, but other than that, the memoir is a personal testament."

"Then why didn't Liesl write hers?"

"I have a theory," Adam said with a smile.

"I'm listening."

"I learned a memoir might be rewritten if it failed to display the accepted ideals of the community."

"Is that what you think happened with Liesl's memoir?" Abbey asked.

"Actually, I do," Adam said. "I believe there was some kind of relationship between Liesl and Lafayette, and when Liesl confessed to it in her memoir, that memoir was destroyed, and the one we have was written to take its place. Look at the last line."

Abbey picked up the memoir once again and read, "She had a lively disposition from her youth yet was not mindless to the most blessed and needful part." She looked up at Adam. "The last six words are underlined."

Adam pulled out a small memo pad and read from his scribbled notes. "The 'most blessed and needful part' comes from the writings of a famous Moravian educator named John Amos Comenius. Comenius saw the world as a labyrinth of confusion where seeking worldly pleasure only resulted in unhappiness. The one needful part was God. Maybe the writer of the memoir is telling us that even though Liesl was tempted to seek happiness in earthly desires, she eventually chose the most needful part."

Abbey tried to contain her excitement. Adam's detailed research and analysis impressed her, and she wanted to believe a connection between Liesl and Lafayette might still exist. But could she trust Adam? She studied his still expression as he waited for her reaction. The Michael experience had made her skittish, but she wasn't going to let that hold her back. She pulled the bookmark from her blue bag.

"According to my grandmother, this bookmark belonged to Liesl. Maybe you could take a look at it?"

Adam carefully accepted the colorful rectangle, holding it with something like reverence.

"I'll do better than that," he said. "I'll show it to Martha Brown at the Kemerer. You know, the Museum of Decorative Arts? Martha's an expert on colonial embroidery. If anyone can tell us more, it'll be her."

"*C'est extraordinaire*," Kera said as she studied Abbey's cellphone photo of the painting with Lafayette, Mrs. Boeckel, and Liesl. "You've learned a lot about Liesl already."

She and Kera sat around a glass coffee table on opposing love seats in Abbey's sunroom, drinking rioja and sharing some excellent aged Manchego cheese. Strings of vintage-style Edison bulbs crisscrossed the ceiling, and in typical Nana-style, the rattan loveseats were covered in a riotous pattern of lavender irises and turquoise-blue columbines. Nana had added the glassed-in room to the back of the Victorian years ago, despite the neighbors' vocal complaints about compromising the authenticity of the historic neighborhood. It was Abbey's favorite part of the house.

"I still can't believe Liesl is real," Kera said. "I honestly thought she was just a legend."

"I feel a real connection with her," Abbey said, taking a sip of wine and swishing it around in her mouth.

"And what about Pete and this new archivist guy? Any connections happening there? Any sparks flying?"

"Hardly. I have no interest in men at the moment." Pete's gentle smile and Adam's handsome cheekbones flashed through her mind, but she was sticking to her story. "Liesl is my new obsession. All I want to do right now is find out more about her."

Kera raised her eyebrows as she nibbled her cheese, and Abbey turned her attention to the afghan draped across the back of the love seat, fingering the faded red, white, and blue checks.

"Remember how Nana always used to call this a coverlet? Such an old-fashioned word."

Kera sighed. "Let's not get sidetracked. I still don't understand why you moved back here. Or why you suddenly have no interest in men."

Abbey figured she knew what was coming, but instead of demanding a confession, Kera reached into her bag, a sack-like woven thing in psychedelic colors, and removed a skinny brown rectangle.

"You didn't!" Abbey cried, immediately recognizing the diamond-shaped pattern of the French chocolatier, Michel Cluizel.

Kera tore away the wrapping on the chocolate bar and

stretched across the coffee table to hand a piece to Abbey. "I did. Sometimes bribery is the only way to go."

"Oh my God," Abbey said as the smooth dark chocolate dissolved in her mouth.

"You owe me now."

Abbey savored the luscious flavor for a minute longer. As much as she hated sharing this story, she knew Kera would wheedle it out of her eventually. And what good did keeping secrets do anyway? Look at Liesl with her hidden messages. More than two hundred years had passed, and Abbey was still determined to solve that mystery.

"Okay, I'll tell you the real reason I moved here. His name is Michael. He was my boss, and he was married. It sounds so pathetic. I never thought I would be stupid enough to get involved with a married man."

Kera broke off a piece of chocolate for herself. "We all do foolish things."

"I wanted to get ahead, to be successful, but I never realized how lonely it could be. I loved the work—I was developing a customer service system that would make life easier for our staff and give clients a more personalized experience. I was making a real difference, but I had to watch my back all the time. Somebody was always scheming to take my job or setting me up to fail so they'd look good. It was sick."

Kera nodded. "That's why I went into teaching. Not that we don't have our own problems. Administrators think running a school is all about rules and paperwork, but at least most of us are there to help the children."

"That's what drove me crazy. Management only cared about themselves. Their next promotion, their move to a bigger house in a better neighborhood. Not to sound all Joan of Arc, but I wanted to look out for people. It became my mission."

"You always were a crusader," Kera said.

It was true. Abbey racked up causes the way other little girls collected Cabbage Patch dolls and My Little Ponies. Saving the whales, drug prevention, recycling. Because of Abbey's badgering, Nana became one of the first Bethlehem residents to start stockpiling plastic bottles, aluminum cans, and glass containers. The sunny July morning Abbey hauled Nana's bright green recycle bin to the curb for the first time marked one of the great moments of her childhood. She still wanted to do good, and she had thought Michael felt the same way.

"Michael joined the company about a year ago, and we hit it off immediately. We had so much in common, our work ethic, even our sense of humor. He would make fun of all the corporate garbage, and yet he wanted to take care of people. At least that's what he led me to believe. I felt safe with him, and I wasn't lonely anymore. He believed in me, and he taught me to believe in myself."

Her voice faltered as she thought back to those early days, still trying to understand how her life had gone off course. Abbey had been working at the firm just over three years when she was promoted to project manager, leaving the armada of small analyst cubicles for an office of her own, complete with four real walls, a door, and one precious window. The promotion also included a new boss pirated from a rival firm in New York. He had a reputation as a shark, and her peers were more than happy to share dire predictions under the guise of looking out for her. Michael Butler, she heard repeatedly, made careers, but he also destroyed them.

Their first meeting took place over lunch in his office, a generous space easily three times the size of hers with white walls and a bank of floor-to-ceiling windows facing the green expanse of Independence Mall. The sleek black desk had to be at least eight feet long with no personal items other than one small framed picture. A massive credenza loomed behind it like a thunder cloud, spanning the entire width of the sizable room and showcasing two silver urns with elaborate double handles. Later, Michael would tell her these were antique rowing trophies from the Schuylkill Navy, an association of rowing clubs located on historic Boathouse Row. Michael belonged to the Vesper Boat Club, and he claimed pulling the oars on the Schuylkill River gave him a better workout than any gym could provide.

Michael's secretary led her to a black pedestal table set for two with sparkling white china. Really, the black-and-white thing was a bit much. Abbey drummed her fingers on the black lacquer. How long would she have to wait until his highness made an appearance? Finally, Michael arrived with no apology and joined her at the table, a dark-haired man with a handsome sculpted face and the elegant bearing of a GQ model born to wear Armani.

While he had somehow mastered the art of seamlessly talking and eating at the same time, Abbey picked at her salad, terrified of dribbling dressing down her new suit, or worse, ending up with a piece of lettuce lodged between her front teeth. Luckily, Michael talked mostly about himself and his plans for the department. His questions to her were routine, and he didn't seem to pay much attention to her answers. Until he asked her what she thought of the firm's management style.

Her brain raced through a minefield of possible responses and finally opted for honesty.

"The best thing management can do is develop a better relationship with their clients and with their own employees. Customers should be the driving force behind everything we do, but instead we treat them like an afterthought, like an inconvenience we're forced to factor into our plans. And top management pretty much ignores their own staff, especially at the lower levels. All the analysts I worked with complained that management never asks for their feedback, never even drops by to see how they're doing."

Michael's expression changed from surprise to amusement and finally landed on something that looked like admiration. Abbey had breathed a sigh of relief; she and her new boss were going to get along just fine.

A few months later, Abbey gave her first presentation to the board, a recommendation to develop a new automated customer service system. The board approved her project, and Abbey became a rising star.

Her new responsibilities meant a lot of long hours, and one night, she was interrupted by an unexpected knock at her office door.

"Sorry to interrupt," Michael said. "Just dropping by to say hello. Doing my part to develop a better relationship with my employees." He smirked and looked around. "So, this is where the magic happens. I'm amazed you can get anything done in this cramped space."

"It's not so bad," Abbey said, thinking of the cubicle she used to occupy.

"My top project manager deserves better than this." Michael placed his hand on her shoulder and rested it there longer than necessary. He added a gentle squeeze, something she knew the firm's "Sexual Harassment in the Workplace" guidelines would not condone. Okay, this was getting out of control. She needed to figure out a graceful way to dislodge his hand. But before she could make her move, he abruptly released her shoulder, mumbled good night, and left.

By the end of the month, she was moved into a new office on a higher floor with two floor-to-ceiling windows.

On a Friday night a few weeks later, Abbey went clubbing with her friend Sherry and some other analysts to a popular after-hours haunt. Stone stairs led to a dimly lit underground space with shiny wood floors, exposed red brick, and deep red curtains that hung from the ceiling like billowing sails. Part industrial reuse and part bordello, the overall effect generated a dangerous vibe she found strangely appealing. The small dance floor beckoned, and she let the music take her, turning her body to liquid as all her sharp edges dissolved.

When the song ended, she saw Michael standing at the bar watching her. *Quite a coincidence, isn't it, Abs?* Her inner voice clearly wasn't buying it.

She felt his presence at their table even before she heard the soft scraping sound of the chair he pulled up slightly behind hers. As she turned, her knee brushed his, setting off a jolt that traveled up the back of her leg to areas better left undescribed.

"I was such a fool. I should have walked away," Abbey said, offering Kera more wine before filling her own glass and gulping down half of it. "He told me later he thought I brushed his knee on purpose. Such a cocky bastard! He also said seeing my face so flushed from dancing made him wonder how I'd be in bed. Which means—"

"He had you in his sights, right from the beginning." Kera shook her head and took a large gulp of wine herself.

At the end of the night, Abbey had joined her friends in a shared cab. As the taxi pulled away, she took one last look at the club entrance and saw Michael. Tall and elegant as always, but without the usual executive confidence or the steeliness of the corporate shark. This man looked lonely, his face downcast like a little boy left alone on the playground. And she'd felt sorry for him.

"I started looking forward to our weekly status meetings with just the two of us," Abbey admitted. "And those meetings began feeling strangely intimate. He had this device at his desk to automatically close his office door. I guess to save him from having to walk across the room."

"Perks of the rich and unexercised," Kera said.

"It sounds absurd, but the door-closing ritual became almost sensuous. I knew I had no right to develop any romantic feelings for him, but after that night at the club, I felt as if I had seen the real Michael no one else knew about. I had these ridiculous fantasies, and I just thanked God that he didn't think of me that way. But then everything changed."

He had rescheduled their weekly morning status meeting to five p.m., and she recalled feeling uneasy as she walked into his office at such a late hour.

"All clear!" Michael called as he pressed the button to close his office door. It *whooshed* shut behind her as usual, but then she heard the distinctive click of a lock.

"Don't tell me you can lock that door too." Abbey tried to keep her voice steady as a tremor traveled down her spine.

"You aren't afraid to be locked in here with me, are you?" His tone sounded innocent enough, and yet the question sent Abbey into panic mode.

This man orchestrated everything. Even the shiny

trophies in his credenza were perfectly placed to complement the touches of silver in his hair. She force-marched her quivering legs across the room and took her usual seat in front of his desk, trying to hide her shaking hands as she pulled out her status report.

Unfortunately, his wide desk required her to stand up on those shaky legs in order to hand him his copy. As she leaned forward, he grabbed her arm. The status report fell from her grip, and she watched mesmerized as it floated almost in slow motion onto his desk. By then, she felt him beside her. His mouth, warm and minty and urgent, crushed against her lips. *He planned this. This is what he wanted all along.* But it was too late. He gently rested her on the big black desk next to her forgotten status report and a photo of a smiling blond woman.

"That was just the beginning," Abbey continued in a strained voice. "Soon there were clandestine meetings at out-of-the-way hotels. Business trips with adjoining rooms. I knew it was wrong. That photo of his wife haunted me. I never thought I would do something like this to another woman. I hated myself. Of course, he told me he and his wife lived separate lives and were getting a divorce. It was just like one of those sob-sister movies on Lifetime. But I couldn't stop. Being with him became addictive, and I fell in love.

"Then, one Friday night in June, I stopped by a liquor store for some wine. Michael was going to his father-in-law's place in the Hamptons, so I'd be drinking alone. I jumped out of the car and locked the door with the keys in the ignition and the car still running. So stupid. I didn't know what to do. I was too embarrassed to call one of my friends. They'd all be out partying anyway. That's when I realized it was a boyfriend moment, and I didn't have one. I was alone just like always. I knew I had to end it, but I couldn't. My pathetic, part-time relationship with Michael was all I had. Who knows how long it would have continued if I hadn't seen him with his wife."

"You met her?" Kera asked.

"No, at least I was spared that. But I saw them together. Michael had canceled our dinner plans, and I went out after work and drank way too much. Then I walked home, hoping the fresh air would clear my head."

Abbey had stopped outside Jasmine Thai, inhaling the sweet scent of curry and thinking how much she missed the whitewashed walls and the gleaming wooden bar. The restaurant's Thai food had become a staple of her diet, but only as takeout since Michael didn't want to risk anyone seeing them out in public together.

"I actually felt lucky that I wouldn't have to worry about precautions like that much longer. Then, I looked in the window and ducked behind one of the neatly pruned oak trees out front."

Kera held back a giggle. "Oh, Abbey, this sounds like something in a movie."

"Don't laugh. I nearly broke my ankle on the edge of the tree pit. Anyway, I recognized his wife from the photo, and watched as he reached for her hand and raised it to his lips," Abbey said, her voice trembling. "His eyes never left hers as he kissed her fingers, one by one."

Kera joined Abbey on the flowery love seat and put her arms around her friend. "*O mon Dieu.* I am so sorry, Abbey."

"He told me he loved me and that we'd always be together." Abbey took another long sip of wine. "I found out later I wasn't even his first affair. That's why he left New York. Some big scandal involving the wife of a major client. How could I have been such a fool? And how the hell could I go back to working for him?"

Kera remained silent for a moment. "And then Nana saved you."

"She died the following night, and when I found out about the house, I had a way out. A path back into the light." Abbey made a sound like a strangled laugh. "Before my bereavement leave ended, I emailed Michael my resignation. Gutless, I know, but I couldn't risk seeing him again."

"How did he react?"

"I don't know. After I sent the email, I changed my email address, and I haven't heard a word from him since. My only communication has been with Human Resources."

She hadn't even told Sherry where she was going. Abbey still felt guilty about that, but she'd wanted to leave without a trace.

"Anyway, I'm here now and doing fine," she said. "But I'm definitely not ready to get involved again. How could I possibly trust anyone? I can't even trust myself."

Kera folded the empty Michel Cluizel chocolate wrapper into a tiny square. "Seems odd to me that Michael hasn't tried to find you. He doesn't sound like the type of guy who would go down without a fight."

Abbey thought about Michael's competitiveness, about how stubborn he could be when he wanted something. And how determined he'd been when he wanted *her*. Despite all the pain he'd caused her, she still missed him sometimes. Missed that feeling of being desirable to someone.

"I'm sure I'll never see him again," Abbey said with great conviction, even though she couldn't help wondering if it were true.

CHAPTER 13

September 30, 1777

For some reason, Lafayette is curious about my life. I believe reticence to be a virtue but perhaps if I tell him some of my story, my memories will rest in peace.

—Diary of Sister Liesl Boeckel

"Good morning, Sister Liesl," Dr. Glatt said when she opened the front door. "I hope you don't mind this early visit. I must travel to Easton later today and thought I might take a look at our patient before I leave."

"Of course." Liesl gestured the doctor inside. "I was just preparing to check on him myself."

"How is he doing?"

"His wound continues to heal with no signs of complications," Liesl said, leading the doctor up the stairs.

"And his state of mind?" Doctor Glatt asked with a glint in his eye.

"The same. He finds his convalescence quite tedious."

Liesl should have appreciated Doctor Glatt freeing her from the daily chore of caring for Lafayette, but she felt a twinge of disappointment. In spite of Lafayette's occasional boorishness, she had to admit she looked forward to their time together. Despite his worldliness and her lack of it, he had begun to treat her as an equal, listening to her thoughts and opinions with genuine attention. Something she had sorely missed.

Determined to put her time to good use, she filled a wash tub and confronted a pile of dirty linens, most of them used as bandages for Lafayette's leg. As she scrubbed, she reassessed her first impressions of Lafayette. When they met, she had believed all of life was but a lark to him, that he had enjoyed a charmed existence of privilege and ease. Now she knew differently. How difficult it must have been for him to not only lose his parents but also to carry the weight of such overwhelming family expectations. She knew what it was like to have one's life predefined, and the personal cost one paid when duty overrode desire.

She had just begun wringing out the wet cloths when Doctor Glatt found her. "I must commend you on the improved condition of our patient. His wound is healing better than I would have expected."

"He is doing well," Liesl said.

Doctor Glatt lowered his voice. "As we both know, Lafayette is a very demanding patient. However, he has nothing but praise for you and your abilities. He even suggested I should not bother visiting him again."

Liesl raised her hand to her mouth. Not in shock, but because she wished to hide her smile.

"I have heard him spout all manner of nonsense," she said. "I am sure he meant no offense."

That evening, as Liesl climbed the stairs to the sitting room, she thought of poor Doctor Glatt and recalled Lafayette's story about the obedient horse. Lafayette continued to flaunt authority just as he had as a brazen boy. She found his behavior amusing but could not deny that he stirred fresh ideas within her. What would her life be like if she were free to do as she pleased? The thought made her dizzy.

"Hello, dear girl," Lafayette greeted her. "Since I have shared my childhood with you, I believe it is only fair for you to tell me of yours."

"I told you about being in the Little Girls' Choir and singing 'Jesus Call Thou Me' on Christmas Eve," Liesl reminded him. "The rest of my childhood would be of no interest to you."

"That is not true! I have been anticipating this moment all day long. Pray do not disappoint me, as I have precious little to look forward to."

Liesl considered his request. The later years of her childhood had been difficult, and she had never shared the full story with anyone, not even her mother. At the time, Liesl blamed herself and saw no reason to burden her mother with her failings. But now as an adult, she wondered . . . Perhaps revisiting what happened with the Labouress would give her a new perspective, and besides, Lafayette was a difficult man to refuse.

"As I told you, I was very happy in the Little Girls' Choir, but when I reached the age of thirteen, I joined the Older Girls' Choir and everything changed." Liesl paused, noting the strained sound of her own voice. "Do you remember the story of Adelina and Sister Esther Bitterlic?"

"Of course," Lafayette said. "Sister Esther took care of Adelina after her parents died."

Liesl nodded. "Later on, Sister Esther became the head of the Older Girls' Choir and was known as the Labouress."

In her mind, she could still see her, a tall, slender woman of middle years who carried herself with an elegant bearing. Who would have been quite lovely except for a doughy face beginning to jowl.

"I will never forget the first time I met her," Liesl said. "The Labouress had asked to meet with me alone, as she did with all the new girls."

The morning of the meeting, Liesl had stood staring at the powerful flying buttresses of the Single Sisters' House, attempting to bolster her own strength. Joining the Older Girls' Choir meant she would need to start thinking about her future, and she hoped to rely on the Labouress for guidance.

She entered the choir house and climbed the stairs to the worship space known as the Saal. Even though the entire congregation met in the chapel every evening for services, each choir house also had its own place of worship. The Single Sisters' Saal held six rows of perfectly aligned benches in a generous space larger than Liesl expected. She took a seat and looked around.

The plain white plaster walls held no adornment except for a painting Liesl immediately recognized as a John Valentine Haidt. In typical Haidt style, the work depicted the Saviour after the crucifixion with his side wound gaping and bloody. The sight only increased her nervousness, and the Saviour's agonized expression so fully captured her attention, she never noticed the woman silently slipping into the room.

"You must be Liesl Boeckel," the Labouress said in a loud voice.

Liesl flinched, and the old bench creaked loudly, the sound echoing throughout the Saal.

"My, my you are a jittery one. You have no reason to be fearful."

The voice was soothing, but with a slight trace of cunning, and when Liesl looked into the woman's dark eyes, she saw no sign of warmth or kindness.

The Labouress settled herself beside Liesl and described the rigorous life of the Older Girls' Choir. "My girls arise before daybreak to receive the Watchword for the day. Early mornings are spent on chores and school preparation, while the rest of the day is devoted to schooling in the classroom followed by more chores and time for contemplation. We attend the evening service together and then gather here in the Saal one last time for benediction." Switching to a more commanding tone, the Labouress asked, "What skills do you bring?"

Liesl hesitated for a moment, sensing a trap despite the seemingly innocuous question. But why would the Labouress have anything but good intentions?

"My needlework is rather fine," she said finally, "and I have been told I have an aptitude for languages. My mother is a nurse, and I often think I would like to serve as one myself someday."

"That is all well and good, but you will need to learn how to spin. Spinning is our main source of income, and you will want to earn your keep. I shall have you begin by spending time each afternoon tending the sheep." As if the Labouress expected Liesl to object, she added, "Before you learn to spin, you must first acquire respect for the animal providing the wool."

"Yes, Labouress. I am happy to serve in any way you see fit."

"And what is your relationship with the Saviour?"

This careening from one topic to another left Liesl feeling disconcerted, but she had a ready answer. "I have accepted the Saviour as my Lord who died for me and rose again."

"Of course, but have you had a *personal* encounter with the Saviour?"

Liesl bowed her head, and her heart filled with sadness.

"No, Labouress, I have not. I have prayed and prayed, but the Saviour has not yet revealed himself to me."

When Liesl looked up, those penetrating dark eyes were scouring her face like a farmer considering the purchase of a mule. And finding the animal not to his liking.

"Well, that is something we must address. I have organized prayer bands, small groups of girls who gather to share their faith through prayer. You will join the group led by Benigna Schemmel, who is an exemplary example of goodness and piety. You would do well to model your behavior after hers, and perhaps in time, our Saviour will find you deserving."

The Labouress rose from the bench, signaling an end to the discussion, and Liesl stumbled out of the Saal, feeling miserable and disoriented. She was so distracted that she walked directly into a Sister approaching her from across the hall.

"That is how I met Sister Adelina," Liesl said, reaching for Lafayette's dinner tray. The hour was late, and she was exhausted from sharing even these easier memories. Before Lafayette could object, she continued, "And that is enough storytelling for one night. You need your rest."

CHAPTER 14

A Walk in the Cemetery

September 2005

When no one responded to the doorbell, Pete assumed Abbey was out and fumbled in his pocket for the key she had given him. It was not unusual for customers to give him a house key so he could come and go, but this was the first time he had ever used Abbey's, and it felt strangely intimate. He hesitated for a moment and then quietly opened the door.

As he stepped into the hallway, he spotted Abbey out in the little garden, oblivious to everything except maintaining her yoga position. The leaves were dropping now, and the patio was carpeted in a modernistic mosaic of reds, oranges, and yellows. Abbey stood at the center of this swirl of color, balancing on her right leg with her left heel pressed into it at a perfect ninety-degree angle. She slowly moved her palms together, lifted them above her head, and stood in perfect stillness.

Observing her now, he saw a touch of vulnerability he'd missed back when he thought she was just another one of those pushy, executive-on-the-way-to-the-top types, obsessed with work and the things money could buy. Sure, she could be bossy, and she had expensive (not to mention sometimes questionable) taste. But, she loved history, and her face had lit up when she talked about travel. *And* she baked him sugar cookies. She looked so alone there in the garden, he felt a sudden surge of protectiveness, until just as suddenly, she morphed into warrior pose, and Pete laughed out loud. Abbey Prescott was definitely capable of taking care of herself.

When Abbey looked up from her pose, Pete immediately apologized for entering her house, but she brushed him off. "I gave you the key, and I didn't answer the door. You had every reason to come in. What's the plan for today?"

"Actually, I just wanted to take a quick look in the attic. The chimney appears to be in good shape, at least from the outside, but I want to schedule a guy to clean it out, and I'd like to inspect as much of the structure as possible before I get him in here."

She nodded. "No problem."

Pete glanced into the now familiar dining room before following Abbey up the steps. "What happened to the *iconic furniture* in the dining room? What did you do, loan it to a museum?"

"I sold it."

"Really? I thought you loved that modern designer stuff."

"I do, but those pieces don't fit the decor of this house. And I like sitting in the parlor. Those Queen Anne chairs are more comfortable than they look. Besides, I could use the money."

"Abbey Prescott watching her pennies. Pretty soon you'll be buying your clothes at Wal-mart."

"Right. I don't see that happening, but I do have to budget. Especially now that I have this expensive handyman on the payroll!"

Abbey led him past her bedroom, and he felt his face redden as she caught him looking at her bed. *Get a grip, Schaeffer.* It's not like this was the first time a female client had led him past, or even into, her bedroom. A handyman went wherever the job took him. But just like using her house key, seeing *her* bedroom unnerved him.

Abbey opened a door, releasing a musty odor.

"I loved rummaging around in this attic when I was a kid. Kera and I played up here for hours, dressing up in Nana's old hats and dresses. I wonder if those old clothes are still here," she said, as he followed her up a set of worn steps.

Dust motes danced in the sunlight that streamed from the dormer window, but the space was surprisingly orderly—not the usual chaos he found in people's attics. Maybe Abbey had inherited the organization gene from her grandmother.

And maybe it was time to start thinking less about her and more about the job.

Abbey watched with relief as Pete headed straight to the chimney and began his inspection. She'd been alarmed when she caught him checking out her bed, but it wasn't like she thought he might be a crazed rapist. It was more her own reaction that worried her. He looked so cute when he blushed, and it had tickled her that she'd rattled him. For a second, she'd felt attractive, even sexy. And she knew how dangerous that could be.

The attic hadn't changed a bit, and she headed straight for an oval floor mirror covered in dust and opened a box stacked next to it.

"I don't believe it!" she cried, pulling out a green-and-white gingham dress and a droopy white bonnet with a sad-looking yellow daisy. "This was my favorite outfit."

She plopped the saggy hat on her head and held the faded dress to her chest. Unable to see much in the dirty mirror, she wiped the dust off as best she could. Turning from side to side she giggled at her reflection like a little girl.

Then, leaving the hat and dress, she moved on to the rounded corner where the small turret curved like a fairy-tale tower waiting for a princess to let down her hair. Sunlight filtered through the stained-glass windows, casting streaks of color on a sheet-covered object sitting within the circular space.

She pulled off the dusty sheet to reveal an antique cradle

made of solid walnut with a heart carved into the headboard and a barely discernible date painted on the age-darkened wood, 1770. Built when Liesl was alive. She slid her fingers along the side of the cradle and stared at the small space where an infant would lie. An unfamiliar motherly instinct seized her—followed by the panicky thought that with no relationship in sight, motherhood might pass her by.

"This part of the chimney looks fine too," Pete announced, but her attention had shifted to a low bookshelf positioned along the back wall.

"Nana stored all her old photos in here," she said, running her fingers across the old, familiar bindings. She grabbed a well-worn photo album and sank to the floor in a cross-legged position, proving just how much yoga could do for a girl. Pete joined her in a much less elegant crouch, his shoulder almost touching hers.

She opened the album and pointed. "Look, here's a picture of Nana and Pop-pop on their wedding day. Wasn't she beautiful?"

Abbey leafed through the album, one dark page after another. The photos were held in place by corner tabs that gave each picture a slightly formal look, like portraits hanging in a gallery. Sometimes dried-out tabs gave way and photos dropped into her lap. Abbey saw Pete struggling not to follow their trajectory and suppressed a smile. He was trying so hard to be good, which only made him more appealing. Or would have, if she allowed herself to think that way.

She paged past pictures of her grandparents as

newlyweds, arriving eventually at photos of her mother as a baby, a little girl, and then a long-legged teen.

Abbey abruptly closed the album. "Do your parents live around here?"

"They moved down to North Carolina two years ago, on the coast, near Wilmington. Not that they stay there much. They're living the good retirement life, and right now, they're in the middle of an around-the-world trip."

"That was always my dream. To just pack my bags and take off."

"That doesn't sound like you, MPM. How would you live without a plan?"

"Okay, I would have a basic plan but no return plane ticket. Can you imagine the freedom of that?"

"I can," Pete said with a dreamy look.

"If you could travel anywhere in the world, where would you go?" she asked.

"Egypt," Pete said without a moment's hesitation.

"Are you kidding me? I've wanted to go there ever since I saw Nefertiti's statue in Berlin."

They were silent for several minutes, somewhat stunned by yet another common interest.

Abbey recovered first. "Do you have any brothers and sisters?"

"You sure are full of questions today," Pete said without sounding the least bit annoyed. "I have one sister, Kate, who lives on the beach in North Carolina with her husband and two great kids."

"And what about you? Have you ever been married?

"Nope. One of the unintended consequences of having such happy parents is you set a very high standard for yourself."

"Your sister got past that."

"Yes, and her perfect marriage just makes it all the more difficult for me," Pete said with a shake of his head. "And what about your family?"

Abbey ignored the question and asked another one of her own. "Would you like to go for a walk?"

A slow—and Abbey had to admit—sexy grin spread across Pete's face. "Sure, just give me a couple minutes to pack up my stuff."

Abbey waited on the front porch, thinking about Pete. Was it possible for a happy family life to be as much of a burden as an unhappy one? Funny that she and Pete had ended up in the same lonely place, even though their reasons couldn't be more different.

"Where are we headed?" Pete asked as he loaded his toolbox into the back of the pickup.

"I'd like to look for Liesl's grave. Apparently, she's buried in the old Moravian cemetery."

"A walk in a cemetery. How could a guy turn down an offer like that?"

They walked down her street past a group of school kids. Two little girls huddled together whispering, while a lone boy straggled behind with a backpack almost as big as himself. Pete gave him a high five, and the little boy beamed.

"Actually, cemeteries have always intrigued me," Pete said. "They tell you a lot about people and their history."

"So you're interested in more than just old buildings?"

"Of course. I like to know who lived in them too."

Abbey pushed open the wrought iron gate and entered a peaceful spot with a proud assembly of white oaks, tulip poplars, and maples. Unlike most cemeteries, here the tombstones were laid flush with the ground, creating neat rows of low-lying tablets—like a garden of worn stepping-stones marking a bumper crop of souls.

"The Moravians call this God's Acre," Abbey said. "According to the guide at the museum, the flat stones represent the Moravian belief that all people are equal in life and in death."

"I like it," Pete said. "Too many cemeteries look like somebody held a competition to see who could build the largest monument."

A long-ago memory niggled at Abbey's brain. Nana had brought her here, and the two of them had walked among these graves together, under these same stately trees that loomed overhead like leafy centurions guarding the faithful. In fact, Nana had a favorite spot: a slight elevation on the other side of the cemetery, which she claimed offered the best view in all of Bethlehem.

As a girl, Abbey had run from grave to grave, laughing as she conjured up images to match exotic names like Salome Mau and Magdalene Schweisshaupt or feeling true sadness as she read the tombstones of infants who had died at birth or children who were felled by disease before reaching their teens. She also sought out adventurers like Thomas Langballe, who was born in Denmark, and Juliana Wapler who traveled across land and sea from Germany. For an extra challenge, Abbey had hunted for the less common graves of Indians and African slaves who were identified by one name only, such as Benjamin, a.k.a. Schabet, of the Wampanoag people and Andrew, simply described as Negro.

Today, however, her mission focused on one grave only.

"I have a map, but it's not a very good one," she said, pulling out the bad Xerox copy. Louisa had circled Liesel's grave with a red pen, but the map lacked an overall layout, which meant Abbey had no way to pinpoint the exact section where Liesl was buried.

She wandered aimlessly among the stones, kicking stray leaves as she went. Pete followed without complaint, as intrigued by the inscriptions as Abbey had been as a child. Finally, she sank down on a park bench.

"This is ridiculous. Would you like to take a look?" she asked as Pete sat down beside her.

"This is one poor excuse for a map," he said. "Maybe if we walk along the main pathway, we can scan the end stones for a name in Liesl's row."

The two of them forged on, step by step, stone by stone. Her eyes watered from squinting at the barely decipherable inscriptions until, at last, she spotted a name that sounded familiar.

"Sarah Pyrlaeus!" she cried. "If this map is correct, Liesl's grave should lie along this same row."

Abbey walked down the row, struggling to read the faded names. Elisabeth Ockertshausen then Mary Cist. The cemetery map shook in Abbey's hand. Liesl should only be one grave away.

And there it was:

ELIZABETH BOECKEL
BETTER KNOWN AS
LIESEL BECKEL
BORN DEC. 16, 1754
DIED OCT. 1, 1831
NURSED GEN LAFAYETTE
FROM SEPT. 17, 1777 TO
OCT. 18, 1777
SHE BECAME THE
VILLAGE NURSE

Abbey and Pete stood motionless, both of them lost in the sweetness of discovery. It was only a stone, but it proved, once again, that Liesl had existed and confirmed her connection to Lafayette. Abbey read the epitaph over and over, committing it to memory. Then she pulled out her cellphone and took pictures from every angle. Solid proof.

"Very impressive," Pete said, "but . . ."

"But what?"

"Well, it's just that her tombstone looks bigger and newer than those around it. Hers also has a more detailed inscription."

"I noticed that too. And look at the more modern spellings of Elizabeth and Beckel. I wonder if the Beckel family replaced the original marker."

"And added the reference to Lafayette."

"Exactly. The family seemed quite proud of Liesl's connection to him, so it's possible they wanted to keep the story alive."

"Which doesn't mean the story isn't true," Pete said with a certainty that made Abbey want to hug him.

She squatted above the cool marble and rubbed the rough-cut lettering as she whispered, "Liesl, I am here."

After one last look at Liesl's headstone, she led the way across God's Acre and up a short set of brick steps to Nana's favorite spot. The view from the top remained unchanged, encompassing the Old Bell House with its humble belfry and just beyond, the Central Moravian Church topped with a dramatic cupola that Nana always insisted was the same height as the building itself.

They stood in silence, relishing the stillness. The sun had drifted lower, creating a softer, more diffused light. The time of day photographers called the golden hour. The Central Moravian Church proved the picture takers right with its gleaming copper top and its cream-colored stucco bathed in a warm, shimmering glow that contrasted sharply with the darker stone of the Old Bell House.

"Nana loved to come here," Abbey said. "She would bring me to this very spot and tell me stories about the early Moravians. But I never really appreciated history until my mom took me to Europe the summer after I turned sixteen."

"Nice birthday present."

"It changed my life. When we arrived at Charles de Gaulle Airport, I was shocked everything was written in French. Signage, advertisements, books, newspapers. I don't know why I was surprised, but it was like stepping into a different world."

"I know exactly what you mean," Pete said. "Being in another country feels surreal."

"I wanted to learn everything about France. The history, the language. Just walking the streets thrilled me. I couldn't believe it when a girl sailed by me with a baguette and a bouquet of fresh flowers sticking out of her bike basket. Like something out of a movie."

Pete nodded. "What I like most is that even the simplest things are a challenge. Like opening your hotel room door with some oversize key from the eighteenth century."

"Or shopping in a grocery store. One time I thought I was buying butter, but it was a big block of lard!"

Pete laughed and leaned against the wrought iron handrail. "And what about the squatty potty?"

"Oh my God. The first time I saw one was in Italy. I honestly thought the toilet was broken. I figured someone had removed the toilet bowl and left this square thing behind. I checked every stall looking for a real toilet, but they were all the same. It finally dawned on me that the ceramic square with the hole in the middle *was* the toilet. My mom laughed until tears rolled down her face."

They were losing the light now, adding a sense of intimacy.

"From what I saw in the photo album, you look a lot like her," Pete said.

Abbey shook her head. "She was the beautiful one."

"How did she die?"

As soon as the words were out of his mouth, Pete looked as if he wished he could swallow them back. Abbey's first reaction was to ignore his question completely. What right did he have to ask her about something so personal, so painful? But as the seconds ticked by, and she watched Pete grow more and more uncomfortable, she started to feel sorry for him. More than that, she realized this was a story she wanted to share.

"My mom was diagnosed with breast cancer soon after we got back from Europe. She suffered so much, through radiation and chemo, but she never gave up. And she never lost her sense of humor. Even when her hair fell out, she joked that she looked like Yul Brynner's sister. We thought she had beaten it, but when I took her in for her six-month checkup, Doctor Burger asked me to join Mom in her office. The cancer had spread into the lymph nodes, the liver, and the brain. The doctor wanted to discuss more treatments, but Mom just shook her head and said, 'No more.' Anyone else would have been frightened or angry, but she was just sad. She grasped my hand and held it tight saying, 'It'll be okay, Abbey. It'll be okay.'"

Abbey took a shaky breath and finished the story. "It wasn't okay at all. She died three weeks before I graduated from high school. She was only forty-four."

"I am so sorry, Abbey."

Everybody said those words, but Pete's eyes held a deep compassion that convinced her this was not just a case of saying the right thing. She could tell he really meant it. And for the first time in months, she felt as if she weren't alone.

CHAPTER 15

October 1, 1777

It has always been easy for Father to find fault with me, but in recent days, he has become more critical than ever. I fear I have no hope of pleasing him.

—Diary of Sister Liesl Boeckel

"I do not understand the Labouress," Lafayette said as she changed his dressings the following morning. "The woman you described sounds very different from the one who cared for Adelina."

"I cannot explain it," Liesl said. "Sister Adelina believed the Labouress was an angel walking upon this earth, and the whole community admired her piousness. However, she showed me no motherly concern at all. Instead, she was distant and critical and left me feeling unworthy. It saddened me that this stern, unfeeling woman was meant to be a major guiding force in my life."

"How did you manage?" Lafayette asked.

Liesl took a seat in one of the wooden chairs. It was a relief to finally share her pent-up feelings, especially with someone from the outside world. Someone who might understand.

"I delighted in the hectic daily routine, and with no time to spare from dawn till dark, the days passed quickly. I excelled in my schoolwork and finally mastered spinning yarn on the Great Wheel. Unfortunately, the Labouress could never walk past me without a criticism about the crispness of my apron, the quality of my penmanship, or the overtwisted state of my yarn."

The worst time of the week was when she met with the Labouress for a confessional practice called "speakings." Every Friday, Liesl would arrive in the Saal feeling nauseous at the thought of facing yet another cataloging of her failings. The Labouress repeatedly stated that it was her duty to lead Liesl to the infinite grace, faithfulness, and mercy of the dear Saviour. But Liesl never felt further from the Saviour's grace then she did during those sessions.

The Labouress continually badgered Liesl to become more like Benigna. She even excluded Liesl from the hourly intercessions, prayers normally performed by every member of the congregation, insisting only true believers could pray for the redemption of the world. Rather than helping her deepen her faith, the Labouress had constantly stressed the need for Liesl to defend herself from Satan.

Liesl turned to Lafayette with a defiant look. "The more

I listened to the Labouress, the more I wondered if Satan might not appear in any form. Even that of a Labouress."

Lafayette chuckled. "As well you might."

"I kept those heretical thoughts to myself, of course," she said, "but I was fortunate to find comfort in the company of another. I told you I became quite close to Sister Adelina, but she was not my only confidante."

Much to Liesl's surprise, she and Benigna Schemmel had become good friends. Their beds sat side by side in the dormitory, and the two often whispered together before going to sleep. Benigna had been born in the Ohio Territories, the only child of two devout missionaries. While her parents were busy with the local Indians, Benigna was entrusted to an old Chippewa woman named Abequa, a kindly soul who lovingly cared for Benigna but did so in almost total silence. Fortunately, her father had taught Benigna how to read, and her Bible became the lonely girl's truest companion.

When Benigna was ten years old, the family moved to Bethlehem. At first, the thought of living in a choir house with other girls terrified her. Eventually, however, she became more at ease around other people, finding comfort in their shared faith. She especially loved attending the evening service when the congregation would raise its voice as one in song.

Liesl and Benigna attended the daily prayer band meetings together as the Labouress instructed. Benigna led the small group of girls and encouraged each of them to contemplate the suffering of the Saviour and draw ever nearer to the one true invisible Friend. Although Benigna was every bit as pious as the Labouress proclaimed, the girl was a gentle soul who never judged Liesl in any way.

When Liesl paused, Lafayette said, "Please continue. I do so enjoy your stories."

Although the storytelling relieved her mind, it was not easy delving into the past. Especially since even the most innocent memories carried with them the knowledge of what was to come.

"I have other things I must attend to that are more important than telling stories. But, I have brought you something to help pass the time."

She reached into her basket and placed a pen, an inkwell, and several sheets of paper on the table.

"*Merci beaucoup*!" Lafayette cried, as he grabbed the pen. "I shall begin immediately."

"Brother Eugene's shed is on fire!" Brother Samuel shouted when Liesl answered the loud banging at their front door. Brothers and Sisters were already streaming into the street as Brother Samuel dashed off to the next house.

Liesl alerted Mother Boeckel, and they barged into the sitting room where Lafayette sat engrossed in *The History of Greenland*. He set aside the book and appeared to notice the ruckus outside his window for the first time.

"What is happening out there?" he asked, attempting to stand up for a better view out the window.

"Sit down," Liesl commanded. "You will harm your leg and prolong your convalescence with such foolhardiness." Why did he always have to tax her patience? For a moment, she considered strapping him to his bed.

Mother Boeckel's hands fluttered like baby birds attempting flight. "Nothing for you to worry about, sir. That careless Brother Eugene has accidentally set his shed on fire."

Defiant as always, Lafayette stood by the window, using the sill and the back of his chair for support. "At least it is only a shed."

"A shed can set the whole town afire," Liesl said, but her bigger concern was Brother Eugene. The brokenhearted look on his face after she refused to marry him still haunted her.

She grabbed the two leather-covered fire buckets with the name Boeckel clearly painted on the sides. "I trust you can avoid further injury until we return."

"*Oui*, Nurse Boeckel, I shall follow your orders implicitly," Lafayette said with a mocking bow. He pushed his chair closer to the window and lowered himself into it with a grimace of pain.

As the two women raced out of the room, Liesl muttered, "He would rather damage his leg than follow my instructions. Quite the arrogant one, don't you think, Mother Boeckel?"

"That man is a wounded soldier and your patient. You must learn perseverance, my girl. But I will concede the French are different."

When they reached the cistern, the Brothers and Sisters had already formed two perfectly parallel lines to pass buckets of water. On one side, the men filled them and hefted the heavy loads toward the fire, while across from them, a line of women quickly whisked the empty ones back to the cistern.

Liesl positioned herself at the head of the row of women, closest to the fire. The air was unseasonably warm and drenched in humidity, as if the elements had become confused, thinking this was mid-July rather than the first day of October. The intensity of the blaze caused sweat to stream down her face as she grasped an empty bucket from Brother Samuel and immediately passed it to Mother Boeckel on her left. The women moved like one organism with multiple appendages, silently passing the buckets as quickly as their hands allowed.

Brother Samuel dumped bucket after bucket of water onto the flames climbing the rear wall of the shed, but despite the continuous dousing, the fire raged on. The smoke from the shed was thicker now, and the fumes made Liesl's throat burn and her eyes tear. She turned toward the front of the building and spotted movement at the smoky doorway.

"Is that Brother Eugene?" Liesl said.

"It is only smoke," Brother Samuel replied, barely

looking. "Please concentrate on passing these buckets down the line."

Liesl ignored him, focusing her blurry vision on a shadowy form just inside the shed.

"I can see Brother Eugene trying to escape the flames!" she cried, and without another thought, ran toward the burning building.

"What are you doing?" Brother Samuel shouted as he reached out to stop her, dropping a full bucket of water and splattering her shoes.

Undeterred, Liesl brushed him off and ran forward, ignoring the screams of Mother Boeckel and the shouts of the men. She watched Brother Eugene fall to his knees, choking and coughing. If he lost consciousness he would die.

The smoke rose up like a shimmering wall blocking her path. Lifting her apron to cover her nose and mouth, she plunged through the searing heat. Her eyes were useless, and she felt rather than saw the slumped figure.

"Brother Eugene, I am here!" she cried, although she got no response from the motionless body. He groaned as she pulled at his arms, but his weight was too much for her. Suddenly, two of the younger Brothers broke through the smoke and helped her drag the soot-covered man to safety.

Liesl snatched the next full bucket from a stunned Brother Samuel and sprinkled the cool water on Brother Eugene, who lay on the ground, coughing and moaning.

"Don't worry, Brother Eugene you are safe now," Liesl said as she lifted her skirt and ripped strips of fabric from her chemise. She dipped the strips in the cool water and applied the soothing bandages to his face. Luckily, his clothing had not caught on fire, and he soon revived.

Clasping her hand in his, he rasped, "You may have refused to marry me, Sister Liesl, but I am forever in your debt. I would have died if not for you. May the dear Saviour keep you in his loving care always."

"I am glad to see you are still with us. Let me wrap some bandages on those hands."

Doctor Glatt arrived soon after and joined her at Brother Eugene's side.

"You have done well, Sister Liesl," the doctor said as he noted the improvised bandages covering the worst of the burns. Then he called to a towheaded boy who nodded with a serious expression before running off in a blur of skinny, fast-pumping arms and legs. Soon, a wagon arrived to carry Brother Eugene to the hospital for further treatment. By the time the injured man had been trundled off, his shed was nothing but a steaming pile of blackened timber.

"What were you thinking?" Mother Boeckel cried, her face blotchy from smoke and anger. "You could have died. And look at your clothes. You have damaged your skirt and your shoes. And your chemise is in tatters!"

Just then, Liesl spotted her father running in their direction, his face contorted with worry. However, any paternal concern soon vanished when he noticed her disheveled state. "Liesl, you will return home immediately.

We will discuss your indecorous behavior in private for you are at present in no condition to be seen in public."

Liesl stomped home, taking out her frustration on her poor shoes. She had not even begun washing her face when her father burst into the kitchen.

"Why must you always make a spectacle of yourself?" he cried, eyes blazing. "Your dear mother would be ashamed."

"I like to think Mother would be proud of me for saving a life," Liesl replied, her anger rising to match his.

"Your mother knew how to properly conduct herself. She would never have brought shame upon this house."

"What would you have had me do? Stand by and allow Brother Eugene to die because I was concerned about the state of my clothing?"

Father Boeckel pounded his fist on the kitchen table. "Watch your tongue, girl! You are a woman, not a man, and you would do well to remember your place in this world. I am your father, and I will not tolerate your impudence."

But what was her place in this world? Must she never be allowed to have an opinion of her own? She longed to rage at his unfairness, but the lifelong lessons of obedience reined in her anger. "I apologize, Father."

Father Boeckel nodded and left the room. As soon as the back door closed behind him, she raced up the stairs. At least one person in this house might appreciate what she had done.

She charged into the sitting room, alarming Lafayette,

who, for once, appeared speechless. He simply stared, and she pictured what he must see: her flushed and sooty face, her eyes rimmed in red, her Haube plastered to her head even tighter than usual, and a shred of white muslin hanging from the bottom of her skirt.

"I have been worried about you," he said at last. "I . . ."

"The fire is out!" she announced. "And I saved a man's life."

"How did you do that?"

Liesl recounted the story, while Lafayette listened with an unusually serious expression.

"You are a very brave young woman."

"I am glad someone thinks so. Father accused me of shaming my family. And all Mother Boeckel talked about was the damage to my chemise!"

"They do not see you like I do."

Liesl felt her face turning even redder than it had from the fire and quickly changed the subject. "Could you see the bucket brigade from your window?"

"I could indeed. Quite interesting. I have not seen a bucket brigade in operation since I was a boy. The fire engines of Paris are designed with intake valves to draft the water from the Seine directly into the belly of the fire engine."

"Of course, Paris is well ahead of Bethlehem in everything. After all, we are just a backwater in the wilds of Pennsylvania."

Lafayette ignored her sarcastic tone. "Where is your source of water?"

"We have six cisterns around the town, all fed by a spring near the Menakasie Creek. Today, our water came from the cistern behind the Sun Inn."

"And how are the cisterns filled?"

Liesl puffed with pride. "Our waterworks pumps the water up the hill to our town, a distance of over ninety vertical feet."

"Ninety feet?" Lafayette repeated. "I don't believe our French engineers have mastered more than fifty."

"Aha! So, our small community has outdone the mighty minds of France!" She clapped her hands in excitement. "No doubt you are finally impressed."

"Pumping water ninety feet is very impressive indeed," Lafayette said, although his voice sounded doubtful.

"*Merci*, monsieur," Liesl said, bobbing with a mock curtsy before turning more serious. "You must forgive my silliness. Father always reproaches me for my frivolous nature."

"And how right he is. Back to your ministrations, Nurse Liesl!" Lafayette bellowed. "We will not have you shaming the medical profession with your foolish antics. Bring on your tinctures of wormwood, your poultices of cow dung, your unguents of ground rattlesnake fang!"

Lafayette's eyes twinkled with merriment, and Liesl had to cover her mouth with both hands to hold back her laughter. Gaiety was a rarity in this somber house, and neither Mother nor Father Boeckel would be amused.

Suddenly, Lafayette's expression changed, becoming

more thoughtful. His gaze locked on to hers and lingered there longer than propriety would permit.

That night, Liesl lay awake in her narrow bed. Although her body ached with exhaustion, sleep eluded her. Impressions from the day flitted through her mind like a swarm of midges darting above the Menakasie Creek: the arid smoke of the fire and the moans of Brother Eugene. Followed by the moments of gaiety with Lafayette and a feeling of lightness so long forgotten. His words repeating in her head: *They don't see you like I do.* Suddenly, the reprimands of her father were of little consequence. It seemed that *she* no longer saw herself the same way either.

CHAPTER 16

The Embroidery

October 2005

"I need you to stay in the parlor with the door closed," Pete said when he found Abbey in the kitchen, sipping a cup of coffee.

"Why would I do that?" she asked.

"Because I want to surprise you."

"I hate surprises."

"You won't hate this one."

She reluctantly agreed, and once the parlor door was firmly shut, he retrieved his masterpiece from the truck.

He stepped back to admire his work, satisfied the trip out to Lancaster County had been well worth the effort. The antique barn beam he'd acquired from an Amish farmer perfectly complemented the simple stone of the fireplace. And the grain of the white oak added a richness and character to the room. He couldn't wait to see Abbey's reaction.

He heard music coming from the parlor, so at least she'd found a way to entertain herself. When he opened the door, Abbey was seated in front of the antique piano, her sandy-colored ponytail bouncing in time with the lively music.

"Mozart, right?" he asked after she completed the piece.

"'The Turkish March.'"

"You play really well," Pete said, thinking about how much he still didn't know about her.

"My mom taught me. My dad even bought us matching pianos so we could play duets." She lowered the keyboard lid. "This piano is a beauty, but it needs a tuning badly."

"Sounded great to me."

"Am I free to leave now?" Abbey asked. "Or did you plan on locking me in the bathroom? Maybe chaining me to the stove?"

"Don't tempt me," Pete said as he gestured toward the doorway.

Abbey entered the office and stood in the center of the room, staring at the fireplace in silence. Just as Pete started to feel apprehensive, she ran over to the mantel and caressed the smooth wood as if she were petting a cat. "I don't believe it. Where in the world did you find this?"

"I have my ways," Pete said, and felt his face flush with pride.

"I don't know how you do it. It's exactly what I wanted."

"Glad it meets with your approval, MPM. Maybe now you'll forgive me for locking you in the parlor."

Abbey laughed. "You can lock me up anytime for something like this!"

She sounded breathless, and the way she looked at him pretty much knocked the wind out of him too.

"Seriously, this is the best surprise ever!" she said, moving toward him. But then, the telephone rang, and she gave him one of her thousand-watt smiles as she ran from the room.

His euphoria deflated like a birthday balloon kept too long after the party. For an instant, he'd been sure Abbey was going to throw her arms around him and give him a big hug. He shrugged his shoulders to shake off the ridiculous thought.

Time to cut the crap, Schaeffer, and get back to work.

"Drinking a beer, I see." Adam's face lit up as he spotted the frosted glass in her hand.

He was late again, so Abbey had figured she might as well get *some* pleasure out of this meeting and succumbed to a Valley Golden Ale. But she wasted no time crushing his hopes.

"I can't stay for long. Sorry, I have a dentist appointment." She made a point of looking at her watch. "In just over an hour."

Adam slid his tall frame into her side of the Brew Works booth, and Abbey got a whiff of a fresh soapy scent, as if he'd just gotten out of the shower. When he called to say he had information about the bookmark, he'd insisted on meeting her for lunch once again. She gave him high marks for perseverance, but the poor guy had no idea what he was up against.

They ordered sandwiches, and Abbey immediately got down to business. "What did you find out?"

Adam placed the bookmark in front of them. "I knew Martha Brown could help us, although I now know more about eighteenth-century embroidery than any self-respecting man should." Adam paused, perhaps hoping for a word of appreciation, but she just looked at him expectantly.

"Your bookmark is an example of tambour embroidery typical of the 1700s. A tambour was a small drum, and for this type of embroidery, the fabric was held in place with a round frame that looked much like the head of a drum. A special hook punched through the material, caught the thread from beneath, and drew it up to create a linked, chainlike stitch. By working rows of chained stitches closely together, this method could produce shaded colors with great depth, variety, and subtlety. Like you see here." He pointed to one of the tulips whose petals pulsated with varying shades of red.

"According to Martha, who as I told you is an expert in these things, this work surpasses the best traditional pieces she's seen. Unlike most, your bookmark combines fine handwork with tambour embroidery. While the flowers were created with the hook and tambour, the vines and leaves were made with a needle. The stitching is so delicate, Martha said she couldn't imagine how fine a needle would have been required to create it."

"Is that all?" Abbey asked, making no effort to disguise her disappointment.

Adam looked at her with an amused expression. "Well, there is one other odd aspect of this particular piece."

"Don't keep me in suspense, Adam. Tell me!"

"Martha believes a bit of cross-stitch was added on top of the tambour embroidery."

"Where?" Abbey asked, moving her half-eaten sandwich aside to lean in for a closer look.

Adam removed a small magnifying glass from his shirt pocket and placed it over the blue dahlia in the center of the bookmark.

"Right there. Do you see it?" He took her hand and wrapped her fingers around the handle of the magnifying glass. "Two entwined symbols were added to the edge of that outside petal. I think both symbols are the letter 'L.'"

"Oh my God!" Abbey cried as she gave Adam an exuberant hug. "You brilliant man. Do you know what this means? L and L. It has to stand for Liesl and Lafayette!"

"Could be," he said, looking happier than she'd ever seen him.

"I can't thank you enough." Abbey threw some bills on the table and forced him out of the booth. "Sorry I have to leave you like this. I'll give you a ring soon."

"Would you like a beer?" Abbey asked, holding up two bottles. Pete looked surprised but readily agreed. She figured he wasn't the kind of guy to turn down a cold one.

"A neighbor gave me a six-pack as a housewarming gift. I've never tasted it before," she said, handing him a frosty bottle of Yuengling.

A late-day beam of light created shadows across the project plan spread out on the sunroom coffee table as they tilted back their bottles in unison, taking long, satisfying sips.

"I'm more of a wine girl, but this isn't bad," she said. Second beer in one day. Who knows? She might become a beer drinker yet.

"I'm pretty much a beer man, as you might have guessed, and this just happens to be my local favorite." Pete cradled the beer in his large, capable hands as he launched into his project update. "The building inspector thoroughly examined the fireplace, declaring it safe and compliant with city building codes."

"That's great news," Abbey said. "I can't wait to use it when it gets colder."

Pete started to review the tasks required for restoring the walls, the next phase of the project, but Abbey interrupted. "I'm thinking about expanding the office project."

"What do you have in mind, MPM?"

The nickname had grown on her, and now, instead of being annoyed, she couldn't help smiling every time he used it. Maybe it wasn't the nickname itself, but more the tone of his voice when he said it.

"I'd like to create a library nook in the back corner with shelves to hold my books."

"It would interrupt the flow of the plaster walls."

"Yes, but I always wanted my own library. And a place to display some bookmarks from my collection."

"You have a bookmark collection?" Pete asked. He tried, but failed, to suppress a chuckle.

"You can laugh, but some day when we're all reading books on electronic devices, my bookmarks will become collector's items."

"Whatever you say. I can already picture you on *Antiques Roadshow*. Tell me more about this idea of yours."

"Try to envision a corner of the room lined with rows of books, some of my bookmarks displayed nearby, two easy chairs, and a table large enough for two coffee cups."

"Why two chairs and two coffees?" Pete asked in a voice that sounded strangely hopeful.

"In case I have company. Kera and I could sit there together. And who knows? Maybe you'll stop by and we can drink beer in the library nook."

"Fine with me, MPM. Let's add the nook to the project plan."

Abbey was surprised by his ready agreement and quickly

scribbled some notes on the plan before he could change his mind.

After they finished reviewing upcoming tasks, Pete stretched out his legs and said, "I'm going to be out of town for a few days the week after next."

Abbey kept her head lowered, so she didn't have to look him in the eye. She tried to pretend she was only mildly interested, but unwanted images of Pete going off on some romantic getaway made her feel queasy.

"Where are you headed?" she finally asked.

"New York. For business. Can you believe I'm taking the bus? I wanted to take a train, but I'd have to drive to Jersey, and that's too much hassle."

"I love the train," Abbey gushed, recovering from her momentary nausea. "My mom and I used to ride the train into Center City for marathon shopping sprees. I'd come home loaded with bright yellow Strawbridge's shopping bags. I always got a window seat, so I could watch for each stop. My father told me about a mnemonic to help me remember the stations: 'Old maids never wed and have babies' which stood for Overbrook, Merion, Narberth, Wynnewood, Ardmore, Haverford, and Bryn Mawr. But to make it even easier, he came up with his own mnemonic: 'Old Man Nutley wishes Abbey happy birthday." Abbey giggled just like she had the first time she heard it.

"Who the heck is Old Man Nutley?" Pete asked.

"It was our nickname for this eccentric guy who rode

around the neighborhood on a rickety bicycle wearing an old leather football helmet. Old Man Nutley rode so slowly he barely kept the bike upright, and he screamed obscenities when we raced our bikes, which, of course, only made us ride faster and closer."

"Your dad sounds like a pretty cool guy."

Abbey's stomach clenched with a rush of mixed emotions. "He can be."

"Does he come to visit often?"

"Not exactly. He didn't even come back when Nana died. He flies all over the world for his work, but he couldn't manage a trip to Pennsylvania for his mother-in-law's funeral."

Abbey still couldn't believe he had let her deal with the funeral alone. But why break his pattern of always disappointing her? She pictured her father's face, his raven hair tinged with just the slightest touch of distinguished gray, his restless brown eyes darting every which way, always searching out new opportunities and plotting ways to get the upper hand. Sadly, his personality was better suited for work than home. Sadder still, he had never devised a winning playbook for building a relationship with his only daughter. So, he had left the field.

"I'm sure he had a good reason," Pete said.

"Really? Do you want to know his excuse? The twins had the flu. He told me Mallory simply couldn't cope on her own."

Abbey could feel the old familiar anger pulsing through

her. As if Mallory ever took care of those kids herself. After all, she had an au pair. And how ludicrous to suggest Roger Prescott would be the slightest help with two sick little boys. But then again, maybe he was different with his second family. Maybe his dormant parental instincts had finally kicked in.

"I'd still like to meet him," Pete said.

"Well, I doubt he'll be in the neighborhood any time soon." Abbey's tone made it clear the subject was closed. The thought of her father in the same room with Pete was absurd. He'd take one look at Pete's calloused hands and stained jeans and immediately relegate him to the ranks of the great unwashed, a demographic Roger Prescott preferred to stay as far away from as possible.

Anxious to talk about anything else, Abbey asked, "Do you remember the bookmark I showed you? The one belonging to Liesl Boeckel?"

"Of course. You still trying to find out if Liesl was getting it on with Lafayette?"

Abbey rolled her eyes. "Martha Brown at the Kemerer examined Liesl's bookmark and found two tiny letter 'L's' embroidered inside one of the flower petals. I think the letters stand for—"

"Liesl and Lafayette," Pete finished her sentence. "Sounds like Liesl *was* smitten."

Pete couldn't have looked more pleased if he'd made the discovery himself. But then, he always responded with genuine interest to everything she had to say, including all that family stuff she normally didn't talk about. Pete was one of those rare people who listened but never judged.

She decided to take another leap of faith.

"There's more. I found a piece of paper inside the bookmark. It looks like messages written by two different people. I think the writing is in French, but the script is so flowery and old-fashioned, I can't read it. "

Pete tipped his head back to swig the last of his beer. "Your Liesl is quite the mystery woman."

"And I am determined to figure her out. I'm sure Adam could translate the messages, but I'm a little nervous about sharing them. Do you know him?"

Pete stared at a space somewhere past Abbey's left ear. "Not well, but he is a respected member of the Moravian community."

Not exactly a ringing endorsement. Still . . .

"What if this is the proof I've been looking for? It could be a love letter from Lafayette. Can you imagine? This could be a major historical discovery."

Pete leaned toward her and squeezed her hand. "I think you're really onto something, Abbey. I'm happy for you."

For a moment, she thought he might kiss her—and even worse, she thought she might like it. *Get it together, Abs.* The possibility of a Liesl and Lafayette love affair must be making her giddy. If she wasn't careful, she could be drawn into an unlikely romance of her own.

CHAPTER 17

October 2, 1777

The good Moravian brothers bewailed my passion for war, but, while listening to their sermons, I was making plans to set Europe and Asia aflame.

—*Memoirs of Lafayette*

Lafayette's twelfth day in the Boeckel household began as it always did with the morning service consisting of the Watchword for the day and the usual harangue from Frederick. While Frederick continued to preach ad nauseam about the delights of discipleship, he had expanded his repertoire to include a new subject: the depredations of war. Lafayette had no doubt to whom this message was intended, and he silently fumed as Frederick thundered on about war darkening the soul and inflicting a moral injury on society.

Lafayette was always careful to present a respectful

countenance, but on this day, his anger overcame his restraint.

"Frederick, may I speak with you?" Lafayette asked at the close of the service.

The man looked less than pleased but nodded in a distracted, impatient manner. "Of course. I trust your lodgings and care are adequate?"

"Considerably more than adequate. I have no complaints whatsoever, sir. Your daughter Liesl is exceptional. You should be very proud."

"My pride in my daughter is no concern of yours. If that is all, I will leave you, for I have pressing work at the farm," Frederick said as he headed for the door.

"My concern, sir, is with you and your position regarding the revolution."

Frederick turned. "Go on," he said in a tone that encouraged exactly the opposite.

But Lafayette would not be stymied. Even though he knew this man was his host and deserving of respect, some things could not be countenanced.

"When a government violates the rights of the people, insurrection is the most sacred and the most indispensable of duties," Lafayette said.

"Do not speak to me of what is sacred. You are a foolish young man who knows nothing of life or duty."

Lafayette straightened in his chair and adopted his most defiant expression. "I know it is the will of God for this nation to be free."

"And how is it that you presume to know the will of God?" Frederick shouted. "A heathen who denies his host the most basic courtesy. I do not have time for this. I agreed to allow you to recuperate here in my home, and I shall abide by my word, but I will not tolerate your impertinence."

And with that Frederick left.

Lafayette would have followed him if he were able. Frederick was almost as insufferable as his father-in-law! Not only did he lack respect for the revolution, the man ruled his family like a despot, and Lafayette had never tolerated tyranny. He particularly disliked the way Frederick treated Liesl, never acknowledging any of her considerable accomplishments.

Still fuming, Lafayette found he had no patience for reading; the intrepid Moravians struggling to survive in a land of ice and snow would have to wait. Instead, he embarked on a bold letter-writing campaign, bombarding his contacts within the French aristocracy with entreaties for France to form an alliance with America and go to war with Britain. He even wrote to Prime Minister Maurepas, outlining plans for the French to attack the British in the Caribbean, Canada, India, and the China Sea. In jest, Lafayette suggested they might sell the furniture at Versailles to underwrite the expense.

Lafayette's mood became fouler still when he received word that the British general William Howe had captured Philadelphia. It was no surprise since Philadelphia had been at great risk for some time, and yet he was still incensed. If only he had not been injured, perhaps he could have turned the tide in favor of the patriots.

He consoled himself with the knowledge that the victory had not been the glorious success the British expected. Most of the military supplies had been safely removed, and although still considered the capitol, Philadelphia no longer served as the seat of the new government. Congress had relocated, and the business of the new nation was being conducted without interruption in the city of York, some one hundred miles to the west.

His mood brightened even further as he thought of Liesl, who would be coming to care for him soon. She truly was remarkable, whether her father thought so or not. How many young women would have the courage to save a man's life? Lafayette admired her spirit and her stories brightened his dreary days.

The sun's strong rays warmed the back of Liesl's dark blue vest as she left the house with her shopping basket tucked securely under her arm. Although the crisp autumn air whispered the promise of cold nights to come, the sun seemed intent on making good use of every long day remaining.

She needed to purchase yet another cone of sugar from Sister Dorothea at Horsfield House. Now that Mother

Boeckel was baking a sugar cake nearly every other day, her sugar usage had increased threefold. Liesl only hoped Father would not look too closely at the household expenditures, at least not until Lafayette had returned to the battlefield.

Earlier, she had heard raised voices, and Lafayette had been unusually subdued when she made her daily ministrations. She was not at all surprised by the rising tension between the two men. Lafayette's growing vexation with her father's daily lectures had become obvious, and she knew Father would praise the day Lafayette departed from their home.

She felt a sudden pang at the thought of Lafayette leaving but quickly dismissed the feeling. It was never a good idea to become too attached to patients. Once healed, they returned to their normal lives and never gave their caregivers another thought.

It was nearly time for the Ritual of the Great Cake, and she did not want to be late. To save time, Liesl cut through the orchard behind her home. The fruit trees, planted in perfectly aligned rows, were overloaded with reddening apples. The fresh smell of ripening fruit filled the air and filled her mind with visions of sweet, flaky pies.

She moved rapidly across the uneven ground, carving her way through a hazardous terrain strewn with stones and pruned tree limbs. Needing to watch each step to avoid twisting an ankle, she might have missed the movements among the trees off to her right, if not for the smell. The rancid odor announced the presence of soldiers even before they came fully into view.

Stealing apples, no doubt. These soldiers felt entitled to appropriate whatever they liked.

There were three of them, two large burly men and a short, skinny one with a pockmarked face, all in need of a good swiping with a wet rag. As they drew closer, she realized the stench was not just from uncleanliness but also from drink, most likely rum or whiskey. Beer, wine, and hard ciders were common enough drinks in Bethlehem; however, spirituous liquors were considered intemperate. Not that these men were likely to be restrained by temperance of any kind.

She moved more quickly, still minding her steps to avoid stumbling. She prayed they would ignore her, but the largest of the three, a barrel-shaped man with a scraggly, unkempt beard, blocked her path.

"Well, boys, what do we have here? I do believe this gal is an authentic Moravian maid."

"That's right," the skinny one chimed in. "They told us last night the ones with the pink ribbons are ripe for the taking."

Liesl tried to stay calm as her mind raced through various scenarios, most of them ending in horror. She knew she was no match for three battle-hardened men, and a plea for mercy held little prospect of success. Her only chance was to distract them and run. She offered up a quick prayer, asking the Saviour to protect her. Then, she leaned over as if feeling faint, dropped her basket on the ground, and grasped a heavy palm-size stone. When she straightened, she threw the stone with all her might. The missile hit the skinny fellow squarely on the side of his jaw, and the man howled in shock.

Without looking back, Liesl turned and ran. One of the men laughed as she crashed through the rows of apple trees, mindless of the branches that tore at her clothes or the stones that scraped her shoes and pummeled her poor feet. Nothing mattered other than getting to the safety of the street.

Liesl arrived home breathless and disheveled. Mother Boeckel looked ready to scold her until she saw Liesl's dirt-streaked face.

"What has happened?"

Liesl recounted the incident as Mother Boeckel wiped the dirt from her face with a damp cloth and helped to remove her damaged shoes and sweat-soaked clothing.

"You were very lucky," Mother Boeckel said, giving Liesl an awkward hug. "None of us will rest easy until every last one of those soldiers is gone."

"This army cannot depart soon enough to please me," Liesl said, shaken but still defiant. "My dearest wish is that our lives would return to the peace we enjoyed before they ever set foot in our town."

Mother Boeckel nodded in agreement and then added in a confidential tone, "I think it best if we not tell your father what happened. But you must be vigilant. You must promise me to walk only on the streets and lanes and to venture elsewhere only if other Brothers and Sisters are present."

"I promise," Liesl said.

"Well, it appears you are unharmed, but you must lie down. I will fix you a large cup of tea with an extra spoonful of sugar. And I will also inform Lafayette that there will be no Ritual of the Great Cake today."

Liesl tried to sleep but every time she closed her eyes, she saw the faces of the drunken soldiers and smelled their rancid odor. She did not attend the evening service but assured Mother Boeckel she was capable of removing Lafayette's dinner tray. No doubt Lafayette would be concerned about her.

And yet when Liesl entered the sitting room, moving with a slight limp, Lafayette barely looked up from his correspondence. "Have you heard the news from Philadelphia?"

Liesl nodded. Mother Boeckel had told her about the fall of the city just moments before, although the last thing she wanted to think about was the war. Or the soldiers fighting in it.

"I feel so helpless," Lafayette said. "I should have been there fighting side by side with Washington."

Liesl felt a surge of anger. How like him to think of no one but himself. In frustration, she shoved one of the wooden chairs, causing a loud scrape. Lafayette finally looked at her more closely and alarm spread across his face as his gaze rested on the scratches marring her cheeks.

"Dear girl, what has happened to you?" Lafayette cried.

"I am fine," Liesl insisted, although she was consumed by an unaccustomed anxiety. The full impact of what had happened, and what *could* have happened, was only starting to sink in.

"Has your father done something?" Lafayette demanded with a fierceness that seemed to surprise him as much as it did Liesl.

"No, of course not. If you must know, I was on my way to the market for some sugar, and instead of following the road, I walked through the apple orchard. I wanted to save some time, so I would not be late for the Ritual of the Great Cake."

"*Sacré bleu!* What happened?" Lafayette shouted.

"If you calm yourself, I will tell you." she said. And then she did.

"You came to no harm?" he asked for the third time.

"As I have told you, I am fine."

"And you hit the skinny one with a rock?" Lafayette reiterated, his voice filled with equal parts disbelief and admiration.

"I have told you I did."

"If I were not in this condition, I would find those three, and I swear they would feel the full measure of my wrath!" Lafayette pounded the arm of his chair. "I am grateful you got away, but I would see them well punished."

"Someone told them about the ribbons. They knew I was a maid," Liesl said quietly.

"What are you talking about?"

"The ribbons we wear. Red is for girls, blue is for married women, white is for widows, and pink is for Single Sisters like me. The skinny soldier saw my pink ribbons and told the others the ribbons meant I was available to them. As if I were a . . ."

Lafayette's face turned scarlet, and he reached for his writing supplies with the air of a man ready to do battle. "I shall write a letter to the head of the Continental Army here in Bethlehem. Not only that, I shall write a letter to George Washington himself, for he must be apprised of these matters directly. I promise you, dear Liesl, you will never, ever be treated like this again."

Lafayette's fierce protectiveness both surprised and comforted her, and as she walked slowly down the stairway to the kitchen, she realized her anger and anxiety had diminished. While no letter could rectify such a horrific event, she was touched by Lafayette's desire to help and his acknowledgment of the awful wrong done to her. So much of her life was about hiding her pain: keeping secrets from her father, suppressing her grief for the good of the community. No one had ever wanted to fight for her before.

CHAPTER 18

The Visitor

October 2005

Yuenglings had become a part of their weekly routine, and two identical condensation rings decorated Abbey's glass coffee table as she and Pete reviewed her project plan. Everything was on schedule, and best of all, Pete no longer questioned the value of the meetings or her involvement.

"I got a middle-of-the-night call from my mom again," Pete said when they'd finished reviewing the plan. "I'll be glad when they're in a closer time zone."

"Where are they now?" Abbey asked.

"Australia. Headed for the east coast to snorkel the Barrier Reef."

"They really are having a trip of a lifetime."

Pete's expression changed, and he looked uncomfortable. "I wanted to apologize for asking you questions about your parents. I didn't mean to pry."

"Don't worry about it. You never pry. That's one of the things I like about you."

She was surprised to see Pete's face redden even though he tried to hide it behind the Yuengling bottle. She'd only seen him blush like that once before, and something about it made her want to share more about herself.

"I was born north of Philadelphia, near Willow Grove. We moved when I was twelve, and nothing seemed right after that. When my father made partner at his international accounting firm, we sold our little house and moved to a mansion in Bryn Mawr. I missed our old house, but I did love the ballroom. When we first moved in, I told Nana we had a ballroom the size of a football field. It was a good size but not that big."

Abbey pictured the open space with its shiny hardwood floor, giving her twelve-year-old self plenty of room to whirl and shimmy as her narrow boyish hips gyrated to the pulsating beat of Bon Jovi. Her mom had never gotten around to furnishing (or cleaning) the ballroom. It smelled of dust and old perfume, and the many mirrors, which reminded Abbey of a French palace, gave her lots of opportunities to check out her technique. She had danced with abandon, like no one was watching. Because no one ever was.

"I danced in that ballroom every day after school," Abbey said.

"Sounds like a lonely life."

"When I complained the house was too big, that I felt lost in it, my dad got me walkie-talkies."

Pete shook his head. "I'm guessing the walkie-talkies didn't really solve the problem."

"The house was a ridiculous size for three people let alone just two, which happened more and more as my dad flew all over the world." Now it was Abbey's turn to hide behind her beer bottle. "Sorry for sounding like a poor little rich girl. Most people think money solves problems, but sometimes it makes things worse."

They moved on to safer topics and drank another round of Yuengling. Abbey hated to see him leave, and by the time she walked him to the door, the sky was already getting dark.

"Thanks for the beer," Pete said.

"Any time." Abbey paused. "I shouldn't have bored you with stories about my childhood."

"No worries, MPM," he said. "Nothing about you bores me."

That night, Abbey felt strangely restless. Even a Nordic thriller she'd grabbed from the Moravian Book Shop's new arrivals table failed to provide the usual escape. Talking to Pete had dredged up memories she usually kept under wraps, and she had trouble falling asleep. Even bunching up the blue comforter all around her didn't help.

When she finally drifted off, she dreamed of being trapped in a place where corridors stretched out in front of her as far as she could see, and staircases led to one identical floor after another. She woke up shaking at the ungodly hour of three o'clock and only slept for short stints from then on, spending most of the night watching the slow blink of her digital alarm clock.

The following morning, Abbey dragged herself into the shower. The restorative powers of hot steam helped, along with a cup of Original Donut Shop. She sipped the hot coffee and admired her handbag slumped on the granite countertop. It really was the prettiest shade of blue.

She was ready to give the new book another try when the front doorbell rang. Probably just Pete arriving early, but as she headed for the door, she made a mental note to buy a spy hole.

"Hi, Abbey." Michael Butler, her former boss and one-time lover stood on her front porch.

This can't be happening.

He looked taller, maybe a bit slimmer. With his perfectly coiffed hair and sleek Armani suit, he looked like he'd just completed a photo shoot. But he stood so still, he might have been a department store mannequin—all except for his dark eyes sparking with emotion.

She tried to hide her alarm. "What are you doing here, Michael?

"Is that any way to greet an old friend? A very dear old friend?"

"How did you find me?" Her hands were clenched so tightly, her fingernails felt like paring knives cutting into her palms.

"A little detective work and a buddy in Human Resources. I had a meeting up this way so I figured I'd stop by to see how you're doing."

"Well, now you've seen me. I'm doing fine. You can go."

"Aren't you going to invite me in?"

"No, I'm not." A bit more silver flecked his temples, and she wondered if she were to blame. The thought didn't bother her one bit.

"Why the hostility? It's not as if I left *you* and disappeared without a word. Besides, I've come a long way. The least you can do is ask me in."

Michael yanked open the screen door, and she instinctively stepped back. Not because she was intimidated, but because of the sensations his familiar woodsy scent still aroused.

Now that he had crossed the threshold, Michael took charge as always. "Nice place," he remarked as he walked down the hallway, peeking into each room. "I never really envisioned you as the historical-home type, but this place has potential. You can probably fix it up and flip it. Ah, here's the kitchen. A cup of coffee would be nice, Abster."

Abbey bristled at the nickname she'd once loved—she was definitely not his Abster anymore! She moved to the far side of the granite island. "One cup of coffee and then you'll go. Do we have a deal?"

"You know how I love it when you're bossy," Michael said with a familiar smirk.

She was tempted to throw the Keurig at him, but

instead she scanned the K-Cup carousel and chose his favorite, Dark Magic.

"I like this kitchen," Michael said, sounding like a prospective homebuyer. "A bit old-fashioned but cozy."

Abbey reached beneath the cupboard and grabbed the Apollo and Daphne ceramic coffee cup. Before she realized what was happening, Michael made an end run around the granite island and came up close behind her.

"I've missed you," he said, stretching out his arms to encircle her from behind.

Abbey shoved him backward and stepped on the toe of one of his shiny Hugo Boss oxfords. "Get away from me!"

"What is wrong with you?" Michael asked, as if she had violated some basic rule of civility.

"I saw you!" Abbey shouted. "I saw you with your wife, and I know you lied to me."

"What are you talking about? I don't know what you think you saw, but—"

"I *know* what I saw, Michael. I'm not getting involved with you again. Not now. Not ever."

Accumulated rage surged through her body like a fever, but at the same time, she couldn't deny a knee-jerk feeling of desire. She trembled with the force of the warring emotions, but this was no time to show weakness. Drawing upon a lifetime of self-control, she looked him in the eye. "We're done, Michael. You need to leave."

Maybe he sensed her ambivalence, or maybe he was

even more of a prick than she'd imagined, but he grabbed her by the shoulders and spun her around. The coffee cup fell to the floor and shattered. Abbey stared in disbelief as Daphne's graceful arm skittered across the floor. Michael pressed her bottom against the island, bending her backward as he kissed her neck and nibbled on her ear, something she'd always loved.

Michael was right about one thing. All that rowing on the Schuylkill had really paid off. Abbey tried to push him off her, but she was no match for him.

She freed her left arm and stretched it across the cold, hard granite. Shoulder screaming, she skimmed the unyielding surface until her hand connected with soft leather.

She lunged backward to grab hold. A maneuver Michael apparently took as consent because now he was trying to unzip her jeans. Luckily, Abbey had left her bag open, and she tipped it over. Wallet. Keys. Checkbook. Tissue pack. *Why the hell did she carry around so much junk?* At last her fingers grasped what she was looking for.

She lurched toward Michael with a violent twist and held the hot-pink vial of pepper spray in front of his face.

"Are you fucking kidding me? You're going to mace me?"

"Get out of here, Michael. I mean it." Abbey's voice shook, but there was no mistaking the menace in her tone as her finger hovered above the trigger of the Mace dispenser. Michael released her and shot her one last furious, incredulous look before striding down the hallway and storming out of the house, slamming the old screen door almost hard enough to knock it off its hinges. Abbey followed closely behind him, just in time to see Pete pull up.

Pete started to climb out of his truck and then hesitated. "Abbey, if this is a bad time, I can come back."

"No, not at all," Abbey said. "He's just leaving." She couldn't believe Pete had to witness this.

"One last thing," Michael said, turning back toward her with a pained look. "I never lied to you. But maybe you lied to yourself."

Michael glanced at Pete. "Getting it somewhere else I see. That explains a lot. Not one to let the grass grow under your butt."

Abbey wanted to punch him.

"Well, it was nice to see you again, Abster. By the way, we have an opening in our Manhattan office that would be a perfect fit for you. You should give Sherry a call to set up an interview."

"Sherry?"

"Yeah, Sherry. She works for me now. And by the way, she's pretty pissed at you too." Then he turned to give Pete a long, hard look. "Did Abbey tell you she sleeps with married men?"

"Goodbye, Michael," Abbey hissed.

Michael shrugged his elegant shoulders, slid behind the steering wheel of the silver S-Class Coupe in one languid motion, and then lowered the window. "Married *bosses* by the way. This one will do anything to get ahead." Michael revved the engine and laughed bitterly. "God save us all from ambitious women!"

"Nice guy," Pete observed after Michael roared down the quiet street.

"I'm so sorry," Abbey said, suddenly feeling as if she might collapse.

"Abbey, are you okay?" Pete asked. "You look like you need to sit down."

Putting his arm around her, he led her back into the house and out to the sunroom. She saw him glance at the shattered coffee cup on the kitchen floor as they walked past, but he made no comment. A darkening sky had left the sunroom in shadows, and once Pete settled her on the closest love seat, he flipped on the overhead bulbs. Abbey started shaking uncontrollably, and without saying a word, Pete grabbed the afghan and wrapped it around her.

His eyes locked onto hers. "I'm going to make you a cup of tea. I'll only be a minute, and I'm only seconds away if you need me."

Abbey nodded and curled into a ball. As she listened to the comforting sounds of Pete in her kitchen, she traced the red, white, and blue checkered pattern on the afghan, willing her heartbeat to slow down. She was furious at Michael and even angrier with herself for letting him into her home. For allowing him into her life in the first place.

Once she finished the self-flagellation, she noticed cramps in her fingers and loosened her death grip on the Mace, eventually setting it on the coffee table. She almost wished she *had* maced him, but Michael's expression as she waved the pink container in front of his face was vindication enough. She'd never seen him look so scared.

By the time Pete returned with chamomile tea, Abbey had managed to sit up, although she still kept the afghan bundled around her shoulders. She murmured a grateful thank-you as she wrapped her hands around the welcome warmth of the steaming cup.

Pete sat on the opposing love seat and picked up the Mace dispenser, rolling it back and forth in his large hands. "Abbey, I have to ask. Did he hurt you?"

"You mean did he rape me? No. But not for lack of trying."

After several soothing sips of tea, Abbey said, "I did work for him, but what he said was ridiculous. I'm fully capable of getting ahead on my own."

"I have no doubts about that."

"He was getting a divorce, but that's no excuse. I still can't believe I got involved with a married man. That I thought I loved him. When I inherited the house from Nana, I quit my job and came here to get away from him, to make a fresh start."

Pete nodded. "Bethlehem is a good place for second chances."

Abbey stood and dropped the afghan on the love seat. "Thank you for the tea. I feel much better now."

"Are you sure you're alright?"

"I will be."

Pete stood up too, but he didn't seem to know what to do next.

"Forget about working today," Abbey said. "I'd really like to be alone."

"Okay, if that's what you want." Pete still looked uncertain, but she didn't want him to feel responsible for her. At that moment, she didn't want him feeling *anything* for her.

"I'll see you next week," she said, and remained standing until she heard the front door open and close. Then, she sank back down on the love seat.

The confusion on Pete's face as he left gave her a twinge of guilt, but it couldn't be helped. If nothing else, her relationship with Michael had taught her one thing: passion made her reckless. She wasn't going to make that mistake again.

CHAPTER 19

October 3, 1777

When I think of His endless mercies, I feel the blood of the Saviour overstream my being. I fall down at His feet, my eyes flowing with a thousand tears, imploring Him to forgive my sins through His precious blood.

—Diary of Sister Benigna Schemmel

After their heated conversation, Lafayette made no attempt to hide his dislike for Frederick, and his host responded in kind. The following morning, the two men uttered only the most perfunctory morning greetings before Frederick launched into his usual morning tirade.

Lafayette ignored Frederick's ranting and concentrated on Liesl instead, who looked remarkably composed despite the events of the previous day. When he thought of those soldiers, anger washed over him along with a deep sense of guilt. It was only because of his selfish craving for sugar cake that Liesl had been in that orchard at all. If anything had happened to her, he would never have forgiven himself.

As soon as the morning service ended, Lafayette asked Mother Boeckel to post several letters for him, including his missives protesting the treatment of the women in Bethlehem. He had also composed a letter to Adrienne, explaining how she must respond to questions about the plight of the revolution. He wrote, "People will say the Americans are beaten, that the taking of Philadelphia, the capital of America and the bulwark of liberty, was a final blow. These people are simpletons. You must tell everyone the Americans will make the British surrender sooner or later."

He missed his wife with her quiet ways and sweet nature, and yet, he was guilty of thinking of her less than he should have. The best parts of his days occurred at midmorning when Liesl came to change his dressings and the early evening when she returned to retrieve his dinner tray. The times when they were alone together.

A short while later, she entered his sitting room as usual.

"You appear to be fully recovered," Lafayette said. "I trust that is so."

"I am fine," Liesl said as she knelt to change his bandages.

"My letter to George Washington will be posted today, and I can assure you, he will act appropriately."

"I am certain he will, but I prefer not to speak of the matter."

"As you wish," Lafayette said, wondering if such an attack could be so easily forgotten. Certainly, *he* would not soon forget.

"Since you have been an exemplary patient," Liesl said without a trace of sarcasm, "I have brought you a present."

"I love presents!" Lafayette cried.

Liesl reached into her basket and handed him a small rectangle that shimmered in his palm.

"You made this?" he asked, studying the embroidery.

"I did."

"The colors are exquisite. The flowers are so well realized I believe I can smell their luscious scent. Your accomplishments, mademoiselle, are remarkable."

"It is for you to mark your place in *The History of Greenland*."

"Of course, *un marque-page*. Thank you, dear Liesl. Believe me when I tell you this gift will be most treasured. I will think of you every time I look at it."

Alone again, Lafayette stared at the bookmark, unable to take his eyes off the graceful curves of the broad-petaled tulips and the finely rendered daisies leading to the centerpiece of the work, a blue dahlia. As vibrant as the dahlia was, it was restrained by the intertwining stems surrounding it, as if it were being held captive by the foliage, a prisoner trapped within a silken snare.

That evening when Liesl entered the sitting room, Lafayette made a show of carefully placing his new bookmark in *The History of Greenland.* Then, he turned to her with an expectant look.

"I believe it is time for you to return to your storytelling," Lafayette said. "You must tell me more of your time in the Older Girls' Choir and your friendship with Benigna."

"Surely, you have more important things to occupy your mind than the unremarkable lives of young girls."

"Not at all," he said. "Your stories provide a respite from the worries of the present. And you have left me most curious about the Labouress. You must tell me more about her."

Liesl hesitated, for every story brought her closer to events she dreaded. But now that she had started down this path, it seemed she could not turn back. Lafayette would never rest until she told him more, so she took her seat and returned, once again, to that time so long ago.

"Within a few weeks, I began to notice changes in Benigna's behavior. She had become very quiet and withdrawn. She no longer turned toward me at bedtime but rolled the other way and feigned sleep."

Benigna had trouble concentrating on her lessons and appeared to have retreated to some dreamy state. She had lost her appetite as well and became alarmingly thin. When Benigna wore only her shift at bedtime, Liesl could see the clear outline of her rib cage against the thin material.

Benigna's face had a sallow cast and her once lively eyes were dull and wary. Liesl became even more uneasy when she heard Benigna crying and mumbling to herself in the middle of the night.

Fearful for her friend, Liesl decided to confide in Sister Adelina.

"You must tell the Labouress," Sister Adelina said.

"I doubt she will listen to me."

"It is the only answer," Sister Adelina insisted. "The Labouress will appreciate your concern."

But that is not what happened.

Liesl arrived for her weekly trial of speakings, determined to tell the Labouress about Benigna's worrisome behavior despite her misgivings. Finally, the Labouress swept into the room, listened distractedly to Liesl's paltry confession, advised her of some additional responsibilities, and stood up to leave.

"Please, if I may have one more moment," Liesl said in a voice quavering with nervous tension.

"Be quick about it, girl. I have important matters to address."

"I am worried about Benigna," she said, and her voice gained strength as she enumerated her concerns.

"I can assure you Benigna is fine. She is undergoing the ecstasy of the Saviour. Something you are unable to imagine and will undoubtedly never experience for yourself."

"I believe she is ill and needs our help."

The dark eyes of the Labouress sparked with anger. "Have you earned a medical degree that I am unaware of? Do you presume to understand what care Benigna requires better than I do? Return to your duties, Liesl Boeckel, and never question my judgment again!"

Two weeks later, a jagged spear of lightning awoke Liesl before dawn, and she found Benigna's bed empty, the bedding cold. Liesl quietly slipped into her shoes, wrapped a blanket around herself, and left the dormitory. Flashes of lightening helped her make her way through the dark corridor until she found Benigna in the Saal, prostrate on the floor, sobbing as if her heart was breaking.

Liesl drew closer, and Benigna cried out, "Oh, Jesus, my friend in times of need, I thank you from my heart for all the pains of your soul and for your martyrdom until death!"

Kneeling, Liesl tried to calm her, but Benigna was like one possessed. She scratched at Liesl's face and screamed.

"Get behind me, Satan!"

Terrified, Liesl ran down the stairs and into the small room belonging to Sister Adelina. Liesl tried to be as quiet as possible, but the floor creaked, and Sister Adelina struggled to sit up, groggy but awake. "What is it? Is something wrong?"

"Sister Adelina, I am sorry to disturb you, but you must come with me. Benigna is in trouble. In the Saal."

Sister Adelina quickly lit the candle she kept by her bedside and grabbed a coverlet.

When they entered the room, Benigna was no longer alone. A tall slender figure in a long black cape was helping Benigna to her feet.

Seeing Liesl, the Labouress snarled, "Liesl Boeckel, this is no business of yours. Return to your bed immediately!"

Liesl shivered as she recalled the sound of the Labouress's hate-filled voice. Then she stood, offering a clear indication that her storytelling had ended.

"You cannot go now!" Lafayette cried. "You must tell me what happened next."

"I must leave," Liesl said. "The hour is late."

Lafayette gave her a despondent look, but Liesl remained adamant. She had no wish to torment him, but she could only bear to tell small portions of her story at a time.

CHAPTER 20

Wine and Thai

October 2005

Pete sat at the bar in McCarthy's pub, draining the last of his Guinness. The previous three days in New York had taken their toll, and he decided to call it an early night. He looked forward to getting back to his regular work schedule, especially Abbey's project. He'd thought about calling her every night while he was away, but things had been so awkward the last time they'd been together, he didn't want to push it.

It was hard to forget the rush of fury that had surged through him that day Michael showed up. If the guy had been within reach, Pete would have maced him himself. Or worse, much worse. Afterwards, every particle of his being had wanted to put his arms around Abbey, but instead, he'd sat there, rooted in place on the opposing love seat— until she asked him to leave. He told himself it was nothing personal, just her way of dealing with what had happened, but now he wasn't sure where things stood.

As he walked back to his truck, he stopped to glance in the window of the wine bar called Corked. He'd never been inside, not a place for a beer-drinking man. And yet, he had to admit the blue lighting gave the place a sexy ambience. As did the long legs on full display at the bar in the back—legs belonging to a woman with familiar sandy-blond hair whose head was bent down, almost touching, her equally familiar auburn-haired companion.

Abbey stared at the twinkling lights embedded in the bar countertop at Corked, ignoring her companion. She already regretted meeting Adam at this fancy wine bar. His idea, of course. But she'd needed to get out of the house to distance herself from the memories of Michael and to stop thinking about Pete. How Pete had wrapped the afghan around her shoulders and made her tea. And how she'd shut him out, mistreating the one person who least deserved it.

The waiter handed them an extensive wine menu, and she immediately perked up. Like Abbey, Adam was a bit of a wine connoisseur, and the two of them pored over the wine choices together, debating the merits of pinot noir versus cabernet sauvignon and the Old World wines of France versus the New World wines of California. They finally decided on four half glasses. Two whites: a

New Zealand sauvignon blanc and a Russian River chardonnay. And two reds: a French pinot noir and something called the Prisoner Red Blend, a Napa Valley combo of zinfandel, cabernet sauvignon, syrah, petit syrah, and charbono.

Adam moved his chair closer than Abbey thought necessary, and anyone observing the two of them would assume they were on a date. Which they were not. And yet, she had to admit he looked very smart in a charcoal-gray cashmere sweater that contrasted nicely with his coppery hair. He was a decent guy, and he had been a big help with Liesl's bookmark, which is why she'd decided to have him translate Liesl's messages. That, and the fact she had no idea who else to ask.

Once they finished off the white wine, Abbey reached for the Prisoner Red Blend, and taking no prisoners herself, abruptly shifted into business mode.

"I want you to look at something else for me," Abbey said, digging into the Brahmin. "The top seam of Liesl's bookmark was open, and I found this piece of paper hidden inside it. It's written in French, I think. I can't manage the handwriting, but I bet you can."

Reverting to his scholarly self, Adam reached greedily for the small bag. He stared at the tiny elaborate handwriting, squinting to see through the plastic. "Yes," he said finally. "I believe I can."

Abbey took it back, careful to avoid damaging the paper inside. "First, I need your promise, your solemn oath, you will not share these contents with anyone but me."

"Of course not." Adam pushed his glasses higher on his nose and folded his arms across his chest. "I'm a professional archivist. I do not divulge confidential information, and I do not appreciate you questioning my integrity."

Calm down, buddy. No need to act like I'm attacking the sacred code of ethical archivists. He was being ridiculous, but she needed his help.

"I didn't mean to offend you, and I do trust you," she said, holding the paper out to him. "It's just that these messages may solve a mystery more than two hundred years old and that makes me nervous."

"Don't worry," Adam said as he caressed the plastic bag. "I'll let you know the moment I'm finished."

Abbey ended her evening with Adam early, which had been surprisingly easy since he couldn't wait to go home and start translating. Seemed like giving Adam the messages was the one surefire way to get rid of him!

Back home, Abbey cradled Liesl's bookmark in her hand and toyed with the idea of calling Pete. He was probably back from New York by now, and she missed him. But she wasn't sure what she wanted from him—or what she had to give.

She stared at the blue dahlia with the embroidered letter L's and wondered if Liesl had fallen in love with Lafayette. He would have been unlike anyone she had ever met, so it would be natural for her to be intrigued by him. But

Lafayette was a married man, and Liesl was a Moravian Sister raised in a strict society. Would Liesl have risked everything to follow her passion?

Gazing at the riotous flowers, Abbey realized her compulsion to find out what had happened between Liesl and Lafayette was increasingly tempered by a growing sense of responsibility for this woman who had reached out to Abbey through the centuries. If Abbey did unravel Liesl's secrets, what would she do with her discovery? And more important, what would Liesl want her to do?

The following night, Kera breezed into Abbey's sunroom, looking like an escapee from a hippie commune in her black leggings and flowing emerald-green tunic. Abbey had invited her for dinner, promising an update on the latest events in her crazy life. The only subject off the table was Michael. She and Kera had already dissected his reappearance during a late-night phone call, and Abbey never wanted to talk about it again.

As always, Kera brandished a bottle of wine, but this time the bottle held a white. "I know we're red wine freaks, but my personal sommelier Nolan tells me gewürztraminer is the way to go with Thai food."

"How did you know we were having Thai?" Abbey asked.

"Because I know you. You don't cook. You love Thai

takeout, and a new Thai place just opened on Main Street. Besides, I'm a bit of a psychic."

"Well then, with your special powers you probably already know what I ordered, but just in case you're having an off night, let me give you the rundown." Abbey gestured to the assortment of plastic soup containers and foil pans with clear plastic lids arrayed on the coffee table. "For soups, we have tom yum goong and tom kha gai. And for our entrées, I got pad thai with shrimp, drunken noodles, and massaman curry with chicken."

"I love it all, but massaman curry is my weakness."

"Apparently, you're not the only one with a sixth sense. I got a double order of the curry, so you can take one with you."

"You're the best!" Kera gushed as she reached for the corkscrew.

Abbey and Kera attacked the food like penitents breaking a fast. As they ate and drank, Abbey brought Kera up to date on the secret messages she had given Adam to translate.

"I love the idea of hiding messages inside a bookmark. Very romantic," Kera said. "Do you think something was going on between Liesl and Lafayette?"

"I do," Abbey said, waving a forkful of noodles.

"And how about what's going on between you and Adam and Pete?"

"You make it sound like a ménage à trois!"

"Not my words!" Kera said with a laugh. "Wasn't there

some old song about having two lovers and not being ashamed?"

"I don't know the song, and I certainly don't have two lovers. In fact, I don't even have one."

"Well, that's just sad. Tell me more about Adam."

"He's very competent at his job, and he's been a big help to me with the Liesl research. Not bad looking either, dresses well . . ."

"But?"

"But what?"

"I know you, Abbey. You're hedging."

Abbey had to admit Kera *was* good. "He's nice enough, but I'm just not attracted to him. There's no connection—no zing. And now that he has Liesl's messages, he's forgotten all about me. Anyway, he's definitely not a contender."

"And Pete?"

"What about him?"

Kera shook her head in exasperation. "I sense some zing when you talk about *him*. Is he a contender?"

"He's a handyman."

Kera looked like she wanted to say more, but instead she shared her latest third grader story. She had asked the kids to bring in a book from home, and one little boy brought in *My Horizontal Life*.

"Isn't that the book about one-night stands?" Abbey asked, and then quickly added, "I read the review."

"Oh, right, just the review. Anyway, that's the one."

"What did you do?"

"I wrote a little note: 'Might be a bit mature for the third grade.' Then I added a cute smiley sticker and sent it back home."

Abbey laughed so hard she started to hiccup, which only made Kera start laughing all over again. They were still giggling when they exchanged double-cheek kisses on the porch. But then, Kera's expression turned serious.

"Pete's a really nice guy," Kera said. "Handyman or not. Don't forget that, okay?"

CHAPTER 21

October 4, 1777

My childhood memories are bittersweet, a mix of wondrous joy and painful frustration. I often think about what I might have done differently, but a person cannot change who she is.

—Diary of Sister Liesl Boeckel

Frederick had barely completed the morning service when a loud knock at the front door sent Mother Boeckel scurrying downstairs. Lafayette heard a deep voice followed by loud creaking on the steps.

"A General Pulaski wishes to see you," Mother Boeckel said, as she ushered a man into Lafayette's sitting room. The soldier was outlandishly dressed in the style of a hussar, with an enormous amount of gold braiding and a helmet topped with a horsehair plume.

Lafayette leaped to his feet, spilling Liesl's bookmark and *The History of Greenland* onto the floor. "*Mon bon ami*

Kazimierz! How good it is to see you again."

"I am pleased to see you as well," Pulaski said. The men embraced as Mother Boeckel quietly left the room.

"How is your injury?" Pulaski inquired, looking down at Lafayette's leg with concern. "Perhaps you should not be standing."

"I am making a remarkable recovery," Lafayette said, but he did take a seat and gestured for his visitor to sit in one of the small wooden chairs. "I have you to thank for my being here at all. No doubt, myself and many others would have fallen at Brandywine if you and your horsemen had not covered our retreat."

Pulaski slid his chair closer to Lafayette. "But you were the true hero that day, jumping off your horse and ordering those panicked soldiers to stand and take the charge from the enemy. The men still talk about your valor. In any case, I was only doing my duty. As you know, I came here where freedom is being defended to serve it—and to live or die for it."

"We are much alike," Lafayette said. "I knew that from the moment we met. But tell me, when did you last see Washington? I am much in need of news."

"I met with our commander but a few days ago. He was well and quite pleased that I had plans to visit you. He sends his best regards with a fervent wish for your full recovery. He is hopeful you will rejoin him soon."

"As am I. I feel quite wretched sitting here when I should be fighting by his side."

"You shall be there soon enough," Pulaski said, patting his friend on the shoulder. "I have some personal news as well. Washington has named me brigadier general of the American cavalry, and I have at my command four regiments of dragoons numbering a little over five hundred men."

Lafayette congratulated his friend, but he could not dismiss the envy that made his thoughts run wild. Pulaski was older than he, that was true, but was not Lafayette every bit as capable? Ever since he was a boy, Lafayette had burned for his own command. He assessed Pulaski and his dashing good looks. Why should this Polish upstart be so blessed?

But then, thinking of Liesl's steady composure, he reminded himself of his own considerable blessings. His current circumstances were nothing but a brief postponement. Leading men into battle for the cause of liberty was his destiny, and he would not be denied. The Lafayette who first arrived on America's shores would have railed at his fate, and perhaps even spoken harsh words to his friend, but Lafayette was no longer that man.

"I am truly happy for you," Lafayette said. "You will be a fine commander."

Pulaski reached for the bookmark lying on the floor and studied the embroidery. "Where did you get this?"

"It is a gift from the Moravian Sister who tends to my wound."

"I see," Pulaski said with a wink.

"I would not have you making incorrect assumptions,"

Lafayette said. "But it is a fine piece of work, is it not?"

"I have never seen such exquisite embroidery. I will inquire if the Moravian Sisters here in Bethlehem might create a banner for my legion. Imagine this, Lafayette, a banner in the deepest shade of crimson with gold lettering bearing the Latin inscription *Unita virtus forcior.*"

"Union makes valor stronger. It would suit you well, my friend."

Liesl sat by the hearth, completing some much-needed mending for young George Frederick, whose breeches needed constant attention. In truth, she had never seen a child so hard on his clothing.

She looked up as heavy steps descended the stairs and got a quick glimpse of an overdressed officer before hearing the click of the front door. Liesl hoped Lafayette had enjoyed his visit, even though it had interfered with her tending to his leg. Perhaps the officer had given him something else to think about besides her life story.

But the moment she entered the sitting room, Lafayette beseeched her. "Please tell me what happened after you discovered the Labouress in the Saal with Benigna."

"Let me care for your leg, and perhaps then I will tell you more," Liesl said.

"*Je préfère* you tell me now. It was unkind of you to leave me last night without finishing the tale."

"And it was unkind of you to allow your visitor to interfere with your medical care."

"I apologize, but my visitor brought me much needed news. You do understand we are at war."

"As if I could forget," Liesl said. "The war does not change the fact that your bandages should have been changed much earlier."

"Do not be angry with me, my dear nurse. You must know I would rather spend my days with you than with any visitor I can imagine."

"Even George Washington?" Liesl asked, her good humor returning.

Lafayette laughed. "Now there is my charming girl. I beg of you, please tell me more of your story."

"There is little left to tell. I did not see Benigna for several weeks. When she returned to the Older Girls' Choir, she was very quiet. She no longer slept in the bed beside me, and she did not resume her role as leader of the prayer band. In fact, she did not participate in our prayers at all. She spent most of her time tending the sheep. She never spoke of that night in the Saal, and I never asked her about it."

"And the Labouress?"

"She never spoke of it either, although she stopped being critical of me. In fact, she acted as if I did not exist at all. Even our weekly meetings lasted only a few moments. She appeared to have given up on me entirely."

"I am glad. It saddens me to think of the misery she caused you."

"My life did become easier. The years passed without any further incidents, and at age nineteen, I joined the Single Sisters' Choir. Although it was difficult for me to leave Sister Adelina, I welcomed my release from the domination of the Labouress."

Liesl described her last days in the Older Girls' Choir, which included a request from Sister Adelina to see her privately. Liesl had not entered Sister Adelina's room since that fateful night when she sought help for Benigna, but any doleful thoughts flew from her mind as Sister Adelina embraced her.

"I shall miss you," Sister Adelina said as she released her. "You will be close by, but I will not see you as often when you are a Single Sister. You are a good girl, Liesl. Never forget your Saviour loves you and so do I. Do not judge others harshly for we all have our failings and our weaknesses. We must have patience with each other, just as the dear Saviour has with me, with you, and with us all."

"Patience has never been a strength of mine," Liesl said with a small smile. "But I believe I have found my calling. After much prayer, I have decided to become a nurse like my mother."

Sister Adelina nodded. "That will suit you. You will be able to put your energy and intellect to good use."

"If I cannot have the all-consuming relationship with the Saviour that I once sought, at least I can serve the Saviour in my own way."

Sister Adelina took Liesl's hands in hers. "I am sure the

Saviour holds you in his embrace and guides you on your path, but I might be able to offer a bit of help. I will talk to Doctor Oberlin. He has plans to train several medical assistants. I will ask that you be included."

On her last day in the Older Girls' Choir, the Labouress summoned Liesl to her private room, a place few girls ever entered. The tiny cell, no larger than a pantry, offered barely enough room for a single virginal bed and a small wooden desk. Seated behind that desk, the Labouress gave Liesl only a brief nod and continued to busy herself with inventory papers. No doubt she kept a record of every knife, fork, and spoon in the kitchen. And every piece of chalk in the schoolroom.

The claustrophobic bedchamber also held one small pupil's chair, which is where the Labouress gestured for Liesl to sit. The chair was quite low, which meant the Labouress loomed above her. Rather than being intimidated, Liesl welcomed the opportunity to survey the Labouress's lair.

Although located on the second floor of the Single Sisters' House, the solitary window was firmly shuttered, preventing even the slightest ray of sunlight from brightening the dismal space. A single candle flickered on the wooden desk, providing just enough light to read and write but utterly failing to alleviate the gloominess. The desk was cluttered with small pieces of embroidery and several woodcarvings. Probably gifts from grateful girls. Liesl sincerely hoped the Labouress did not expect one from her.

A painting hanging above the desk provided the somber room's sole decoration. The macabre picture depicted a young girl inside a chasm that had been slashed into the side of a hill like an open wound. The girl knelt in prayer as blood poured over her head, streaming down her body and running in rivulets across the hillside. In an odd contrast, the top of the hill bloomed with a profusion of beautiful, oversize flowers. Liesl tried to concentrate on the flowers, avoiding the bloodied young girl below, who looked almost like a fetus in a womb.

"The painting is called *Prayer in the Sidehole*," the Labouress said in the melodic but cunning voice that always reminded Liesl of the serpent in the Garden of Eden.

"It is provocative," Liesl observed.

"As captivating as your artistic opinions may be, I did not invite you here for an evaluation of my painting. I must tell you that you will receive medical training from Doctor Matthew Oberlin."

Liesl beamed. For once, she felt true gratitude toward the woman. "Thank you, Labouress!"

"I do not accept your thanks, for this was none of my doing," the Labouress snapped. "Sister Adelina went directly to Doctor Oberlin without my consent. The first time she has ever disregarded my authority." The dark eyes glimmered with loathing. "It would appear your evil nature is capable of corrupting even the purest of souls. First Benigna and now Sister Adelina."

The wild rush of anger pervading her being must have

shown in her face because the Labouress laughed. A hoarse sputtering sound devoid of any joyfulness that made Liesl recoil with revulsion.

"You will move on to the Single Sisters' Choir, but do not think for one moment that you have escaped me. For I will be watching. I will always have my eyes on you."

With that, Liesl ended her story, and Lafayette shook his head in wonder.

"I shall never understand why the Labouress treated you so abominably," he said, "but how delightful you were able to study medicine. Tomorrow you must tell me all about your training."

Liesl sighed. Apparently Lafayette's curiosity knew no bounds, but she was exhausted from dredging up so many memories.

"Good night, monsieur," she said.

Later, sleep eluded her as she pondered the power of memory. She had never permitted herself to dwell on the past. Much like the weathervane atop the Bell House, the winds of time pressed her forever forward. Sharing her childhood with Lafayette had been harmless enough, but she had never told anyone the full story about Matthew. Those memories were buried so deep, did she truly want to resurrect them?

CHAPTER 22

The Kiss

October 2005

"How was yoga class?" Pete called from the dining room as Abbey closed the front door. She'd discovered a yoga studio within walking distance of her house and signed up for a late-afternoon yin class. Great stretching and good for contemplation too. It had helped her realize Pete's friendship meant a lot to her, and since she still felt embarrassed by how abrupt she'd been the day of the Michael incident, she wanted to make amends.

"I'm feeling very mellow," Abbey said. "How's the nook coming along?"

"Come on in and take a gander. I want to be sure this is what you had in mind."

Two tall bookshelves hugged the walls in a back corner of the room, their empty shelves crying out for literary occupants. Abbey ran her fingers across the mitered edge of one of the oak shelves. "Beautiful. Just the way I envisioned it."

It was uncanny the way Pete was able to take her ideas and create exactly what she wanted. How had he managed to find the perfect oak to complement the rough-hewn mantel?

Still staring at the bookshelves, she said, "I have leftover Thai. Care to join me?"

Pete responded with that slow grin Abbey found so appealing. "Can't go wrong with Thai."

He followed her into the kitchen, where she set the table with paper plates and plastic silverware along with some napkins from the restaurant.

"Not exactly a classy table setting," Abbey said.

"Looks fine to me. You want beer with this, right?" Pete asked as he pulled two bottles of Yuengling out of the refrigerator.

Abbey arranged the microwaved leftovers on the granite countertop buffet-style.

"Help yourself," she said, feeling suddenly awkward as they filled their plates and sat across from each other at the small table. They hadn't sat here together since the first day they met, and they no longer seemed like the same two people. For one thing, she no longer thought of him as the hired help.

"This is great Thai," Pete said as he stabbed some drunken noodles with his fork. "Thanks, Abbey."

She tried to ignore the rush of pleasure she felt whenever he said her name. "It's just leftovers, but I wanted to thank you for helping me out the other day. . ."

Her voice petered out as she remembered that afternoon. She wanted to say more, but the words stuck in her throat.

"No problem," Pete said. "I'm just glad I happened to come by."

Abbey regained her composure. "I also need to tell you I'm going to have to reschedule our project meetings to work around my new job."

"You got a job?"

"Don't sound so surprised. A girl has to earn a living, you know."

"What's the job?" Pete asked, his voice sounding strange, almost nervous.

"You are looking at the new reading program coordinator at the Moravian Book Shop."

Relief flooded Pete's face. "You got a job at the book shop?"

"Yes, that's what I just said. I'll put in some hours each week as a cashier, but my main job will be developing a series of free reading programs. A story hour for preschoolers once a week and an after-school pre-teen book club."

"How did all this happen?"

"Well, I'd been thinking about this bookstore near my old office in Philly. They offered wonderful reading programs for kids, and every time I walked by their display windows, I would check out what the kids were reading next. I pitched a similar reading program idea to Madeline, the owner of the Moravian Book Shop, and she loved it. Hired me on the spot. I already have a list of books for the older kids to read, and Kera volunteered to be my first guest reader for the preschoolers."

Pete beamed. "Those kids will be lucky to have you."

"The salary is a pittance, but it'll pay for groceries. And beer!"

They sat in companionable silence.

"How's the research on Liesl going?" Pete asked, and once again, his voice sounded strained. Abbey wondered if he might be coming down with something.

"I gave the messages to Adam to translate, but I haven't heard anything yet. I've been wanting to ask you about Adam. I know almost nothing about him."

Pete took a long swig of beer. "Adam's a pretty private guy, but I can tell you the gossip I heard from old Mrs. Dotter, if you want."

"I swear that woman is frightening. Tell me."

"According to Mrs. Dotter, Adam's father left when he was just a baby. Then when Adam was a senior at Moravian College, his mother died in a car accident. Mrs. Dotter is convinced alcohol was involved. Anyway, Adam inherited the house, and after that, the Moravian community became his family. Mrs. Dotter says the board members at the archives are like surrogate parents."

"That's sad," Abbey said.

"Are you and Adam dating?" Pete asked suddenly.

"Of course not. Whatever gave you that idea?"

"I walked by Corked last Friday night and saw the two of you huddled together at the bar."

"What were you doing? Stalking me?" she blurted out and immediately felt her face burn with shame. For some reason the idea of Pete being jealous rattled her. "I'm sorry, that was a stupid thing to say. I don't think you're a stalker, and I have no interest in Adam Wright. We met for coffee and drinks a couple times, but that was business. I'm pretty sure his only interest is in Liesl, not me. Anyway, after all the drama with Michael, I've sworn off men."

"We're not all like Michael, you know," Pete said softly.

Abbey's legs shook as she stood to clear the dishes. What she really needed to do was clear her head. It was becoming impossible to ignore Pete's interest in her, and she wasn't sure what to do.

Pete joined her at the sink and tried to cover a yawn.

"Sorry. It's not the company, believe me. My mom called me in the middle of the night. She forgot about the time difference again. They were all wound up because they saw Uluru. You know the famous red rock in the center of Australia?"

"I've seen photos. It looks incredible."

"Mom said pictures don't even come close to capturing how big and how red the thing is. Their only disappointment is they haven't seen a kangaroo yet."

"Your parents sound pretty great."

"They are." Pete's gentle brown eyes never left her face. "It must have been hard when your mom died."

"It was the worst," Abbey said. She hadn't planned to say anything more, but the memories came rushing back.

"Mom refused to waste any more time in the hospital and asked to spend her remaining days at home. Hospice provided everything: a hospital bed, medications to control the ever-present pain, and a woman named Mrs. Shrum who cared for her twenty-four/seven."

Her mom ate little and slept more. On a good day, she liked to reminisce about the old house on Hamilton Street where she lived as a newlywed and Abbey's first trip to Europe. That trip seemed like a lifetime ago to Abbey, but her mom's eyes had glowed as she relived every cup of coffee at every café, every painting in every museum, and every time Abbey's face had lit up at some new discovery.

"My dad set up a stereo system in Mom's bedroom," Abbey said, her voice shaking with emotion. "The strains of Bellini filled the house at all hours of the day and night. The music stayed with us until the end."

Abbey could still picture herself and Nana sitting on either side of the bed, each of them holding a wraithlike hand while her father hovered nearby. Her mom was unable to speak, but she had looked at each of them with such love that thinking about it made Abbey's eyes fill with tears.

"The funeral and my high school graduation were excruciating," Abbey said. "I stumbled through both of them like a sleepwalker. I was lost. It was as if my mom owned the only map to my future, and now that map was lost forever. Then Nana scooped me up and brought me home to Bethlehem and somehow managed to get me moving again. I spent most of the next four years either at college or wasting my summers toiling away at boring corporate internships arranged by my dad. But through it all, Nana was always there for me. My dad traveled more than ever, so I seldom saw him. And when I did, it was like I reminded him of all the things he was trying to forget. Then, a year after the funeral, he announced he was moving."

Her father's exact words still echoed in her head. "I need to make a fresh start. You understand, don't you, Abs?"

No, she did not, and she never would.

"Everybody deals with grief differently," Pete said quietly.

"Well, *he* certainly did! He sold our house and left for the West Coast where he met and married Mallory."

"Do you still talk to him?"

"Occasionally. At first, he called me every Sunday night, but ever since the twins, not so much. He doesn't want me in his life anymore."

"I doubt that."

"He left me," Abbey whispered, her lower lip quivering. "He moved away and left me all alone."

"You're not alone now," Pete said with a tenderness that made her shiver. He carefully placed a serving bowl in the sink and stepped toward her with equally careful movements.

Abbey tried to suppress her panic. This was the last thing she needed, especially so soon after Michael. But

Pete was right, not every man was like that. Maybe it was time to stop fighting her feelings for Pete and find out where this might go. She looked up into his kind brown eyes, and her fear slowly evaporated.

He finally reached her, and Abbey never flinched, not even when his strong arms enveloped her. Or when a rush of warmth pulsed through her as he held her close. She was no romantic, but her first thought was that he felt like home.

She turned her face to his, and he kissed her, gently at first but with increasing passion.

"I'm not sure I'm ready for this," Abbey said in a shaky voice as she pulled away.

Pete took her hand and placed it over his heart. "There's no rush. I'll be here."

After he left, Abbey gripped the front of the kitchen sink, reliving the soft warmth of his mouth on hers and the surge of anxiety that had raced through her as his passion ignited her own. She hadn't lied when she told Pete she wasn't ready, but the truth was she had no idea if she ever would be.

CHAPTER 23

October 5, 1777

It is well we cannot see the future. I still remember when I believed all things were possible and that happiness was within my grasp.

—Diary of Sister Liesl Boeckel

Lafayette stood by the window, testing the strength of his injured leg. Outside in the crisp October air, the covered heads of the Sisters passed by, clustered together like bouquets of white tulip buds, while the Brothers in their worn leather breeches headed south toward the industrial quarter. And the soldiers, easily identifiable by their coarse clothing and coarser demeanors, clogged the street.

Lafayette's constrained circumstances weighed even heavier on his mind since his visit with Pulaski. His wound was healing but not nearly fast enough, and he could not have felt more imprisoned if he were manacled and chained to the wall!

His only saving grace was the sweetness of his jailer. Liesl and her stories gave him as much pleasure as reading a beloved book, like Voltaire's *Candide* or *Persian Letters* by Montesquieu. He would never have expected a simple Moravian girl to have led such an intriguing life, and he was anxious for the next chapter.

At that moment, Liesl interrupted his cogitations as she entered his room, carrying something new in her basket.

"What magic elixir have you to offer me now, fair maiden?" he asked, returning to his seat. "I would gladly quaff your nastiest concoction if it would gain me my freedom."

"You must be patient," Liesl said, repeating the same advice she gave him every morning. "Today, I will treat your leg with sunflower oil. It is an effective ointment used by the Indians."

"Is this something you learned from your Doctor Oberlin?"

"That is correct," Liesl said as she removed his bandages and applied the lotion.

"I am anxious to hear more about him, for I believe your stories are the best medicine of all." A pained look crossed her face, and for the first time, he wondered if this storytelling might be difficult for her. "Of course, if you prefer not to share any more memories, I understand. I would not wish to make you uncomfortable."

Liesl stood quietly for several moments before settling herself on the small wooden chair. "I suppose I cannot deny you something that improves your well-being."

Lafayette smiled with relief. "You will never know how much your stories mean to me."

"I was one of nine medical assistants," Liesl said, "and our first assignment was to gather herbs. The apothecary garden supplied many of the ingredients Doctor Oberlin needed, but some herbs could be found growing in the wild."

During her first foray into the forest, Liesl had entered the woods with the other newly selected medical assistants, each one carrying a woven basket or a flaxen sack. It was springtime, and the forest floor was a patchwork of every shade of green the great painter of the world had ever created. At each turn, new life struggled out of the rotting leaves, pushing its way up through the deep, dark soil and into the light.

"Be careful where you step," Doctor Oberlin said as he led them deeper into the woods, moving through the trees with grace and confidence as if he were a woodland creature himself.

The only sounds were a woodpecker tapping steadily on a nearby tree, and an awkward fawn crashing through the underbrush as it struggled to follow its mother.

Dr. Oberlin stopped by a cluster of deep-green serrated leaves at the base of an old oak tree and gestured for the group to gather around him. "This is lemon balm," he said. "You can recognize it by its square stem and distinctive leaf pattern." Crouching down, he removed one of the leaves, tore it in two, and sniffed at the ragged halves. "It also smells like a lemon."

He passed one piece to the closest assistant, and then he extended the other to Liesl. As she took it, her hand brushed against his long, elegant fingers, and she tried not to blush. She was unaccustomed to being in the company of men and being close to him filled her with a strange combination of pleasure and unease.

After collecting several branches of the lemon balm and placing them carefully in his sack, Doctor Oberlin said, "Spread out to see what you can find, and if you discover anything of interest, let me know."

Liesl followed the path of the deer up a slight incline, the ground under her feet cushioned by fallen leaves and pine needles. As she breathed in the green freshness of living things, she marveled at how very lucky she was to have been chosen for this work.

Halfway up the slope, she spotted a tall plant covered with purplish leaves.

"Doctor Oberlin," she called, "I have found something."

The doctor moved quickly to her side and exclaimed, "Do you know what this is?"

"I believe it is blue cohosh. I recognize it because my mother sometimes used it in a tincture to aid women during childbirth."

"You are correct," he said with a broad smile. "It seems you have inherited your mother's talent for medicine. This is a fine specimen of the blue cohosh plant, and it is an herb I particularly need since my supply is quite low."

Pleased with herself, Liesl smiled in return. No one

would ever describe Doctor Oberlin as handsome, his plain features were unforgettable except for disconcerting green eyes flecked with gold, which seemed to sparkle with approval as he looked at her.

He tore off a branch and held the stem between his fingers. "The leaves may cause skin irritation, so avoid them as much as possible. Collect as many branches as you can carry but leave at least half of the plant for future growth."

When another assistant called for him, he started down the slope but then looked back. "Well done, Liesl!" he said.

Once the baskets and sacks were overflowing, they all returned to the narrow front room of the apothecary, which was housed in a small stone building on the street just below the Gemeinhaus. Bunches of drying herbs hung from the ceiling, and an impressive bank of wooden shelves stretched along one wall, displaying a vast assortment of medical instruments, scales, and powders. A center shelf proudly displayed distinctive blue-and-white Delftware jars from the Netherlands, and below that, forty-five wooden drawers, meticulously labeled in Latin, identified the plants and herbs stored within, ranging from *B. Juniperi* (juniper berries) to *Sem. Anisi* (star anise).

Liesl's mother had told her medical care was a priority from the earliest days of the Moravian community. Beginning with Doctor Meyer, who arrived within months of the settlement's establishment, Bethlehem always had the services of a proper physician trained in Europe. Few colonists had access to such learned medical expertise and providing care to non-Moravian neighbors became a lucrative venture. Her mother said Doctor Meyer could often be seen racing out of town on his horse, saddlebags stuffed with medical paraphernalia, on his way to deal with an emergency in the surrounding area. How proud her mother would be that Liesl had become a part of this longstanding tradition.

"Join me here in front of the compounding hearth," Doctor Oberlin said as he moved to the far end of the room near some distilling equipment, surrounded by a collection of variously sized mortars and pestles. His tall and lanky frame bent over the brick compounding hearth as he examined the collected herbs, describing the curative powers of each one.

"Ah, here is the best find of the day. An excellent supply of blue cohosh discovered by our Sister Liesl," he said with a nod in her direction.

She stared at the stone floor in an effort to appear modest, even though Doctor Oberlin's words filled her with pride.

Liesl paused her narrative and shifted in her seat. "That was just the first of many lessons. I soon mastered the process of grinding herbs with the mortar and pestle, even though it left my arms aching and sore. Under the direction of Doctor Oberlin, I prepared pills and powders and even learned how to create basic tinctures by combining herbs and alcohol."

"It sounds as if you found your calling," Lafayette said.

"Yes, I believe this is the work I was born to do."

Liesl had gladly devoted every available moment to her medical education. On many a late night, she could be found at a schoolroom desk, huddled over the latest textbook loaned to her by the doctor, struggling to decipher the German text by candlelight.

She began by focusing on the theory of humors, which postulated that the body contained four basic substances controlling both personality traits and health. Blood indicated a sanguine temperament, sociable and creative; yellow bile denoted an energetic but short-tempered character; an excess of black bile would render a person melancholic, although a normal measure resulted in thoughtfulness and independence; and phlegm signified a gentle personality, relaxed and kind. To avoid illness, an individual needed to maintain a proper balance of all these humors. Any imbalance required treatment with a combination of dietary changes and herbs.

Each morning, Liesl joined the other assistants as Doctor Oberlin reviewed assignments and discussed the progress of patients. One day, he asked her to stay behind as the others left to begin their duties.

"How are you progressing with your study of the humors?" Doctor Oberlin asked, gesturing toward the large leather-bound book in her hands. "Have you learned the basic temperaments associated with each?"

"I have, sir."

"Excellent! And what humor do you suppose most applies to me?" he asked with a glint of amusement in his peculiar golden-flecked eyes.

Liesl blushed but maintained his gaze. "I would say black bile, sir."

"That is correct, and I believe the same could be said of you."

Unsure how to respond to such a personal comment, Liesl lowered her head and held out the textbook. "I have completed the chapters you recommended, and I wish to return this in case other students have the same interest."

"None of the others are as dedicated as you are, Liesl. You may keep the book and begin a study of pneumatic theory. That is, if you wish to do so."

"Yes, sir. I would like that very much. Thank you, sir."

"It is my pleasure, but I would prefer it if you did not call me sir. It makes me feel like an old man. Besides, we are colleagues now."

"Yes, sir. I mean yes, Doctor Oberlin."

As Liesl walked toward the Sisters' House to monitor Sister Susanna's asthma, she thought about her conversation with Doctor Oberlin. She admired him greatly and enjoyed working by his side more than she cared to admit, but she had never dared to hope he might develop feelings for her. Now that hope kindled within her, although she tried to quash it, reminding herself he had merely said they were colleagues. And yet, those green-gold eyes had seemed to sparkle just for her. She clutched the heavy book to her chest, attempting to still the pounding of her heart.

The next morning, Doctor Oberlin looked unusually grave.

"I have received word of a smallpox epidemic in Philadelphia. As you may know, smallpox is a highly contagious and potentially deadly disease. Given our proximity to Philadelphia, we must take steps to prepare for the likelihood that we will have cases here.

"Beginning today, you will notify me immediately of any patients exhibiting high fever, one of the first symptoms of the illness. Nausea and vomiting may also be present. Another common symptom is a rash with flat red lesions displaying on the face, arms, and legs. Any patients exhibiting a rash of this type must be quarantined immediately.

"Smallpox is difficult to treat, but we do have one tool at our disposal. Several years ago, our own Doctor Otto introduced an inoculation for smallpox. Called 'variolation,' the procedure involves taking pus from an infected individual and inserting it under the skin of a healthy person. I have been inoculated along with a small number of our community. Perhaps some of you have been as well."

No one responded, and Doctor Oberlin was unable to hide his disappointment. "The inoculation provides lifetime immunity but may cause a mild case of the disease. There is only a small chance of death; however, some individuals develop painful sores that can lead to severe scarring. I offer the inoculation to any of you who desire it. This decision is a personal one, and I will not attempt to persuade you in any way. To avoid the risk of infection, I will insist you leave the care of smallpox patients to me, unless of course, you choose to receive the inoculation."

The nine medical assistants stood in silence, some staring at the floor while several shifted nervously from one foot to the other. Finally, Liesl stepped forward.

"I will have the inoculation," she said, even though the thought of permanent disfigurement terrified her. If she were going to become a nurse someday, she must be prepared to take risks. Doctor Oberlin nodded and looked at her with admiration, which made her even prouder of her decision.

A few weeks later, Liesl was awakened from a sound sleep by Sister Adelina shaking her gently but relentlessly. "Wake up, Liesl. Wake up! Doctor Oberlin needs your help."

Liesl dressed quickly, and Sister Adelina tucked several blond hairs out of sight inside her Haube.

"Fortunately, our Sisters slumber deeply," Sister Adelina whispered conspiratorially.

"However, we do not wish to disrupt their much-needed rest. Do make sure Doctor Oberlin returns you before daybreak."

A black carriage with a small, enclosed compartment was waiting outside, its two black horses snorting impatiently. Liesl had never ridden in such a thing and had no idea what to do next. A man she supposed to be the driver suddenly materialized and lowered a folding step from beneath the carriage door. Liesl may have remained rooted in place if not for Doctor Oberlin's familiar voice emanating from within the invisible confines of the conveyance. "Please hurry, Liesl, we must be off."

Hurtling herself into the darkness, she joined Doctor Oberlin on a narrow, high-backed seat. She was immediately engulfed by his scent, mostly herbal but with a muskiness that tickled her nose and made her hands shake.

"What is the emergency? And where have you obtained this carriage?" Liesl asked, her voice sounding overloud in the small space. She was unaccustomed to being in such proximity to a man and tried unsuccessfully to edge closer to the door.

"A suspected case of smallpox at the Seip farm," Doctor Oberlin replied. "It could not wait till morning, so Tobias Seip sent his carriage. I hope you will forgive me for disturbing you at this hour, but you are the only assistant who has been inoculated."

Liesl had received her inoculation two weeks earlier and suffered no ill effects of any kind. However, she had never cared for a smallpox patient before and had no idea what to expect. She wondered why Doctor Oberlin was unable to handle this emergency by himself as he usually did, but she said only, "I am glad to be of service."

When the carriage turned onto the road toward Easton,

the driver gave the horses full rein. Outside the small side window, silhouettes of trees flew by, and the jostling inside caused its passengers to bump against each other repeatedly.

"I apologize for the rough ride," Doctor Oberlin said, his eyes never leaving the road in front of them. "But I fear we may already be too late."

The carriage finally came to a halt in front of a small farmhouse whose windows flickered with candlelight. Doctor Oberlin grabbed his medical bag, and Liesl carried a case filled with small glass vials, each one holding a different, neatly annotated remedy. Tobias Seip opened the farmhouse door and immediately ushered them into a small back bedroom where his daughter Jane lay on a sweat-soaked bed. His wife sat nearby, caressing her daughter's small hand.

Jane's face and arms were covered with red lesions. When Jane gulped for air, Liesl glimpsed the rash on her tongue and in her mouth as well. Liesl turned to Doctor Oberlin and realized by his grim expression that there was little to be done.

He addressed the parents in his most gentle voice. "She is in the hands of God now."

The four of them prayed for a miracle as the mother sobbed quietly, and Jane struggled for breath. Liesl could do little more than wipe Jane's brow and pour small amounts of water mixed with cooling germander into the young girl's ravaged mouth. Finally, with a great constriction of the chest, Jane fell into eternal sleep.

"I had never witnessed such a tragic death of one so young," Liesl said to Lafayette, and turned away. "I was so distraught that as we walked back to the carriage, I fell to the ground, exhausted and overcome by grief. Doctor Oberlin had to lift me up and help me into the carriage."

Lafayette studied the sadness etching furrows across Liesl's face; it was a grief that went even deeper than the tragic death of a child.

"Did you care for him?" he asked.

Clearly flustered, Liesl said, "Will your questions never end? You are without a doubt the most inquisitive man I have ever known."

And then she left the room.

Liesl struggled with her memories for the rest of day. Helping Mother Boeckel prepare a chicken pie for the midday meal only reminded her of working next to Matthew at the compounding hearth, formulating medications together. And when she hung out the wash, she found it impossible not to think of Matthew's gentle hands on the night Jane died when he had picked her up and tenderly placed her inside the carriage, carefully tucking a soft blanket around her as if she were a child.

She had not told Lafayette the rest of the story, for some remembrances were meant for her alone. Once she and Matthew were settled in the carriage, the driver had returned them to Bethlehem at a much slower pace than their breakneck arrival, and the gentle rocking of the carriage had soothed her. Without considering the inappropriateness of her behavior, Liesl had rested her cheek against Matthew's shoulder. As they reached the outskirts of town, Liesl had abruptly straightened and attempted to apologize, but Matthew had taken her hand and solemnly kissed her fingers whispering, "Please do not be sorry. For you see, dear Liesl, I intend for you to be mine."

That evening, Liesl arrived in the sitting room, determined to deflect the conversation from her life to Lafayette's. She needed a respite from memories that threatened to overwhelm her.

"I have spoken enough of myself," she said before he could utter a word. "Tell me more about your life in Paris. Surely, you did more than just go to school."

Lafayette studied her face for a moment, and she prepared herself for an argument, but then he said, "I much preferred school to the required graces of the court, for my awkward country manner and a certain self-respect made it impossible for me to adapt entirely to the ways of the nobility. The endless dinners and parties were a trial. Once Queen Marie Antoinette favored me with a dance at one of her grand balls, but I spoke so little and moved so clumsily she laughed at me! I was quite humiliated and avoided such entertainments whenever possible."

"I have never danced," Liesl said.

"Never? Even as a child?"

"Father believes dancing is a sinful activity designed to awaken unholy desires."

"I have never heard such balderdash!" Lafayette cried, shaking his head so furiously Liesl feared his wig might fly off. "Would you like me to show you?"

"I cannot. Father would be outraged. Besides, you must not impede your recovery with reckless movements."

"I promise I will attempt no fancy footwork, for I am an inept excuse for a dancer, and my skills will not be improved by this leg injury. But I would happily teach you a few steps. It will do me good to have some exercise."

Lafayette rose awkwardly from his chair and stood directly in front of her. "This dance is called the allemande. Let me show you how it begins. First, we join our hands, your left to my right."

When their hands touched, Liesl felt an unexpected tremor. Perhaps her father was right about the sinfulness of dancing. She only hoped Lafayette had not noticed.

"Now, with our hands still joined, turn left under my right arm and circle around," Lafayette instructed with obvious pleasure at being in command.

As Liesl completed the circle and came back face-to-face with Lafayette, she realized they were closer than they had ever been. Her heart pounded, and his breath quickened as well. No doubt, inactivity had left his body unaccustomed to any form of exertion. If only she could claim a similar excuse for her breathlessness.

"Very good, mademoiselle. It is possible that with you

as my partner I might yet redeem myself on the dance floor." Then he muttered softly, "*L'amour apprend aux ânes à danser*."

Love teaches even donkeys to dance.

Liesl gave him a sharp look. "Monsieur, you forget yourself on two counts: failure to behave like a gentleman and failure to recall that I am fluent in your language."

Before Lafayette could reply, Liesl pulled her hand from his and left the room.

That night, Liesl lay in her narrow bed, trembling as she relived every second of the dance. Despite the powerful effect that dance had on her, she was certain it meant nothing to Lafayette. After all, in Paris men and women routinely attended balls where they were free to touch and laugh and hold each other close. How different from her circumspect world where men and women were seldom together except at service, when they were forced to sit on opposite sides of the chapel.

Liesl resolved to forget about the dancing and made a vow to never do anything so foolish again. She whispered her prayers and asked the Saviour to forgive her unsuitable behavior. But when she closed her eyes, all she could see were their two hands joined as one.

CHAPTER 24

The Argument

October 2005

"The space looks terrific," Kera said, as she entered the Moravian Book Shop's second floor activity room. "I love the posters."

"Thanks," Abbey said. "I had to do something to liven it up."

She had prepped for this day by plastering the dull walls with book jacket art—everything from *Goodnight Moon* to *Harry Potter and the Sorcerer's Stone.* She'd also delivered flyers to all the Main Street businesses, which seemed to have paid off as a stream of preschoolers and their mothers filed into the room.

Abbey welcomed everyone and helped to position the eight preschoolers in a semicircle around Kera at the front of the room. One little girl cuddled a teddy bear, and a towheaded boy sucked his thumb while grasping the worn corner of a faded Cookie Monster blanket. As Kera started to read *We're Going on a Bear Hunt*, Abbey moved to the back, joining several mothers who sat on folding chairs and whispered softly to each other.

All eyes were on Ms. Kera as she read in a singsong voice, "*Splash splosh, splash splosh, splash . . .*"

So far so good.

And then a man's voice rang out. "Samantha? Come to Daddy!"

The little girl with the teddy bear stood up, her eyes round with terror. She ran to the back of the room screaming, "Mommy! Mommeeee!"

Samantha's mother wrapped her arms around her little girl, but she was shaking almost as much as the child. She was a pretty woman, if you ignored the bruise-colored circles under eyes.

"I have a restraining order," she whispered.

"No goddam restraining order is going to keep me from seeing my own child!" the man shouted in the hoarse voice of someone whose bosom buddies were cigarettes and beer. He needed a shave, and the bottom button of his flannel shirt had popped open to reveal a patch of hairy belly. His eyes flitted wildly about the room as his beefy hands curled into fists.

Abbey quickly stepped between the man and the terrified mother and daughter.

"I am going to have to ask you to leave," Abbey said in her best authoritative voice, her hands on her hips. She hated bullies, and she had no intention of allowing this blowhard to ruin her first reading session. An unbidden image of Derrick Trolinder came to mind, strengthening her determination even more.

"I'm not going anywhere without seeing my daughter!" the man yelled.

Samantha wailed, and Abbey could hear several of the other children whimpering. As she contemplated her next move, she saw Kera pull out her cellphone.

Abbey stepped closer to the man, blocking his view of her friend. "You're scaring the children. You need to leave now."

"Who's gonna make me? You?" the man jeered, his face contorted by an exaggerated smirk.

"Why are you here?" Abbey asked in a more conciliatory tone, hoping to distract him until the police arrived.

"I think I made that clear," he said, a vein bulging in his forehead. "What are you stupid? I. Want. To. See. My. Daughter!"

Nothing made Abbey angrier than being called stupid. Especially by an idiot like this guy. But she had to remain in control, so she took a deep breath. "Maybe you should deal with this when you're calmer."

"And maybe you should stay the hell out of it!" the man growled.

Abbey was getting nowhere with this brute. She thought of how Pete might handle the situation and changed her tactics.

"Why did your wife get a restraining order against you?"

she asked in a voice that actually managed to sound sympathetic, even though everything about this man made her want to slap him silly.

"Who knows?" the man moaned. "The stupid cow is crazy. I never laid a goddamned hand on her or the girl."

"Please refrain from using profanity in front of the children," Abbey said, adopting her prissiest tone, which sounded like Mary Poppins without the British accent.

"Sorry, ma'am," he sneered but looked at her with new interest. "Who are you anyway?"

"My name is Abbey Prescott. I'm the reading program coordinator here at the bookstore." Abbey glanced behind her and was glad to see everyone had clustered in the back of the room. They all seemed calmer now. Even Samantha.

"Well, la di da. Sorry to interrupt your *program*, but I have my—"

The wail of a siren swelled in the distance.

The little towheaded boy let his blanket slip from his grasp and jumped up and down yelping, "Police! Police!"

"You called the cops? You bitch!"

The man rushed toward Abbey with his hand raised. Thank God she had taken that Defense for Divas course. Grasping his arm, she propelled him forward using his own momentum against him. The man stumbled and fell over a folding chair just as two police officers entered the room.

The officers dragged the man up off the floor and out to their squad car—no easy task since the guy kicked and cursed the whole way out of the shop. No doubt her little reading group had picked up some new vocabulary.

She worried about the reactions of the mothers, but thankfully, they commended her on her handling of the tricky situation. Most even said they would come back for the next session, including Samantha's mother, who gave Abbey a teary hug and thanked her over and over.

Kera gave Abbey a big hug as well. "Nicely done. Even the cops were impressed. One of them said you should consider a career in law enforcement."

"Not likely," Abbey said. "Besides, you were the one who called them."

"Yes, but you were the one who faced down that bully. What an exciting start to your story hour. I'd be glad to come back any time."

The following day, the book shop was much calmer. In fact, it had been deadly quiet all morning. With nothing else to do, Abbey grabbed a well-worn feather duster and whacked it around the children's nook. She had just reached the Amelia Bedelia books when she realized fingerprints were more of a problem than dust. She was thinking about finding a soft cloth to replace the duster when someone touched her arm.

"What are you doing here?" she blurted at Pete, sounding annoyed rather than pleased. She noted with relief that his jeans and navy pullover were decent enough, although he still looked slightly disheveled.

"Sorry, I didn't mean to startle you," Pete said. "I just wanted to see the working girl in action. And I thought you might want to go out to lunch."

Abbey had been so busy with her new job that she and Pete hadn't had a real conversation since the night of the kiss. She'd thought about him a lot, but for some reason, she didn't like seeing him here. In public.

"I can't. I only get a half an hour."

Madeline called from across the room. "Abbey, go ahead. It's been slow all morning. Have a nice long lunch with your young man."

Abbey bristled at the "your young man" but grabbed her bag and followed Pete out to his truck. The inside was cleaner than she expected, immaculate even, not a speck of dust on the dash or a smudge of anything on the floor mats. She wondered if it was always like this or if he'd recently had the truck detailed. If she hadn't been so irritated, she might have been touched. Instead, she reminded herself mixing business with pleasure was always a bad idea. Look what happened last time.

"Ever been to the Bayou?" Pete asked.

"No, what's that?"

"The Bayou Southern Kitchen and Bar. My top pick to eat around here."

"Where is it?" Abbey asked. "I don't want to take advantage of Madeline."

"You worry too much. I'll have you back in an hour."

Abbey tried to relax, but the whole situation had caught her off guard. She crossed her legs and jiggled her left foot as Pete drove north on Broad Street. By the time he pulled onto a side street, her left ankle had achieved maximum torque. Pete finally parked in a lot across from a large stucco building with café tables sprouting bright red umbrellas, lined up out front. Very European. She worked hard not to look impressed.

The inside of the Bayou was appealing too, with shiny wood floors and exposed red brick. A skinny waiter with a skimpy goatee greeted Pete with a big smile and a warm handshake.

"My man, how's it going?"

"Just fine, Julian. How are you?"

"Getting by. And how are you, darlin'?" Julian asked, casting an admiring look in Abbey's direction.

Before Abbey could answer Pete said, "This is Abbey."

Something about the way he said her name made her blush. She ducked her head and followed Julian across the crowded restaurant to a small two-person table in a corner.

"So, what are you drinking?" Julian asked her.

"Just water for me. I have to get back to work."

"Work can wait," Julian said with a laugh. "I'm thinking you need a beer right about now."

"Well, I'm really more of a wine drinker."

"Now you've cut me to the quick!" Julian imitated a dramatic stab to his heart. "Given that you like that *other* beverage, I would suggest a glass of Founders Rubaeus. It's a fruit beer."

"Why not?" Abbey said. "But can we see the menu? I don't have a lot of time."

Julian gave Pete a look as if to say, *What's with her?* But Pete just shrugged.

"To save time, I'll order for both of us," Pete said. "We'll start with brussels sprouts and then Bayou mac & cheese and NOLA shrimp. We can share. Sound okay?"

Abbey just nodded, feeling overwhelmed and out of control.

"How are things at the bookstore?" Pete asked.

"Good. Assuming I don't get fired for this long lunch."

"Abbey, relax. I promise I'll have you back in an hour. Here's Julian with the beer already. Everything's going to be fine."

Abbey took a sip of the raspberry beer. Julian was right—it was pretty tasty. She took a deep breath and wondered why she felt so anxious. She was a cashier. It wasn't like she was on the verge of achieving world peace or finding the cure for Alzheimer's.

The food arrived, and it was delicious, especially the roasted brussels sprouts. The company was even better. Pete entertained her with stories about his childhood, like the time he and his buddies got caught skinny-dipping in a local quarry. Abbey even relaxed enough to tell Pete about her story hour.

"No wonder the local police want to recruit you!" Pete said when she finished.

"It was no big deal."

Pete saluted her with his beer. "Officer Abbey Prescott, she always gets her man! But seriously, you were really brave. You could have been hurt."

"Nice of you to worry about me, but I can take care of myself."

"Believe me, I've seen how capable you are, but everybody needs someone to look out for them."

Abbey couldn't disagree with that. What a relief it would be to have someone take care of her for a change.

They were having so much fun, she almost forgot about the time, but Pete had his eye on the clock. He took care of the bill and hustled her out to his truck.

"Thanks," she said. "I'm really glad you talked me into this."

"No problem. I'm hoping it will become a habit."

"What do you mean?"

"Sometimes it's good to loosen up a little bit, and I'm just the man to help you out with that."

Her first instinct was to come back with something sassy, but she was getting tired of defending her independence. And besides, maybe he was right.

Pete got her back to the bookstore only a couple minutes over the hour he'd promised. Before she hopped out of the truck, he asked, "Would you like to go for a walk later? We could meet at that spot you like near the cemetery."

"Sure," Abbey said. "See you there about five thirty."

Madeline grinned and gave her a knowing look,

obviously having already decided Abbey and Pete made a good match. Abbey ignored her and got back to work. Really, she had no time for this nonsense.

When she got home, Abbey threw on a pair of stretch pants and sneakers and then jogged over to the cemetery. Pete already stood at her favorite spot. With his face turned away from her, she observed his solid build and wind-ruffled hair. He *was* attractive and a good guy too, someone a girl could rely on.

The view was the same as always; however, the sun had deserted them behind a canopy of lumpy gray clouds. Even the stone of the old Moravian buildings looked darker and danker as if something sinister had sucked away their natural warmth. Abbey joined him and hugged herself to ward off the shivers.

"Are you cold?" Pete asked. He took off his jacket and gently helped her into it.

"Thanks," she said as she cuddled into the soft flannel. It still retained his warmth, along with a slight scent of sandalwood.

"You really know how to pick the views, MPM. Even on a day like today, this is an ideal angle to appreciate the Central Moravian Church. Did you know that when it was completed in 1806, it was the largest church in Pennsylvania?" Pete continued almost as if he were talking to himself. "It's a bit of an architectural wonder. The building has foundations six feet wide and six feet long, and the rooftop is supported by triangular trusses that run the entire length of the attic. That's what makes the inside of the church so open and airy. No interior pillars or beams."

"You know an awful lot about the church," Abbey said.

"I drew up the blueprints for the whole structure last year."

"I don't understand."

"The new pastor was concerned because there were no building records. He wanted documentation in case anything ever happened. Like a repeat of the fire in 1941."

"*You* did the blueprints?" Abbey asked with a nervous laugh.

"I'm smarter than I look," Pete said.

Abbey didn't know what to say. This conversation had gone off course, and none of it was making any sense to her.

"I'm an architect, Abbey," Pete said.

"What do you mean?"

"I mean I'm an architect, trained and certified. I worked for Barrister Architects in New York for over seven years. One of the top firms in the city. Won all kinds of awards."

Abbey struggled to make sense of this new information. Why hadn't he told her this before? Especially after she'd shared so much about herself. Her emotions spiraled from confusion to disappointment and ended at something that felt unreasonably like betrayal.

"I don't understand. I thought you were just—"

"Just what?" Pete interrupted in a flat, angry tone. "Just a dumbass handyman?"

"That's not what I was going to say. Why did you leave the firm?"

"I got tired of the corporate hustle. Tired of dressing to impress. Tired of dealing with jackasses who always greenlighted the big commercial cookie-cutter jobs and never gave the small, creative projects a chance. Smooth operators who thought success was all about the right clothes and the right cars. You know, people like your Michael."

"He is not *my* Michael!" Abbey snapped, her own anger building. "And what exactly are you implying? That I'm like that too?"

"No. But I guess I am disappointed you were with someone like him."

"Well, I'm not with him anymore," Abbey said. "And I am so very sorry to be such a disappointment!"

"Let's not do this, okay?" Pete tried to speak calmly, but she couldn't help noticing the angry flush mottling his neck.

"Do what? Talk about all my shortcomings? You're right. Let's not do that. Instead, let me tell *you* something. I don't appreciate being judged by someone so dishonest he didn't even tell me who he really was!"

Pete stared up at the church's belfry for a long moment before turning to her. "You know, Abbey, that's the saddest thing anyone has ever said to me. I showed you exactly who I am."

They stood without speaking but unable to move. Finally, Abbey pulled off his jacket and threw it at him before jogging back to her house alone—past the cemetery, where the natural peacefulness had transformed into gloom, and past the tidy homes whose charm seeped away in the dying light. Pounding the sidewalk harder and harder, faster and faster. Every jolt reminding her of every man who had ever disappointed her. She took the porch steps two at a time and slammed the front door hard enough to shake the finely turned pillars. Inside, she stood in the hallway rigid with anger.

She never should have trusted Pete. It was always the same. Men always let her down.

CHAPTER 25

October 6, 1777

Lafayette has awakened in me emotions that I thought were buried, feelings I never expected to know again. I must call upon the Saviour to guide me and keep me on the right path.

—Diary of Sister Liesl Boeckel

With a frustrated sigh, Lafayette crossed out a misspelled word and pushed his paper and pen aside. It was impossible to concentrate when dancing with Liesl had affected him more deeply than he could ever have imagined. After all, he was hardly a stranger to romance. The French court was rife with liaisons of all varieties, but he had never experienced such desire as this. He was still reeling from the strong emotions that simple contact had unleashed.

However, it was not the dance alone that unsettled him. Hearing Liesl's story of studying medicine and braving the inoculation for smallpox had touched his heart even more violently than the sensation of her hand touching his. He had never known anyone so determined, so fearless. So very like himself. He decided the best course of action was to remind them *both* of his attachment to Adrienne.

When Liesl arrived to tend his wound, Lafayette announced, "Today, I will tell you about my Adrienne and how we came to be married."

Liesl looked relieved, so Lafayette continued.

"As I said before, I was an orphan and a wealthy one at that. An easy target for someone seeking a marriage for his daughter. Especially someone like Jean-Paul-François de Noailles, the Duc d'Ayen."

Lafayette had always understood, if not admired, the powerful Duc. It was well-known the man had a problem—five, to be exact—so it came as no surprise to fourteen-year-old Lafayette when he learned of a proposed match with Marie Adrienne Françoise, one of Jean-Paul's five daughters. Lafayette's wealth already made him a perfect candidate, but his sad circumstances as an orphan with no close family must have appealed as well. Jean-Paul would have assumed he could mold Lafayette into a worthy member of the House of Noailles with no interference from anyone.

"The Duc d'Ayen negotiated a marriage arrangement with my guardian," Lafayette said. "However, his wife had her say as well and insisted the nuptials be delayed for two years until her daughter reached the age of fourteen."

"Fourteen," Liesl repeated. "She was but a child."

"Not at all," Lafayette scoffed. "A girl is considered of marriageable age at twelve. My mother-in-law should never have forced me to wait."

Ignoring Liesl's disapproving expression, Lafayette reminisced about the day his wedding finally took place. Adrienne with her porcelain skin and doe-like brown eyes had made a perfect bride, easily outshining every woman in the room. While the others attempted to outdo one another with elaborate gowns and towering hairstyles constructed from outlandish pastel wigs, Adrienne wore a simple dress of white crepe trimmed with delicate bands of Brussels lace. She carried a small bouquet of orange blossoms, and those same blossoms adorned her gently curled hair as if a shower of petals had been released by the heavens just above her head. All the great families of France were in attendance, and even the king himself, Louis XV, graced the wedding reception with his presence.

"And what a reception it was," Lafayette said, clasping his hands. "We were served one hundred plates of appetizers, thirty platters of roasted meats, and forty-six desserts."

"I cannot imagine," Liesl said.

Seeing her shudder, Lafayette wondered if she might be cold.

"Two years later, when I was eighteen, I received a captaincy in the Dragoons, something I had been promised as a wedding present. But soon my controlling father-in-law set me up in a distinguished but dull job as court flunky to the king's brother, the Count of Provence. Fortunately, I managed to leave that job and return to military life, a move that infuriated the Duc."

"You were not the pliable son-in-law he had envisioned," Liesl observed.

"I was not. And I did not hesitate to be disagreeable to preserve my independence." He paused as he proudly recalled his recalcitrance. "Adrienne and I were happy together, but when news of the first shots of the American Revolution reached France, I gave my heart to America. I became obsessed with the rebels and thought of nothing else but raising my banner and adding my colors to theirs. When Jean-Paul learned of my plans to leave for America, he vowed to do everything in his power to keep me in France. He even persuaded Louis XVI to issue an explicit order banning all French soldiers from volunteering to fight in America's war and directing the arrest of any French soldier attempting to leave the country for that purpose. However, this did not deter me. I bought a ship, renamed it *La Victoire*, and set sail for South Carolina."

Liesl looked stunned. "You defied your king?"

"I had to," Lafayette said. "I believe the welfare of America is intimately bound with the happiness of all humanity. She is going to become the deserving and sure refuge of virtue, honesty, tolerance, quality, and liberty. I was compelled to join her cause."

"You expect a great deal," Liesl said. "I only hope we will not disappoint you."

"I see you have completed your coverlet," Liesl said as she admired Sister Susanna's work. "The yellows and oranges are lovely."

"Thank you, dear girl," Sister Susanna said in a shaky voice. "It is a miracle I was able to finish it, considering the state of my health."

Liesl had often wondered if Sister Susanna might be exaggerating her asthma symptoms, but seeing the sickly woman propped up in her narrow bed underneath the colorful patchwork quilt forced Liesl to chide herself for such an uncharitable thought.

"I brought a mixture of beeswax and cloves to rub on your chest," Liesl said. "I hope it will bring you some comfort."

"You are a blessing to me," Sister Susanna said, loosening the front of her shift.

As Liesl spread the sticky ointment across her chest, Sister Susanna seemed to revive.

"How is your guest?" she asked.

"He is recovering," Liesl said, knowing full well that Sister Susanna longed for more information than that.

"But what is he like? I hear he is quite handsome."

"I would not know," Liesl said. "His appearance is of no interest to me."

"But you are an observant young woman," Sister Susanna

persisted. "Surely, you can tell me if he has an appealing visage. I have heard he is quite tall with the highborn look of an aristocrat."

"You already seem very well-informed," Liesl said as she applied the last of the beeswax. She had grown quite tired of this weekly interrogation.

Sister Susanna sighed. "I do wish you would share a bit of information about the marquis. He is much discussed, and I am most interested in learning more about him."

"I am not in the habit of discussing my patients," Liesl said in a firm voice. Of course, she would never violate the privacy of a patient, but she also despised gossip, which she considered a weakness of her sex.

Liesl placed a small package on the bedside table. "I have also brought you a packet of licorice root for your special tea."

"Thank you, Sister Liesl," Sister Susanna said. "However, I do wish you would trust me enough to speak more freely."

"You are doing well, Sister Susanna. Drink the licorice tea every day, and I will see you next week."

Liesl's second visit of the day proved to be much more pleasant. Sister Johanette Luise's mother took no interest in anything other than her infant grandson, now called Andreas, who was thriving under his grandmother's care. His pink cheeks and happy gurgling filled Liesl's heart with joy, wiping out all thoughts of Sister Susanna and her insatiable curiosity. As she examined the child, so full of promise, she wondered what his life would be like. Would he be constrained by the world he was born into or might he grow up to be more like Lafayette, allowing nothing to stand in his way and trusting his own instincts with unwavering passion?

She was still thinking about Lafayette's supreme confidence when she entered the sitting room that evening.

"Oh my," Liesl said. "What is this?"

Lafayette no longer wore his bright blue officer's waistcoat with the excessive gold trimmings. Instead, he had donned a simple flax shirt and a pair of dark breeches that looked better suited for a shorter man.

"Mother Boeckel offered to clean my uniform and provided me with these clothes. The pants could be a bit longer, but I am comfortable in this simple garb. Do I look like a Moravian?"

Liesl shook her head, thinking no change of clothes could make *him* look plain or pious. Especially since he still wore his white wig, the corkscrew curls looking more ludicrous than ever when paired with the modest clothing.

And yet.

"You look," she said, struggling for the appropriate word, "somewhat humble."

Lafayette laughed. "That would be the first time anyone used that word to describe me."

Liesl tried not to think about how the change in dress made him appear more human—and much more appealing.

"Now that I have told you about my Adrienne, you must tell me more about your Doctor Oberlin," Lafayette said.

Liesl considered refusing, but her past had burdened her for so long, she ached to share the full story with someone. And who else could she tell? She would never again have a confidant like Lafayette, and since he would be leaving soon, she needed to act. With a sigh, she sat once more in one of the wooden chairs and allowed her mind to return to her last day of true happiness.

Liesl started by describing the sweet, fresh scent of the herb garden behind the Single Brothers' House on a day not long after she and Doctor Oberlin had tried to save poor Jane. It was late afternoon, and the sinking sun cut long shadows across the orderly rows of basil, peppermint, and horehound. A three-sided stone enclosure framed the fragile herbs, protecting them from the gusty winds that blew through this open swath of land and creating a private space safe from curious eyes.

In the center of the enclosure, Doctor Oberlin stood alone with his back to her.

Liesl stopped for a moment to observe him unseen. His tall frame might appear awkward to some, but she saw only towering strength. Her gaze lingered on his elegant surgeon's hands, and she blushed as she recalled the night Jane died.

Liesl and Matthew had spoken little since that night other than in the professional manner required by their positions. But every time he stood near her, Liesl could feel her pulse quicken, and sometimes she feared she might swoon—a ridiculous feeling she could never have imagined just a few short weeks ago. When Matthew had asked her to meet him here, Liesl immediately guessed the purpose, but instead of feeling faint, she remained calm and remarkably serene. She believed the Saviour had guided Matthew to her, and she never doubted they would spend the rest of their days together.

Matthew turned as if sensing her presence. "Liesl," he said, as if her name held miraculous powers.

She ran to him and reached up to encircle his neck with her arms.

"I am here!" she said as he lifted her up and swung her around. They both laughed with sheer delight until he finally set her back down.

The gold in his eyes sparkled like sunlight on a forest stream. "Liesl, my love," he said. "Will you marry me?"

"I would be honored," she said, her voice shaking with emotion.

And then, he leaned in to kiss her lips, and she knew they had sealed an impregnable bond. Surely nothing could taint this bliss.

As required, Matthew approached the Elders to request that he and Liesl might be married. The Elders approved of the match, and when Brother John asked Liesl if she would accept Doctor Oberlin's proposal, she agreed straightaway. Now the couple had just one more hurdle to surmount.

Liesl and Matthew were summoned to the chapel for a meeting with two of the Elders. Out of habit, Matthew sat in a pew on the right side of the room while Liesl sat on the left. The familiar surroundings and happy memories of the place provided her comfort. She recalled with special fondness the night many years before when she sang "Jesus Call Thou Me" in front of the entire congregation. She had been nervous that night as well, but all had worked out. Just as she was sure it would today.

Brother Timothy and Brother John took their places on a bench facing the two supplicants. Brother John held a wooden box that Liesl knew contained the three red leather tubes that would decide her future. Each concealed a small piece of paper. The word "YES" was written on one paper, "NO" on another, and the third was blank, which meant more prayer was required before a second query might be made.

Even though Liesl knew of couples whose marital hopes had been dashed by the Lot, she was certain she and Matthew were meant for each other. They would serve the community in a beneficial partnership as doctor and nurse, both dedicated to the well-being of all. And they loved each other with full hearts and open minds. Of course God would grant them their wish.

Brother Timothy began the ceremony with a prayer. "We thank you our dearest Lord and Saviour for thy love and care. And for providing the Lot as a way of speaking to us and guiding us according to thy will. Today we ask for your holy blessing on the marriage between Doctor Matthew Oberlin and Sister Elisabeth Boeckel. Both parties understand the sacred partnership of marriage and have agreed to join their lives as one. They understand as well that the word of the Lot is your word."

Brother John removed the lid and presented the open box to Brother Timothy to make the selection. Liesl held her breath as Brother Timothy chose one of the three red tubes and removed the scrap of paper.

"The answer is no," he intoned in a somber voice. "The Lord has spoken. His word is final and incontrovertible."

Matthew stood and fled the chapel, his face drained of all color. Liesl knew she should leave as well, but she seemed permanently attached to the hard bench. How was this possible? How could her Saviour have deserted her?

"No," she mumbled and then cried out. "No, I cannot accept this!"

Brother Timothy's eyes narrowed. "I understand your disappointment, Sister Liesl, but surely you would not question the word of our Lord."

Before she could answer, Brother John strode forward.

"You must leave now," he said in a kind voice with a hint of warning. He helped her to her feet and whispered, "Please say no more."

"What happened after that?" Lafayette interrupted, clearly mystified. "I do not understand. This Lot prevented you from marrying Matthew?"

"The Lot is the word of the Lord, and no one must ever

question it. I never spoke with Matthew again, and I was no longer permitted to work in the apothecary. In that one moment, I lost everything. At first, people were kind, but I was unable to hide my anger and disappointment. Soon, I started receiving sharp glances from Brothers on the street, and one evening, two Sisters made a show of moving away from me in the chapel. As if I carried an infection."

"I have never understood such narrow-mindedness, such cruelty," Lafayette said, his voice rising in anger. "They had no right to treat you like that."

"Those slights were of little consequence. Within weeks, Matthew was sent to Suriname to care for slaves working on the sugar plantations, and a few months after that, Mother Boeckel came to my room at bedtime. She is not a woman given to displays of affection, but she rested her hands on my shoulders and told me Matthew had contracted yellow fever and died. Then she played her flute as loudly as possible to drown out the sounds of my sobs, so that Father would not witness my lack of control."

"Liesl, I am so sorry."

Lafayette's face displayed such sorrow, that for a moment, she wished he would take her in his arms and comfort her. "The story does not end there. I sat at the bedside of the Labouress when she died."

"The Labouress? What does she have to do with you and Matthew?"

Liesl described how a new doctor had been summoned from Germany after Matthew's departure. Doctor Ulrich, a dour, old man who would have preferred to remain in Stuttgart tending his roses, assigned Liesl to care for the ailing Labouress.

Liesl might have refused, but she was indebted to the man. Soon after he arrived, the doctor had approached the Elders, asking that Liesl join his medical team based on a letter left for him by Matthew. When Brother Timothy questioned the wisdom of the request, Doctor Ulrich had insisted and even promised to take full personal responsibility for Liesl's actions as his assistant. With no further objections, Liesl was immediately reinstated.

"I am pleased this Doctor Ulrich defended you," Lafayette said. "But what about Doctor Glatt? I have told him how accomplished you are. I sincerely hope he treats you well."

"He has been very good to me," Liesl said, and allowed herself a small smile as she recalled Lafayette's words to Doctor Glatt.

"But please continue," Lafayette said. "I am most anxious to learn more about the Labouress and her role in this story."

Liesl picked up the tale once again, recalling her visit to the bedridden Labouress. Her private cell had changed little since Liesl's visit years before. The lighting was still eerily dim, and the horrible blood-soaked painting still hung on the wall. However, the Labouress had shriveled to a mere fragment of her former self. She lay on the narrow bed, her skin the color of dirty gray muslin. The only unchanged aspect of her visage were the penetrating dark eyes that welcomed Liesl with familiar loathing.

"So, you will be the one to send me to my final rest. The Lord does work in mysterious ways."

"I am here to offer whatever care and consolation I can," Liesl said, trying to ignore her hate-filled tone.

"You are still too pretty," the Labouress said, peering up at Liesl. "The pretty ones are always the worst, the ones who need the most watching."

Liesl dipped a soft cloth into a bowl of cool water mixed with apple cider to draw out fever. She wiped the sweat from the wizened brow and said nothing, for she was all too familiar with the ravings brought on by illness.

"I saw you and Matthew in the herb garden, you know."

Liesl squeezed the cloth so tightly, water dripped onto the side of the bed. Was it possible the Labouress had followed her that day? How else would she know about the herb garden? Liesl blushed to think of anyone, especially the Labouress, witnessing such a private moment.

"I don't understand," she said, trying to sound calm.

"You would not be so anxious to care for me if you knew," the old woman croaked.

Liesl leaned forward to wipe the woman's forehead again, but the Labouress grabbed Liesl's hand with surprising strength. "I do not want you to tend to me. I have spent years trying not to think of you. Trying to forget what *you* forced me to do."

Liesl managed to disengage herself from the clawlike

fingers. "You must rest. The fever will soon subside."

"I can never rest!" the Labouress cried. "I have been unable to enjoy a single moment of peace since . . ."

"Since?" Liesl prodded, unable to hide her curiosity.

The dried-out lips of the Labouress compressed into something resembling a smile, although her eyes sparked with hatred. "You will never know! You will never . . ."

Suddenly, her body convulsed and her gray face turned crimson. She panted loudly as she attempted to raise herself up from the bed screaming, "I am proud of what I did. Proud! The angels knew you were not worthy. Matthew was better off without you, even if his life was shortened."

The Labouress collapsed back onto the bed and fell into a stupor. She never spoke another word and died a few hours later.

Finished with her story at last, Liesl gripped the sides of her wooden chair to steady herself. For several moments she remained silent as grief and sadness eddied all around her. Lafayette looked confused but remained silent as well.

Finally, Liesl said, "I cannot conceive her meaning. All I know is my happiness died with Matthew, and I shall wear the pink ribbons forever."

CHAPTER 26

The Conversation

October 2005

Abbey sat alone in McCarthy's pub waiting for Kera. It was early, and the Friday night crowds had yet to arrive. The bartender polished the dark wooden bar with a canary-yellow cloth, and behind him, two waitresses huddled together oblivious to Abbey's early arrival. One of the waitresses laughed and gave the other a hug.

Abbey could use a hug herself.

Nolan would be joining them later, but Abbey had asked for some time alone with Kera first because she needed her advice. The progress in her office suggested Pete was working almost every day, but she hadn't seen him since the argument, and it was obvious he was timing his arrivals and departures to avoid her. He hadn't even shown up for their project meeting. She'd watched the clock all afternoon, listening for his pickup truck and waiting for his familiar tread on her front porch.

At first, Abbey had convinced herself she was better off without Pete Schaeffer, justifying her position by conducting imaginary conversations in which she demolished his credibility and his integrity with eloquent cross-examinations. *Why did you never mention you were an architect? Why did you purposely mislead me?* But by the second day, Abbey started to wonder if she had overreacted. Maybe not sharing his work history wasn't a capital offense.

And yet, she couldn't shake that sense of betrayal. She couldn't bear the thought of another relationship based on misconceptions. Opening up to someone never came easily to her, and how unfair to encourage her to tell *her* story while holding back his own. The whole situation left her angry and confused. Abbey had a plan for everything, but she didn't know what to do about Pete.

She kept coming back to a conversation with her father, who claimed one could tell a lot about a book by its cover. "We all package ourselves one way or another," he'd said. "And the best people always show up in the best packaging. If I interview a guy wearing a Brooks Brothers suit, I know I'm dealing with a serious person who wants to get ahead and knows how to look the part." When she asked about interviewing a woman, his answer was "That doesn't happen often with these high-level positions."

Abbey liked to think this exchange had challenged her to become one of those rare high-ranking women, but maybe she had taken something else away from the conversation. Maybe she did judge people by their packaging.

A flutter of crinkly organza announced Kera's arrival. She looked even lovelier than usual in a multicolored peasant skirt and a shimmery deep red top that made her dark hair shine. Kera glowed like a poster child for happiness, and Abbey felt a momentary stab of jealousy.

They each ordered a beer, and as soon as the cold ones arrived, Abbey related her conversation with Pete, the shocking news that he was an architect, and the argument that followed.

Kera didn't look the least bit surprised.

"You knew he was an architect?" Abbey banged her beer on the table, almost tipping over the glass. "Why didn't you tell me?"

"Why would I? It had nothing to do with the work he was doing for you."

"But he lied to me!"

"I don't see how. He just chose not to mention he was an architect."

"He pretended to be something he wasn't," Abbey insisted. "He betrayed my trust."

"So you trusted him. That's interesting."

"Well, obviously I was wrong. You'd think by now I would have learned."

"Abbey, I really think you're making too big a deal of this. Anyway, I kind of liked the idea of you falling for a handyman."

"I have not fallen for Pete Schaeffer!"

"Whatever you say, but you did like him even when you

thought he was just a handyman."

"You make it sound as if I have something against blue-collar workers."

"Not in general, but I don't see you ever dating one."

"You think I'm a snob?"

"Well, you do like all your designer stuff. And sometimes I think you judge people by their appearance rather than looking deeper," Kera said.

"Like I did with Pete."

"Mm-hmm. But if you're looking for real honesty, I always thought you were careless."

Abbey winced, but Kera continued.

"Maybe because you always got what you wanted, you never valued people as much as you should. Even me."

It was like being under assault. First Pete and now this. "That's not true! I always valued your friendship."

"You know, when we were kids I always hoped to hear from you during the year," Kera said, "but you completely forgot about me as soon as you left Bethlehem. When I was eleven, my English teacher started a pen pal program, and I wrote you a long letter asking you to be mine. Weeks went by until I finally got a reply. Not a letter, but a fancy card with a note, 'I'm not really into pen pals but can't wait to see you in July!'"

Abbey thought back to those days—as much as she'd treasured her friendship with Kera, she *had* preferred to keep it a part-time thing. "I'm so sorry, Kera. You're right. It seemed important to keep the two sides of my life separate. I'm not trying to make excuses. I hurt you, and there is no excuse for that."

"I got over it a long time ago. I only brought it up because I realize now it wasn't carelessness, it was fear. You were afraid of caring too much. Of getting too close. And now it's gotten worse than ever. I see you shutting yourself off from other people."

Abbey's inner self howled. She got along with everybody. She'd even won a teamwork award at work! It must be the difference in their personal experiences that made it hard for Kera to understand. Life could be cruel, and Kera had little familiarity with that.

And yet, Kera had struck a nerve. Abbey no longer created a fortress of sheets and comforters around herself in bed at night. Instead, she had moved on to constructing an elaborate personal defense system with imaginary bulkhead barriers and watertight compartments.

Kera leaned in and lowered her voice. "You're always trying to protect yourself. It explains why you would fall for a married man, someone who could never be totally yours. Why you would leave your friends without a word. And why you would make a federal case out of Pete not telling you he was an architect."

Abbey wrapped her hands around her nearly full beer glass, still cool to the touch. Kera might be right, but self-protection had become a way of life. Sometimes Abbey wondered what it would be like to open up the floodgates, but the fear of drowning was too strong.

"I know you've had a lot of hurt in your life," Kera said, "but you can't let that hold you back. You deserve to be happy. Sometimes you have to take a chance. I don't mean to lecture you, but I do worry."

Abbey straightened. "I can take care of myself."

"Of course you can." Kera gave her a weary smile. "But I have noticed some positive changes since you've been back."

"Like what?"

"Well, for one thing, I've never seen you so relaxed. And I'm really proud of what you're doing for the kids in your reading programs. Anyway, I like the new Abbey Prescott even better than the old one."

"I don't think Pete is too crazy about either Abbeys at the moment."

"Pete's a really good guy. I'm sure you two can work this out."

"I have my doubts, but thanks for being straight with me."

Kera reached her hand across the table to grasp Abbey's fingers. "I think Pete means more to you than you realize. Don't push him away. Give him a chance."

A tall, gangly guy approached their table, and Kera's face lit up as if a stagehand had switched on a spotlight. Nolan. Abbey greeted him warmly, acutely aware of Kera's comments about how she judged people. With his long face, receding hairline, and slightly mournful eyes, Nolan was nothing much in the looks department. But when he smiled, his face lit up with the kind of charisma politicians spent their careers trying to cultivate. And when he looked at Kera . . . well, Abbey would give a large portion of her bank account for a man to look at her that way.

Kera and Nolan were good company, and Abbey did her best to join in the lighthearted conversation, even though she felt bruised from all the truth telling. At the end of the night, she and Kera did their French cheek-kisses, holding on to each other a bit longer than usual. Nolan offered an awkward handshake, but Abbey gave him a hug instead.

"I'm really glad I finally got to meet you. Take good care of my best friend."

Abbey took a shortcut home, ducking into the alley behind McCarthy's. She was so deep in thought, she hardly noticed the smell of rotting cabbages decaying in a dumpster and almost tripped over a Harp bottle. Kera was right. Abbey did try to protect herself, but Kera had no idea how far that self-protectiveness could go.

For the first time, Abbey forced herself to take an honest look at what had happened with Michael. Like rewinding a tape, fragments started coming together. The last time she saw her, Sherry had told her she deserved better, but then she had added "*You* are better than this!" And that first time in Michael's office when he locked the door? She hadn't panicked. The truth was, she'd known Michael wanted her, and she had done nothing to discourage him. She was as much to blame as he was.

Worst of all, as much as she'd longed to hear it, Michael had never uttered the word divorce. He was a jerk, no question about that, but he was right about one thing. He had never lied to her.

She steadied herself against the railing of the Moravian cemetery. She could no longer pretend that Michael was the only villain in this story. Unable to bear the guilt of what she had done, she'd concocted a fantasy placing all the blame on him. Giving her a way to justify her disgraceful behavior and avoid having to admit she was a flawed human being just like everybody else.

Abbey should have been despondent, but instead, she was suddenly filled with a strange exhilaration. She would always be ashamed of her bad choices, but those decisions had been hers alone. She wasn't some hapless victim swept away by frenzied passion. By taking responsibility for her actions, she could finally take control of her life again.

She'd made a royal mess of things: running into the arms of a married asshole and then walking away from a truly decent man. But she could turn this around. All she had to do was forgive herself and hope Pete could forgive her too.

What am I doing here? Abbey had left work early for the sole purpose of catching up with Pete, but now she hesitated. Raindrops streaked the windshield of her new Honda

Civic, creating a wavering view of the pickup truck in front of her. Maybe this wasn't such a good idea after all.

She wasn't sure what to say to him. She just knew she missed his grin and the comforting feeling of being around him. And she couldn't stop thinking about their one kiss, the feel of his lips on hers. It was a sensation she hoped to repeat, which is why she was sitting here trying to find the courage to walk inside her own front door.

Finally, Abbey pulled the hood of her raincoat up over her head, forced herself out of the car, and ran up the steps of her beloved home. Although lately even the Waffle House seemed to be withdrawing its support—the front porch looked lackluster, robbed of its usual cheer by the steady gray rain. Her reflection in one of the windows showed a similar unfortunate transformation. She scarcely recognized the pale, drawn face with the bedraggled hair. No chance of bowling Pete over with her appearance, that was for sure. She hadn't had a good beauty sleep in days.

She took a deep cleansing breath, opened the front door, and called out a hollow-sounding "Hello." All she received in return was a muffled something from within her office.

She straightened her shoulders and walked down the hallway. This was her home after all, no reason why *she* should feel like an intruder. But at the office doorway, she faltered.

"Hi," Pete said with a slight nod, never lifting his head high enough to make eye contact.

He had removed most of the blue carpet, revealing the worn yet beautiful wood flooring underneath, and Abbey realized her project would soon be completed. The thought sent her stomach plummeting like a bungee jumper in free-fall. What if she never saw him again?

"Nice progress," she said.

"Thank you," Pete responded, as emotionless as if he were speaking to a stranger, to someone who meant nothing to him.

Abbey stood pinned in the doorway like Liesl's bookmark stuck inside the shadow box. There was so much she wanted to say, but no words came. Finally, she retreated to her kitchen where she hung her dripping raincoat on a chair and listened to Pete packing up his things on the other side of the wall. Soon he was in the hallway, heading for the front door. Her heart slammed against her chest with every one of his footsteps.

"See ya," Pete called softly.

His voice spurred her into action, and she ran out into the hallway, ready to say anything that would make him stay. But words failed her once again, and she settled for the banal.

"You missed our project meeting on Friday," she said. "Maybe we could meet tomorrow afternoon to get caught up?"

Pete wore a hooded jacket that concealed much of his face, but Abbey could see the pain in his eyes.

"I can't make it tomorrow," he said. "Besides, your project is almost completed."

And then he walked out onto the porch and quietly closed the front door, leaving her there.

The rain pounded against the side of her house with a steady throbbing sound. Abbey was having trouble breathing. She could feel the sea water rising, pressing against the walls of her carefully constructed barriers—the waves gaining height and power.

And then Abbey ran outside, ignoring the rain that soaked through her clothing in an instant.

"I miss you," Abbey blurted out just as Pete's fingers touched the door handle of his truck. "I want to make things right between us."

"Ditto," Pete said. "But you should go back inside. You're getting soaked."

"It's okay. I won't melt." She probably looked like some swamp creature, but she'd come this far—she wasn't going to stop now. "Are you busy tomorrow morning?" she asked, not caring how needy she sounded. "I have the day off. If you come early, I'll make you breakfast."

Pete stared at her for a long moment and then grinned. "Abbey Prescott cooking breakfast. Wouldn't want to miss that. If I agree will you get out of this rain?"

Abbey nodded, and he brushed a strand of soggy hair from her cheek.

"Sounds like a plan, MPM. I'll see you in the morning."

CHAPTER 27

October 7, 1777

My faithful Saviour comforted me during my darkest hour even when I was denied my happiness and all seemed lost. I have risen above my pain, and by exercising diligence and piety, I shall be rewarded with all the blessings doing good for others doth bestow.

—Diary of Sister Esther Bitterlic

"Our dearest Saviour," her father prayed in a particularly loud and harsh voice, "you came to free us from life's temptations. Let us not lose our way and fall prey to the siren songs of the world. Guide us that we may hear your word deep in our hearts and through our devotion and discipleship be rewarded with thy blessings. Amen."

When Liesl opened her eyes, her father was glaring at her. He had been even more short-tempered than usual that morning, barely greeting anyone as he entered the sitting room for the morning worship. And now, she recognized the slight tremor in his left hand that only appeared when he was agitated.

"Liesl, I need to speak with you," he said.

Feeling uncertain, she followed him downstairs to the pantry, a small room containing shelves of kitchen supplies and a spinning wheel.

"I met Sister Susanna as I returned from the farm last night. She suggested I would be relieved when Lafayette returned to the battlefield."

"I am sure we will all be glad when the soldiers leave our town," Liesl replied, choosing her words with care. "But I am glad to hear Sister Susanna is feeling well enough to leave her bed."

"She suggested you might be enjoying the company of our guest more than would be appropriate."

"I do not understand," Liesl said, suppressing a growing sense of alarm. "What would Sister Susanna know of my behavior?"

"Apparently, she is not the only one. Her exact words were: 'Tongues are bound to wag when a young woman shows affection for a handsome young stranger. Particularly a Frenchman!'"

"This is idle talk," Liesl said. "Surely you would not pay it any attention."

"It is my duty to be aware of anything that would bring shame upon this family," her father said, his voice rising in volume.

"Father, I have acted with no impropriety."

"Let us hope that would be so," he said, but the simple words resounded with menace.

Liesl would have shared her father's concerns with Lafayette, but as soon as she entered his room, he met her with a barrage of queries.

"I still do not understand. How could *you* have made the Labouress do anything? And what did she mean when she said she was proud of what she did? What could she have done?"

"These are questions without answers," Liesl said.

"It is a puzzle," Lafayette agreed, "but one that must have a solution."

"I have given it much thought, as you can well imagine, but I must reconcile myself to never knowing," she said, wishing that saying the words would make it so. Lafayette believed he had the power to remedy any problem, and it was true that after his letter to Washington, the soldiers showed new respect toward the women of the town. In fact, many of them crossed the street whenever a Sister approached as if any proximity might be considered a violation. However, some things were beyond even Lafayette's considerable abilities.

After caring for Lafayette, Liesl made her way to the Sisters' House to visit with Sister Adelina. Her friend ushered her into the smallest of the common rooms where they would have some privacy. They sat side by side on a small sofa, exchanging news until Liesl broached the subject utmost on her mind.

"I have often wondered why the Labouress disliked me so much."

"She did not dislike you," Sister Adelina said.

"Please, Adelina, tell me the truth."

Sister Adelina looked down at her hands. "I believe the Labouress worried you were too much like herself."

"I don't understand."

"Many years ago, the Labouress told me the story of her disappointment. I suppose there is no harm in sharing it with you now that she is gone. Of course, she was known as Sister Esther then, and she must have been a beautiful young woman."

Sister Esther had her choice of husbands, but once her dark eyes landed on Jacob Mack, her fate was sealed. Jacob embodied everything she could hope for in a man. He was hardworking and devout, but also handsome in a way that made her heart flutter. Sister Esther knew a Moravian marriage was considered a service to God and that both partners must love God more than each other, but she had no great interest in religion. She was a lighthearted girl more preoccupied with her appearance than her soul. She wanted Jacob, and she would make sure he wanted her. She gave little thought to anything else.

Sister Esther devoted every evening service to showering Jacob with tender glances, quickly hidden behind one of her delicate hands. After just a few weeks, one of the Elders approached her and asked if she would marry Brother Jacob Mack. Of course, she knew final permission to marry must be granted by the Elders, but she was already picturing the day when she would remove her pink ribbons to don blue ones. And the night when she would lie in the arms of Brother Jacob.

"But the union was not to be," Sister Adelina said. "The Lot forbade the marriage, and our Labouress never fully recovered. She was unaccustomed to disappointment and spent hours berating herself for every thoughtless action and every careless word. Wondering whether her failing was her vanity or her tenuous devotion to the Lord."

"But what does this have to do with me?" Liesl asked.

"Let me tell you the rest of the story."

Jacob married and soon became a father to two children, a boy and a girl. Children that Sister Esther believed should have been hers. Despite several offers from suitable Brothers, she never married. In her overactive imagination, Jacob Mack had achieved a mythical status, her one perfect and unattainable love. No other man would ever be good enough, and she became mired in bitterness.

Convinced she had lost her one chance for happiness, she decided to give herself entirely to the Saviour. She led the Little Girls' Choir and later accepted the position of Labouress for the Older Girls, devoting herself to the care of her young charges. She would be responsible for guiding them and keeping them from harm. She would not let them stray. She certainly would not allow them to repeat her mistakes.

"The Labouress believed you were too beautiful and too headstrong. Too much like the girl she had been," Sister Adelina said. "I tried to tell her that was not true, but she remained convinced. And then she told me of her dream."

In the Labouress's dream, two angels entered the chapel during evening service. Neither male nor female, the angels were dressed in white silk that swirled around them as they floated in unison across the wooden planked floor to the front of the room. As they gazed upon the congregation, their faces cast a radiance that filled the chapel with light as at the break of day. Each angel held a small stamp with a handle made of ivory and a metal plate engraved with the Moravian seal depicting a haloed lamb gripping a staff in its right foreleg. A staff topped with a cross and a fluttering flag of victory.

The angels moved among the congregation, pressing the stamps onto the foreheads of the faithful. As they pressed the seal onto each brow, they intoned the words, "*Vicit agnus noster, eum sequamur.*" Our Lamb has conquered, let us follow him.

When one of the angels approached Sister Esther, she gathered up the courage to ask the purpose of the imprint. The angel replied, "Those who have the seal on their brows will soon see the Lord, but for those without faith, the path will be forever blocked. Failing to believe is the greatest of sins."

The angels marked the foreheads of all the Brothers and Sisters. Except for one.

"You," Sister Adelina said.

"And do you believe this dream of hers?" Liesl asked.

"Only in part. I believe in the angels and the sealing of the brows, but I will never believe they would have passed over you." Sister Adelina squeezed Liesl's hand. "I think the Labouress allowed her past to color her dreams and her feelings about you."

Liesl and Sister Adelina spent the rest of the day helping out at the Schnitz House, where they sat in a circle with other Single Sisters, paring just-picked apples at a furious pace. The mindless activity gave Liesl time to think about the story Sister Adelina had shared. At least, she finally understood why the Labouress disliked her, but how unfair to punish her for the Labouress's own failings. Liesl nearly nicked her finger, thinking about all the years of misery that woman had caused her.

Liesl could only conclude the Labouress had suffered from a form of madness. How else to explain her peculiar dream, much less her ravings before she died? Liesl decided to finally put away all thoughts of the woman and vowed to never think of her again.

"Where have you been?" Lafayette sniffed the air as Liesl dragged herself into his sitting room that evening. After spending hours paring apples, her back ached, and her Haube was damp with sweat from the heat of the ovens blazing all day long, drying the fruit.

"You smell of smoke and apples," he said. "Not an altogether unpleasing scent."

"What a discerning nose you have. I have been working in the Schnitz House."

"And what pray tell is that?"

"It is a small building located behind the Sisters' House where we prepare the dried apples we call Schnitz. Dried apples last for many months, allowing us to prepare apple dishes even in the middle of winter. Things like Schnitz pies and Schnitz und Knepp, a mixture of ham, apples, and dumplings."

"I am sorry I will not be here by then. For many reasons, but also because I would have liked to try a piece of Schnitz pie."

Liesl ignored his sad expression and tried not to think about how dull life would be without him. "Apple-picking time is much anticipated, for it offers a rare opportunity for Single Sisters and Single Brothers to be together. The Schnitz House contains but one large room with ovens lining one of the long walls. The Sisters pare the apples while the Brothers manage the fire and lift heavy trays of sliced apples in and out of the ovens."

Lafayette's face drooped even more. "And did a Single Brother merit your attention?"

"Of course not. I have no interest in any of the Single Brothers."

Lafayette looked considerably happier as he reached for his bookmark and waved it in front of her. "The seam at the top of this bookmark has opened."

Liesl reached out her hand. "Let me have it, and I will repair it."

"No, let it be. I rather like it this way, for I can picture romantic possibilities."

Liesl felt an embarrassing warmth creeping up her neck into her face. "A bookmark is hardly romantic."

She walked to the window, hoping he would not see her reddening cheeks, but Lafayette joined her there. He seemed delighted with the reflection of the two of them standing together. Even Liesl had to admit they made a striking pair. The tall aristocrat and the slender Moravian maid, his pale face and her rosy cheeks.

"Your bookmark would be the perfect place for lovers to hide private correspondence safe from prying eyes," Lafayette said.

"I can assure you that bookmark was never intended for such a purpose," Liesl said, her heart racing even as she tried to sound offended.

"And yet, it is ideal."

"I would know nothing about such things, sir."

"You should, mademoiselle, you should."

Liesl noticed a stocky figure standing in the street below and quickly stepped away from the window. She only hoped her father had not looked up at the second-story window.

CHAPTER 28

The Plan

October 2005

"I hope you like pancakes," Abbey said when she opened the door the next morning, wearing a flowery apron over a T-shirt and jeans and topping off the look with a big smile. As apprehensive as she was, she couldn't help being happy to see him.

"Breakfast of champions," Pete said with a smile that matched her own.

The kitchen table was set for two with classic white pottery arranged on French placemats sporting the bright reds, blues, and oranges of Provence. Abbey confidently flipped the last round of pancakes onto a serving platter and placed the dish in the center of the table. As they ate, she took a satisfying sip of Original Donut Shop and cradled her coffee cup in her hands, savoring the warmth as it soothed her nervousness. Honestly, sometimes she enjoyed holding her coffee as much as drinking it.

"These pancakes are really good," Pete said as he swiped at a bit of syrup dribbling down his chin.

Abbey's face flushed with pride. "Old family recipe."

"I like the coffee too. What is it?"

"Original Donut Shop," she said. Apparently, their taste in coffee was one more thing they had in common.

"By the way, where's the Range Rover?" Pete asked. "When I pulled up out front, I assumed you'd run out somewhere, maybe to a breakfast takeout place."

"You always underestimate me."

"In fairness, that was before I found out you were a gourmet pancake maker."

"I traded the Range Rover for a Civic."

"But you loved the Rover."

"I did, but I need something smaller, something with better gas mileage."

"You've changed," Pete said.

"So people keep telling me. I'd like to think I've grown." Abbey stared down at her syrup-covered plate. "I owe you an apology. I did make assumptions about you. I never realized I could be such a snob."

"You can be a little snobby, but that's not the real you. I know that, and I shouldn't have overreacted."

"Don't try to make me feel better," Abbey said, meeting his eyes at last. "I was wrong, and I'm really sorry."

"It's okay," Pete said and patted her hand. "Living on the nonprofessional side of life has made me a bit oversensitive. I've learned firsthand that the smart guys don't always have all the answers, and the supposedly dumb ones often have a lot more common sense."

The touch of his hand was warm and consoling, but Abbey refused to let herself off easy. "I said some awful things I didn't mean. I guess you could say I have some trust issues when it comes to men."

"You don't have to worry about that with me," Pete said with a look that made her insides melt like butter on a hot pancake.

"I know," Abbey said, trying to control the shaking in her voice, "which is why I have to tell you the truth."

Pete's expression changed from comforting to confused, and Abbey rushed on.

"Michael *is* a jerk, but he didn't lie to me. He never actually said he was getting a divorce. I convinced myself it was true to make me feel better, to avoid taking responsibility. I was just as much at fault as he was. I knew what I was getting into. I knew it was wrong, and yet, I did it anyway. I don't want to lie to myself anymore, and I certainly don't want to lie to you.

"So there it is," she said with a deep sigh. "I don't blame you if you never want to see me again."

Her heart hammered in her chest as Pete sat in silence.

"Nobody's perfect," he finally said, "and I'm not big on judging. Besides, I never knew that Abbey. I only know the Abbey sitting in front of me right now, and I definitely want to keep seeing her."

Abbey hardly ever cried in front of anybody, but she

felt a tear slide down her cheek. Pete pretended not to notice, but gave her hand a squeeze.

"You must think I'm a terrible person," she said.

"No, I just think you have terrible taste in men."

"I'm going to have to work on that," Abbey said, wiping her face.

Pete talked about his newest client, an eccentric older lady who insisted on calling him Sonny. And gave her the latest update on his parents who were bargain hunting in the street markets of Hong Kong. Pete acted as if nothing had happened, and she could feel the tension of the last few days leaving her shoulders, sliding down her back, and dissolving into nothingness.

"Any news on Liesl's messages?" Pete asked.

"I mailed Adam a check for the translation, but I still haven't heard a thing. I'm starting to get a bad feeling about him," Abbey said. "You don't like Adam, do you? Every time I mention his name, your eyes get squinty."

Pete hesitated. "I had a bad experience when I first moved here."

"Details, please."

"Adam was one of my first customers. He asked me to repoint a stone wall in his living room. Beautiful fieldstone."

When Abbey raised an impatient eyebrow, Pete refocused on the purpose of the story.

"I did a great job on it, but he stiffed me."

"What do you mean?"

"Our deal was for him to pay half up front and the

other half upon completion. Adam never made the final payment."

"Why not?"

"Didn't want to part with the money, I guess. I know he was satisfied with the work because he referred other customers to me. I kept calling him about making the last payment, and he kept making excuses, but after a while, he refused to take my calls. It was almost as if he thought sending customers my way paid his debt."

"What did you do?"

"What *could* I do? I was new in town, and I didn't want any trouble. I would have warned you about working with him, but I figured since you were paying him, you'd be okay."

"I'm going to call him right now," Abbey said. She dug her cellphone out of her blue bag and tapped in Adam's number.

"What can I do you for?" Adam asked.

"I wondered when you'd have that translation ready for me," Abbey said.

"Soon," Adam replied.

"It's been a while," Abbey said, still trying to keep things civil. "I was under the impression you'd be done by now."

"These things take time," Adam said, sounding bored. "Anything else I can help you with?"

"You can give me the original messages and the translation I paid for," Abbey snapped.

"No need to be rude," he said. "You have no idea what

a revelation this is, do you? This is a discovery that could make an archivist's career."

"Well, it won't make yours. Liesl's story has nothing to do with you and your career aspirations. I might remind you the messages are my discovery, not yours."

"I think I'm entitled to a large part of the credit. After all, I translated her memoir and figured out why it might have been rewritten. I took the bookmark to Martha who discovered the letter L's. And now I've translated the messages."

Abbey allowed herself an instant of satisfaction. "So, the translation *is* completed!"

"I'm thinking of contacting that TV show *History's Mysteries*. I bet they would pay a nice sum for a story like this one."

"No!" Abbey cried, and Pete looked at her in alarm. "No one decides what to do with the messages but me."

"What's that saying? Possession is nine-tenths of the law?"

Anger surged through Abbey like a building imploding. "Give them back or you'll be sorry!"

"I'm in no mood to listen to threats. If you ever want to find out what your little friend Liesl was up to, I suggest you come over here. And perhaps we can come to some kind of arrangement."

Adam's lewd tone made the pancakes curdle inside Abbey's stomach.

"Why you . . ."

At that point, Pete removed the cellphone from her shaking hand and pressed End.

"We'll figure out how to handle this," he said.

Abbey relayed the full phone conversation, and Pete's expression grew grim when she told him about Adam's invitation.

"There is no way you're going over there," he said. "At least not alone."

"What are we going to do?" Abbey asked. "I can't believe I gave him the originals. Adam's not going to give up those messages. He thinks this is his big break."

"And a big payday," Pete said. "The guy sure likes his money. Well, if he won't give us the messages, we'll just have to take them back."

"What are you, some kind of second-story man? Don't tell me you have *another* line of work, I don't know about."

"Very funny. I don't mean steal them, just get them back. Although stealing from a thief sounds like a pretty safe proposition. Who would Adam trust enough to show the messages to them?"

"Maybe a historian or somebody with museum connections."

"Like somebody from the Smithsonian?"

"Do you know somebody at the Smithsonian?" Abbey asked.

"No, but what if someone pretended to be."

"Adam's not an idiot. He could check them out."

"Okay, how about some unknown, but imposing historian?" Pete drummed the kitchen table with his fingers. "Let's get creative for a minute. What would this historian be like?"

"He'd have a special interest in the eighteenth-century Moravian community in America."

"Good. What else?"

"He could be assembling a special collection of artifacts from that period. He would have to be wealthy. Maybe he could be British," Abbey said, getting into the game. "Adam is so pretentious, he'd be a sucker for a British accent. But why would a historian contact Adam?"

"This is where we can use Adam's vanity to our advantage," Pete said. "Our historian can flatter the hell out of Adam. Tell him everybody knows Adam Wright in Bethlehem is an expert on Moravian history. Plus, he can promise to be extremely generous should Adam contact him with any new historical find."

"He just might be enough of a fool to buy it," Abbey said and then she laughed. "You know, this could actually work. We could write a whole script for this impostor historian, but where would we find somebody who could pull it off?"

"You remember my friend Julian?"

"The waiter at the Bayou."

"That's right. Did I mention he's a drama major?"

The rented Lincoln Navigator pulled up in front of Adam's house with Julian behind the wheel, and the other two coconspirators huddled in the back seat, hidden from view by the car's dark windows. Abbey had to admit, Julian certainly looked the part of a dapper British historian. With a new suit and a layer of what he called "old-age make-up," he looked at least twenty years older. Even his goatee looked elegant.

Abbey still couldn't believe they were doing this. The whole plan had come together so quickly, she'd had no time for second thoughts. Julian had been happy to help and kept referring to this as his role of a lifetime. He'd even started calling himself "Sir Julian." His nonchalant attitude worried Abbey, but he had played his part like a pro so far. The phone call had gone exactly as planned, with Adam eagerly agreeing to show Julian the messages.

"Let's go over this one more time," Pete said, tapping Julian on the shoulder to make sure he had his full attention. "Once you get inside, I'll wait ten minutes before calling you on your cell. If you have the messages in your hands, you'll answer yes. And if not, I'll wait another five and call again."

"And if Adam gets suspicious or refuses to show the messages to you?" Abbey prompted.

"I'll get huffy and walk out," Julian said. "But don't worry, he'll show them to me. Adam thinks I'm his ticket to fame and fortune."

"You *were* very convincing on the phone," Abbey said. "Even I would have believed you."

"Thank you, darlin'," Julian said.

Pete squeezed Julian's shoulder. "Thanks again for doing this, buddy."

"Sir Julian Whittington is honored to be of service," Julian said, adopting an aristocratic British accent before switching to his normal voice. "Okay, kids, it's showtime!"

Julian climbed the steps of a historic fieldstone mansion far too big for a single occupant, rang the bell, and disappeared inside.

Abbey wrung her hands as if shaking water off them. "This waiting and wondering is going to make me crazy."

"Everything will be okay," Pete said. "We have a great plan. You're the one who saw to that, MPM."

"Well, you're the criminal mastermind who came up with the idea in the first place."

They sat back and tried to get comfortable. Pete stared at the house and jiggled his phone while Abbey kept her eyes on her watch, tracking the slow-moving second hand as it ticked its way around the dial.

Finally, Abbey said, "It's time."

Pete placed the call, and after four excruciating rings, he said, "Hey, Julian, are we good?" A brief pause. "Okay."

Pete put his phone back in his pocket.

"Well?"

"Let's get in there and recover your messages."

Abbey and Pete charged up the steps and rang the bell.

"What the hell are you two doing here?" Adam asked, but Pete and Abbey ignored him and pushed their way into the living room.

"I believe these belong to you, darlin'," Julian said, and handed Abbey the original messages along with Adam's translation.

"You can't give them to her!" Adam howled, and then he looked more closely at Julian. "Who are you anyway?"

"Just a plain old American dude helping out some friends," Julian said as he removed the pocket square from his suit and started wiping off his makeup.

"Give me back the messages," Adam said, turning to Abbey. "They belong to me now."

"You have no proof of ownership," Abbey said. "I'm the one who found those messages in Nana's bookmark."

"And what proof do you have of that?" Adam asked. "I'm calling the cops. We'll see what they think about this little con job of yours."

"Let's do that," Pete said. "I'm sure they'll be curious about a professional archivist stealing a historical artifact from a family member."

"What are you talking about?" Adam sputtered.

"I'm related to Liesl," Abbey said. "It's well-documented in some of that information you gave me when I visited the archives. A visit, I might add, that was recorded on the archives visitor register. I also have the cancelled checks to prove I paid you."

She paused before delivering the coup de grâce. "I don't even need to involve the police. I can bring my evidence to the board of directors at the archives. Even if they don't believe me, I have a feeling they'll be wondering why you didn't share the messages with them."

Julian headed for the door. "The jig's up, as they say across the pond. Nice almost doing business with you, Adam!"

Adam started after him with his fist raised, but Pete blocked his path. "Don't make things worse. Abbey is satisfied with the recovery of her property, and we can all put this unfortunate episode behind us."

"I want to hear her say it," Adam said.

"Now that I have the messages back, I have no need to complain to the board members or anyone else." Abbey paused and couldn't help adding, "Unless, of course, you force me to."

"Get out!" Adam shouted, his face almost as red as his hair. "Just. Get. Out."

Julian put the Navigator in gear the second Abbey and Pete jumped into the backseat.

"Time to make our getaway before your friend back there changes his mind," Julian said, and then launched into an impressive rendition of "We are the Champions."

Abbey had to admit the guy had talent. She held the papers over her heart and beamed. "I can't believe we did it."

"We make a good team," Pete said.

Abbey sighed happily and looked up just in time to see Julian wink at her in the rearview mirror.

CHAPTER 29

October 8-16, 1777

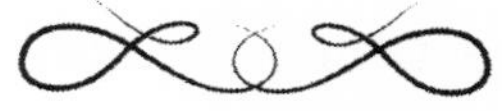

Father is once again displeased with me. How I miss my dear mother, who was always able to look beyond my failings and my weaknesses to see a daughter deserving of her love.

—Diary of Sister Liesl Beckel

The day began gray and overcast with no warming sun to wake the small household. Father Boeckel, of course, convened the morning worship in the sitting room as usual. The dark skies and early hour left Lafayette feeling muddled, but he was awake enough to notice that Frederick was in a particularly ill humor.

At the conclusion of the service, Frederick made an announcement. "Lafayette, I am pleased to observe that your wound is healing well. Since you are much recovered, you no longer require the ministrations of a medical assistant. I am sure you will agree the community would be better served if my daughter cared for patients with greater needs than yours."

Frederick paused, and Lafayette had no choice but to nod in agreement.

"Of course, sir."

"I also release you from attending our morning worship. I am certain you need to spend every moment of your time preparing for your imminent return to the battlefield."

Once again, Lafayette nodded. "Thank you, sir."

Frederick directed his next comments to Mother Boeckel, who seemed as surprised and confused as anyone. "My wife will attend to all of your needs, and contact Doctor Glatt if necessary. She will also deliver and retrieve your dinner tray each evening. Furthermore, sugar cake will no longer be served each afternoon since the cost has become prohibitive."

Poor Mother Boeckel blushed furiously at that last remark and clasped her hands as if praying for forgiveness.

Finally, Frederick turned to Liesl, his face darkening. "Liesl, you will return to your duties with Doctor Glatt, and if your medical services are not required, you will join me at the farm."

Liesl nodded, her face a picture of painful resignation. "Yes, Father."

Lafayette sat quietly as the others fled the room. Liesl and Mother Boeckel averted their eyes from his, the familiar bonds of duty and obedience encircling each woman like the bridle and straps of a horse harnessed to the plow. But Frederick gave Lafayette a look of such smug triumph that Lafayette had to grip the sides of his chair to restrain himself.

Frederick was more cunning than Lafayette would have suspected, and now the man had contrived a way to prevent him from seeing Liesl. The thought left him stricken. Of course, he knew his time in Bethlehem was temporary. Had he not yearned daily to return to the fight? Yet now he felt as if he had been ripped open and an essential part removed, an amputation far worse than any on the battlefield. He could no longer ignore how much Liesl meant to him. How she had transformed him and touched his heart in a way no other soul had ever done.

He pounded the arm of his chair in frustration. He was not a man to be ruled by the will of others. He had not permitted his father-in-law or even the king of France to hold sway over him. He would certainly not be constrained by the likes of Frederick Boeckel!

As her father had predicted, Lafayette focused all of his efforts on returning to the field of battle. Although he still limped, he started leaving the house every morning for meetings where Liesl was sure he happily applied himself to analyzing the latest war news and devising strategies for future campaigns. Lafayette would have no time to think of her at all.

Her father must have seen them at the window and become convinced the gossips had been right all along. How like him to believe the wagging tongues rather than the word of his own daughter. Perhaps he feared for her soul, but more likely his concern was for his own reputation. She vacillated between feelings of anger and relief. Would the forced separation diminish her feelings or merely serve to inflame them?

With Lafayette gone from the house, Mother Boeckel asked Liesl to retrieve his breakfast dishes. She entered the silent sitting room and thought how empty the space was without him. A mild drizzle softened the morning light outside the window, saturating the room with a gloomy gray haze. The fire had gone out, adding to the sense of abandonment. The only sound was Mother Boeckel rattling around in the kitchen below. Even the pots sounded unhappy.

The checkered coverlet she had made years ago lay lifeless on the bed, its shades of red, white, and blue strangely dull and worn. Without his boundless energy and forceful personality, the room felt flat, deserted.

He had left *The History of Greenland* on the upholstered chair, the one she would forever think of as *his* chair. When she picked up the book to move it to the small side table, her poorly placed bookmark almost fell out from between the pages. How odd. Lafayette was never that careless.

Something peeked out from inside the bookmark,

tucked between the fabric and the backing. Recalling their last conversation, Liesl inspected the open seam with unsteady hands. A folded piece of paper had been placed inside.

October 10, 1777
My dearest Liesl, if you are reading this, I am impressed with you as always. Please respond to me. What a marvelous amusement it shall be to communicate with you in this way. Despite the edict of your father, we shall share our innermost thoughts and feelings, hidden in a bookmark. I suggest we write in French for additional safety. Lafayette

Liesl laughed aloud at his cleverness. And his impertinence. But it did not stop her from picking up the pen that lay nearby beside the inkwell and quickly writing a response.

Dear Sir, your amusement has always been of utmost importance to me, and I am gratified that my bookmark has proved to be of greater value than I would ever have imagined. L.

From that day on, Liesl managed to sneak into the sitting room every morning to read the latest message secreted inside the bookmark and add her response. Soon her life had but one purpose: to read the next words written to her by Lafayette.

October 11, 1777
My dear girl, I have received word of my command from George Washington. I am most pleased, but my heart aches at the thought of leaving. I find that my love of America and Americans has become focused on one young woman in particular. The thought of leaving her fills me with despair. My only consolation would be to know that she would miss me, if only but a little. Your faithful servant, Lafayette

Congratulations, monsieur! I know this is the news for which you have been waiting. I am happy for you, although I must admit I am saddened by the thought of your departure. L.

October 12, 1777
My darling girl, have you just admitted that you will miss this most cantankerous of patients? I hope I have not misread your words because I already miss you more than this small slip of paper allows me to say. Please tell me how you spend your days so I may imagine where you are and what you are doing. Your loving servant, Lafayette

I attend morning and evening services, of course, and Father contrives to keep me occupied at all other times. He has me working with him at the farm, collecting chicken eggs, cleaning tools, and other such menial chores. When I am not with him, he has taken to dropping in unexpectedly at the apothecary. It is apparent he no longer trusts me, and perhaps he is right, since I am not sure that I can trust myself. L.

One evening Liesl sat with the other Single Sisters in the chapel, awaiting the start of the service, thinking of the words Lafayette had written. Would he really miss her? Or was she just a novelty of the New World, a trifle enjoyed but soon forgotten?

The chapel always stirred up a host of warring feelings. This had been a place of childhood joy along with the scene of her greatest disappointment. She tried not to think of Matthew, but the painful memories came tumbling back. She relived the moment when her life with him, a future she had envisioned so clearly, had been denied, disappearing forever like the faint smoke from a beeswax candle.

Lost in the past, she failed to see Lafayette enter the chapel, although she sensed his burning gaze. Their eyes locked only for an instant, and yet it was as if the room had emptied of everyone but themselves. She noted his return to full military dress with a pang of sadness. His gold epaulets gleamed in the candlelight, a clear reminder of how soon he would be leaving. She thought his face forever etched in her mind, but he looked more handsome than she remembered, and she realized the pain of losing Matthew had ebbed, replaced by a fresh aching in her heart, caused by a man with a regal bearing and a proud patrician face.

October 13, 1777
My angel. I must address you thus, for that is how you appeared to me in the chapel. Your father had often suggested I

attend the evening service. I am sure he believed it would be good for my soul. However, given current circumstances, he no doubt regrets his invitation. Sadly, I was unable to concentrate on the proceedings for I could not take my eyes off a certain Single Sister. Although she only raised her eyes to mine but once, she must have felt my yearning. What I would not give for a moment in her presence. With love and longing, Lafayette

I had forgotten how handsome you are. Seeing you in the chapel awoke feelings I had thought were dead to me forever. When Matthew died I believed my broken heart would never heal, but now I am so very grateful to the British musket ball that brought you here to Bethlehem. Your Liesl

October 14, 1777
My dearest girl, I bless the British blackguard who fired the musket ball destined for my leg! I swear this to be true even though, as you are aware, I find it hard to voice a single complimentary word about our ancient foe. I am indebted to that unknown redcoat forever. You have filled my heart with joy. Your loving Lafayette

My heart is filled with doubt. I cannot help but think of your wife. I must accept that you are not available to me or to any other save your Adrienne. I am filled with anguish and fear that I have lost my way. Liesl

October 15, 1777
My darling Liesl, Adrienne and I were but children when we wed. I care for her, of course, but I have never experienced true

love. Until now. Do you remember the day of the fire when you called me arrogant? I am sure you did not mean for me to hear you, but I did. And you were right. I was nothing more than a puffed-up popinjay. A man of no substance. While you, my sweet Liesl with your passion and your courage surpassed me in every way. But I have changed. Liesl, my love, you have made me a better man. Your humble loving servant, Lafayette

I have never known what you call true love. I never achieved the oneness with the Saviour I so desired. Then I gave Matthew my heart, but our love had no chance to grow. Surely, written correspondence is not sinful and of no great consequence, but why do I feel as if I am on the brink of something that will change me forever? Your Liesl

October 16, 1777
My beloved girl, do you remember the night we danced? You trembled at my touch. All day and night I am in constant torment, longing to hold you, aching to feel you in my arms. If we were alone together would you put your arms around me, my love? I am passionately thine. Your loving Lafayette

I tremble once again as I write this. I feel as if I would be torn in two between what I know to be right and what I desire. Zinzendorf spoke of a pure act performed with the innocence of Adam and Eve before the Fall. How I long to share that innermost connection when two devoted souls become as one. I am tempted to cross out those wicked words and call upon my Saviour to rescue me. And yet how can love be immoral? How can it be wrong to follow one's heart? Your loving Liesl

CHAPTER 30

The Architect

October 2005

"Pretty clever using the bookmark to hide their correspondence," Abbey said after reading the first of the translated messages aloud. She sat next to Pete on one of Nana's rattan love seats, sharing some celebratory beers.

"What do you think of Adam's translation skills?" Pete asked.

"I have to admit he's good at something."

"Even a broken clock tells the right time twice a day," Pete said, making her laugh.

She continued to read until Pete interrupted her with an exaggerated groan.

"Lafayette actually said he was grateful for the musket ball that tore up his leg? What a load."

Abbey smiled sweetly. "Perhaps you could hold your comments until the end of the reading."

"Just one more question," Pete said. "Who the heck is Matthew?"

"I have no idea. Apparently, Liesl was in love with him, but he died. I'm starting to think my Liesl had a tragic life."

Abbey continued reading the messages in chronological order, even though she was dying to skip ahead.

"Is that it?" Pete asked.

"That's the last entry."

Abbey sipped her Yuengling and stared into the garden, where a couple of Nana's roses still held on to their petals. She wished the messages told her more, but they did confirm her suspicions: Liesl and Lafayette's relationship went much deeper than that of a nurse and her patient. Kind of like her relationship with Pete going well beyond a client and a handyman. She'd never have gotten these messages back without his help, and yet she still didn't know much about him.

"Was it hard for you to leave New York?" she asked.

"The timing was right," Pete said. "The firm was in the midst of a chaotic acquisition. They tried to talk me into staying, but in the end, my leaving suited us both. I got out of there, and they got another seat at the table for an architect from the acquired firm."

"You sound bitter."

"Not about leaving. I just wish I hadn't wasted so many years there. All I did was work. I had no life."

"Corporations will suck the life out of you if you let them. If Nana hadn't died, I'd still be back in Philly, slaving away. Working sixty-hour weeks, answering emails and texts at all hours of the day and night. The thing is, when you're in that corporate bubble, it feels normal."

"Life is much better out of that rat race," Pete said, raising his beer before taking a long sip.

"What brought you to Bethlehem?" she asked, realizing she'd always assumed he was a hometown boy.

"You'll love this, MPM. I did my own research project. Listed all my requirements. Things like small city, East Coast, architectural significance. Bethlehem popped up right away. I spent a weekend roaming the streets in the historic district and across the river. I knew right away it was the place for me."

"I don't even know where you live."

"I have a condo down on the South Side. You know, with the working stiffs."

Abbey had to smile at the not-so-subtle dig, but Pete was right. South Bethlehem had been an industrial hub since the 1800s, manufacturing zinc, brass, iron, and of course, steel. All that heavy industry had demanded unskilled laborers, and a stream of European immigrants had poured into the community. Even today, the neighborhood retained its working-class culture.

"I went to a concert on the South Side one summer during Musikfest," Abbey said. "The ruins of the steel plant provided a backdrop for the stage, and the blast furnaces were illuminated with red and purple lighting. Stunning but also kind of sad. Like looking at extinct metal dinosaurs."

"It's a sad story," Pete said. "Bethlehem Steel was the second largest steel maker in the country. Then in the late 1990s everything fell apart, and the plant shut down. Some say it was competition from foreign steel; others say it was corporate greed."

Pete was quiet for a moment, his soft brown eyes turning serious. Abbey braced herself, dreading anything that might jeopardize their newfound détente.

"You treat me differently now that you know I'm a professional," Pete said.

"That's not true," Abbey protested. She admired him more than ever, but that had nothing to do with his line of work.

"I don't feel much like working. How about going for a ride? There's something I'd like to show you."

"Sure," Abbey said. "Where to?"

"Have you ever heard of Martin Tower?"

"Never."

"That's what I figured, so let me show you one of Bethlehem's most unusual buildings."

They cleaned up the breakfast dishes, working side by side like an old married couple. Abbey couldn't help thinking about the last time they'd stood together in front of this sink, but if Pete gave any thought to their one and only kiss, he kept it to himself.

When they were done, Pete led the way to his pickup, and Abbey hopped into the passenger seat. She hadn't been inside his truck since the day he took her to lunch at the Bayou. The day she first met Julian, her future partner in crime. Who would ever have predicted that? Her life had certainly gotten more interesting. For the first time, that fresh start she'd hoped for when she moved here actually seemed within reach.

Pete drove a short distance west on Elizabeth Avenue and pulled into a parking lot with a perfect view of a high-rise across the street. The dark-gray building with striking white vertical stripes would have been at home in a New York skyline, but it was totally out of place in Bethlehem, dwarfing everything in sight.

"That's Martin Tower?" Abbey said. "Of course I've seen it. It's impossible to miss, but I never knew anything about it."

"You asked me why I moved to Bethlehem. Well, Martin Tower is one of the reasons. It's twenty-one stories high. About one fourth the size of the Empire State Building. Or comparing it with something more to your taste, it's only three-tenths the size of the Eiffel Tower."

"But it looks monstrous."

"That's because it's the tallest building in the entire region—nothing else even comes close."

"Why does it have such an odd shape?"

"This was Bethlehem Steel's world headquarters, and to satisfy their many top executives, they used a cruciform design, which guaranteed every one of them a corner office. The company spent thirty-five million on this baby at a time when they should have been cutting costs instead.

Those guys acted like they were masters of the universe. They even hired attractive young women to do nothing but sit in the lobby, waiting to lead visitors up to the executive floors."

"Power and sex. Always a potent combo." Abbey regretted her words as soon as they flew out of her mouth. Suddenly the confines of the pickup truck felt dangerously intimate, and she found herself thinking about drive-in movies and steamed-up windows. "Who uses the building now?" she asked, moving on to a safer topic.

"It's empty. Grass growing in the parking lot. Six hundred thousand square feet of unused office space. No one knows what to do with it. Apparently, it needs asbestos removal and a sprinkler system. Who wants to spend that kind of money?"

"It's tragic to think of the place rotting away." Abbey stared at the tower, thinking about choices and how making a wrong one can destroy everything.

"It was designed to represent strength," Pete said. "But now, it's become a symbol of arrogance."

"Why did you become an architect?"

"Ever since I was a kid, I always looked at buildings as if they were living things with personalities. Some houses were warm and inviting like puppies ready to welcome you with sloppy kisses. Others were cold and sterile with a look-but-do-not-touch vibe. Later on, I could study a blueprint and envision what it could become. I loved creating environments where people could live and work in buildings that provided functionality but also made them feel good."

"Sounds like you miss it. Do you ever think of going back?"

"To a big firm? Never. But I may join a small outfit in South Bethlehem. I've met with them a couple of times. We still have to hammer out all the details, but I'm hoping I'll be on the payroll soon. Because you're right, I do miss it."

"I really hope it works out for you," Abbey said, still thinking about choices. God knows, she'd made some disastrous ones, but she wasn't going to let that ruin her life. Pete's acceptance of her past proved she could put it behind her. As long as she learned from it first. Maybe the secret wasn't making the right choice every time but allowing herself a second chance when she needed one.

"Would you like to go to the opera?" Pete asked.

"With you?" she said, thinking this might be one chance she wouldn't want to miss.

"That's right. I know you've sworn off men, but this is not a date. It's strictly a cultural experience."

"What's the opera?"

"*I Puritani*."

"Bellini. You sure know how to tempt a girl."

"Don't get too excited. The Metropolitan Opera has this Live in HD series with simulcasts of opera productions. It's only a video of a live performance, but it's at Miller Symphony Hall, in Allentown, and it *is* the Met. What do you think?"

Although Pete tried to make it sound as if the invitation was no big deal, she could see how pleased he was when she agreed to go. To be honest, she had pretty high hopes herself. With any luck, this might be much more than just a night at the opera.

CHAPTER 31

October 17, 1777

Which way shall I choose? Shall I stay upon the path of the righteous or is this temptation beyond my ability to resist?

—Diary of Sister Liesl Boeckel

Her world had become smaller than ever, and Liesl gave little thought to anything other than her bookmark and the contents within. She felt consumed with an unquenchable thirst that only the words of Lafayette could satisfy. Every day, after her father left for the farm, and Mother Boeckel occupied herself with young George Frederick, Liesl stole unseen into the sitting room.

Today, however, her usual anticipation was dulled by the painful thought of Lafayette leaving the following day. She should have been relieved that temptation would soon be beyond her reach, but instead she felt only remorse for a chance not taken. Her heart raced as she carefully removed the folded sheet of paper from inside the bookmark.

October 17, 1777
Will you come to me tonight, my love?

Liesl stared at the short message, reading the eight simple words over and over. Surely, she must have realized it would come to this. Perhaps she had even wished for it. But for the first time, Liesl did not write a response. She carefully folded the paper and returned it to its hiding place.

Lafayette's words reverberated in her mind as she went about her daily chores. *Will you come to me tonight, my love?* She joined her father at the farm, but his stern looks only made her nervous, and she dropped a chicken egg, splattering the ground with cracked shell and oozing yellow yolk.

"What is the matter with you today?" Her father shook his head in exasperation. "You may as well spend your time with Doctor Glatt for you are of no help to me."

As she walked from the farm to the apothecary, Liesl tried to block out Lafayette's question by repeating the Watchword for the day, a simple verse from Proverbs: "Who can say, 'I have made my heart clean; I am pure from my sin?'" But she soon found herself wondering if the verse offered a plea for tolerance or a rationalization for sin.

She knew right from wrong, had been taught from the time she was a child to follow the righteous path, to obey the dictates of the Church and the instruction of her father. A lifetime of teachings bade her to ignore the message from Lafayette. To remain a maid forever. And yet . . .

The walk should have cleared her mind, but as she passed the herb garden, memories assaulted her. A man stood among the herbs, and for a moment Liesl wished she could go back in time, back to that fateful day when Matthew asked her to be his wife.

The man turned, and Liesl recognized Brother John.

"Brother John, you have returned to us," she said.

"I am recently arrived from Germany," he said. "You are looking somewhat distressed, Sister Liesl. Are you well?"

"I am fine," she said, avoiding his probing eyes.

"I have been wanting to speak with you," Brother John said. "The night before I left for Germany, the Labouress called me to her side. You may recall she was quite ill."

"I was with her when she died," Liesl said.

Now it was Brother John's turn to look distressed. "Did she say anything to you?"

"Nothing that made any sense, only the ravings of one with a high fever."

"Oh Liesl, I must share with you the confession I heard from the Labouress. I only pray I am doing what is right."

Liesl stared at him in confusion. Would the Labouress never leave her alone?

"The Labouress saw you and Matthew here in this herb

garden," Brother John said. "And she was determined you should never be together. She told me God would never grant such a wicked, undeserving girl the joy that had been denied herself. I am afraid the Labouress was consumed with an obsessive dislike for you."

"Of that I am well aware, but what else did she say?"

"She told me about the Lot," Brother John said. "She prepared the Lot for us, and she did it in such a way that she controlled the outcome."

Liesl started to protest that this was impossible, but Brother John continued.

"I fear I am to blame," he said, his face burning with shame. "The Labouress had prepared the Lot many times before. Because she was always available, we had come to rely on her for the task. On the day your marriage to Doctor Oberlin was to be decided, I gave her the wooden Lot box, the three red tubes, and three small pieces of paper. The papers are to be prepared following our strict procedures: one with the word 'Yes,' one with 'No,' and one to be left blank, indicating more time and prayer are required. During her confession, the Labouress described to me how she laid the three blank scraps of paper on her desk, dipped the pen in the inkwell and wrote the word 'No' on all three papers. When the ink dried, she rolled each paper into a tight cylinder and carefully placed one inside each red leather tube."

Liesl swayed on her feet, and Brother John led her to a nearby bench.

"Liesl, I cannot tell you how sorry I am, but now that I

have begun, I must tell you the rest."

"The rest?" Liesl dropped her head into her hands. "That woman destroyed my happiness. What more could she have done?"

"The Labouress also prepared the Lot for the decision whether Doctor Oberlin should be sent to Suriname."

Liesl groaned. "No, it cannot be."

"The Labouress told me she prepared the Lot in much the same way as she had for your marriage decision. Only this time she wrote the word 'Yes' on all three papers. While she expressed some remorse over the fate of Doctor Oberlin, she said when he refused to marry any other woman, she had to save him from temptation."

"She was mad," Liesl moaned.

"Liesl, please understand, I could do nothing. I had no proof and who would believe such a preposterous story? I knew she would soon see her Saviour face-to-face and believed that would be punishment enough."

"I do not blame you, Brother John," Liesl said. "I am grateful to you for telling me, but it is as if my heart has broken once again."

"Would you like me to fetch your stepmother?"

"No," Liesl said. "Please leave me now."

Brother John touched her arm in an awkward attempt to console her, but the moment he walked away, she fell to the ground, her mind a jumble of fractured images. Her dear Matthew with his green-gold eyes. And the black eyes of the Labouress, gleaming with malevolence from within her puffy face like two dried-up raisins in a stale and moldy scone.

How could anyone fathom the evil of that woman? She was a lunatic who encouraged Benigna to destroy herself. And then, she not only derailed Liesl's marriage but sent Matthew to his death. Liesl's happiness had been stolen from her, ripped away, leaving her with nothing. Liesl could not bear to think of what might have been if the Labouress had not interfered.

In the midst of all her pain and confusion, Liesl wondered what type of person the Labouress might have been if she had not been denied *her* happiness. It was, after all, the one thing they had in common. But the Labouress had allowed that disappointment to poison her whole life, and Liesl had no intention of becoming like her.

And then, one more thought emerged. *Will you come to me tonight, my love?*

By the time Liesl returned home to help Mother Boeckel prepare the evening meal, she ached all over. She declined to attend the evening service, telling Mother Boeckel she was ill. Which was true. Standing in her small bedroom, her body shook so badly, it was as if she suffered from the falling sickness.

Lafayette lay awake straining to hear any sounds of movement throughout the silent house. All was quiet except for the singing of the night watchman as he went about his duties, scrutinizing the town for any signs of smoke or fire. Lafayette could only hope the watchman would not see the flame that burned within his heart.

Lafayette's emotions swung back and forth between expectation and remorse. Initially, he had been so sure of Liesl's affections that her failure to respond to his message had been of little concern. But now he felt a growing alarm, and he cursed his selfishness. He had no right to ask Liesl to compromise her beliefs or to put herself at risk among her people. Surely a community like Bethlehem would show little sympathy for a girl who ignored the teachings of the Lord to pursue her own desires. If anyone were to find out, no doubt she would be ostracized. He should never have shared his feelings.

Why had he been such a reckless fool? This was not Paris, and Liesl was nothing like the conquests of his youth. Among the elite of French society, sex outside of marriage was not only tolerated, it was expected, particularly for wealthy young men. But Liesl had nothing in common with the giggling girls of the French court who had set their caps for a young marquis. Nor was she like the older women whose ambition masqueraded as lust, women who worked their way through the ranks of the nobility intent only on acquiring personal power.

Liesl was an innocent, a girl who knew nothing of the world beyond the streets of Bethlehem. And yet, this sheltered girl had an intellectual curiosity to match his own and a passionate soul more in harmony with his than anyone he had ever met. How could he have allowed his brutish, lustful nature to tempt such a pure heart? He would never forgive himself for his uncouth behavior and only hoped his darling Liesl would find it within her generous heart to absolve him. He continued to berate himself until he fell into a fitful slumber.

Liesl crept down the stairs and stood outside the sitting room door, dressed only in the white shift she wore for sleeping. The house had grown chilly as the late-night temperature dropped, but her body seemed lit by an inner fire, leaving her impervious to the cold.

She stared at the white surface of the door, only barely visible in the dark hallway. The black hinges on its edge were even more difficult to see, but Liesl knew the distinctive swirl of Brother Anton's blacksmithing work and traced the decorative curl with her finger. This was just an ordinary door. A door like any other she had routinely opened all her life. She had come this far. Why was she so hesitant to go any further?

All the doubts that had haunted her throughout the day suddenly loomed large and indisputable, but knowing that happiness had been stolen from her once before, how could she turn away from this her only remaining chance? She had reconciled herself to living a life alone, but this was an opportunity like none other. She could step outside her circumscribed world for one night. A night she could hold in her heart forever, a memory to sustain her for the rest of her lonely days.

Liesl reached for the lever of the door latch, fingering the lip of its smooth upside-down spoon shape. The clever design allowed the door to open with the press of an elbow. Liesl had used this handy device when her arms were encumbered with medical supplies or trays laden with wine glasses and sugar cake. But tonight, her arms were empty. Tonight, she had nothing to offer but herself.

The eerie howling of wolves gathering at the edge of town broke the quiet. Liesl clasped her hands to her chest and held her breath, listening for any disturbance in the house. Eventually, the wolves tired of their melancholy chorus, and the deep silence of the night returned.

Liesl pushed down on the lever and the door swung open without a sound. She stepped confidently into the doorway, but a creaky floorboard punctuated the air with a resounding crack.

Lafayette awoke suddenly, his eyes blinking as he struggled to see in the dimly lit room. "Is someone there?"

She stood still as he stared and imagined what she must look like in her simple white gown with her blond hair loose, framing her face like a halo.

"You came," he said at last.

"Yes."

"Oh, Liesl," Lafayette groaned. "I did not expect to see you."

"Are you sorry I am here?"

"No, no. I want you beside me more than you can ever imagine, but are you sure this is what *you* want? Please believe I would never cause you pain. Now or later."

"I am certain, but I must ask one thing of you."

"Anything, my darling girl."

"Promise me that after you leave this place tomorrow, we will never meet again. Our time together must remain one single memory, never to be tainted by longing or regret. Let me be sure we will never be tempted again. Promise me you will not return to Bethlehem."

"I promise you, my love."

Lafayette reached out his hand, and Liesl glided toward him like an apparition shimmering in the moonlight.

CHAPTER 32

A Night at the Opera

October 2005

"Wow," Pete said when she answered the door. "Looking good, MPM."

Abbey grinned, pleased that her choice of perfectly tailored winter white pants with a light blue, silky-soft cashmere sweater had achieved the desired effect.

"You're not looking so bad yourself." She noted his tan Dockers with slight creases along each side, telltale signs of a recent purchase. "I think we may be the best-looking couple at the opera."

The early-evening air was cool and crisp like the first bite of the season's best apple, and as she stepped out onto her porch, she shivered. Not from the cold but because her whole body thrummed with anticipation for this not-a-date.

"Your carriage awaits," Pete said as he opened the passenger side door of his pickup and helped Abbey climb onto the elevated seat. She didn't really need his assistance, but she liked the feel of his hand on her arm.

Pete started up the truck, and Abbey laughed with delight as the sound of Roy Orbison's inimitable "Pretty Woman" filled the air. She joined Pete in a raucous sing-along as they sped from Bethlehem to Allentown, past the Civil War monument and into the suburban sprawl of fast food and strip malls.

Once they crossed the Lehigh River, the cityscape became more urban, with tightly packed row homes and bumper-to-bumper street parking, making Abbey grateful her grandparents had chosen the more spacious streets of Bethlehem for their home. Abbey and Pete were just finishing an eardrum-bursting rendition of "It's Over" when they pulled into the parking lot next to Miller Symphony Hall.

"Downtown Bethlehem certainly has Allentown beat in the ambience department," she said, slightly breathless from all the singing.

"That's true. But Allentown is working on a comeback. In fact, this building is actually pretty impressive."

Abbey sighed and feigned a pained tone. "Okay, Mr. Architect. Give me the details."

"Since you asked so nicely, it dates back to the 1800s and was originally used as a food market. By the end of the century, the building was renamed the Lyric and converted to a theater by an architect famous for theater design. A guy named J. B. McElfatrick."

"Never heard of him, and I would have remembered a name like that."

"Not many people know about him, but he's considered the father of American theaters. He built two hundred of them all over the country. This is one of only a dozen still standing." Pete stopped to gaze at the front of the building. "This is called classical block architecture, a subset of neoclassical."

"And neoclassical is . . . You have to realize how little I know about architecture."

"We can change that," Pete said. "Neoclassical design was a reaction to the excesses of baroque and rocco. People got tired of all those flying cherubs, so they returned to the restraint of classical Greece and Rome. Lots of neoclassical buildings look almost like Greek temples. Think of the White House and the US Capitol. But classical block architecture carried the restraint even further."

"I like the high-arched windows, but I'm not usually a big fan of restraint."

She giggled and added, "In architecture."

She'd been thinking of her Victorian turret but realized her comment could be taken more than one way. And felt almost giddy as Pete's face turn red.

The small lobby was elegant and old-fashioned with three glittering chandeliers hanging over the heads of about a dozen patrons. Pete explained that Wednesday nights were encore nights, drawing a smaller crowd than the live broadcasts on the weekends. Only the front rows of the orchestra level were occupied, but Pete led Abbey up a set of carpeted stairs to the second floor where they had the entire mezzanine to themselves. They chose seats in the first row, dead center with a totally unobstructed view.

"Best seats in the house," Abbey said. "Not bad at all."

The stage was bordered with gilded trim like a three-sided picture frame. Four private boxes with elaborately carved half-moon balconies, two on each side of the stage, complemented the simple but appealing design. J. B. McElfatrick had done his job well.

The floor of the stage was hidden behind a large movie screen showing scenes of people arriving at the Metropolitan Opera House. Abbey scrutinized the well-dressed New Yorkers in their urbanite uniforms of understated black, with upswept hairdos for the women and a preponderance of tortoiseshell eyewear for the men. She'd been part of that world once. For a moment, she envied the privileged ones who would watch the opera live, but then she thought how lucky she and Pete were to see the same performance for a fraction of the price in an empty balcony.

Maybe Kera and Pete were right. Maybe she really had changed.

She took a quick look at the program to refamiliarize herself with the opera. The music she knew well, but like most operas, the plot of *I Puritani* was pretty forgettable.

Pete looked over her shoulder as she read. "Can you give me a refresher?"

"Arturo and Elvira are star-crossed lovers on opposite sides of the English Civil War. Like a seventeenth-century *Romeo and Juliet* with the usual misunderstandings and melodrama. You know opera. Silly romantic stuff."

"I do," Pete said. "But I also know it's much better with a pretty girl by your side."

Abbey gave him a sidelong glance. "I never knew you were such a charmer."

Pete grinned and propped his feet on the railing in front of them. "There are still a lot of things you don't know about me."

Soon the rustle of the crowd settling into their posh seats at the Met subsided, and the oboe sounded a single note, signaling the start of the orchestral tune-up. Abbey closed her eyes, relishing the swelling cacophony as all the different instruments chimed in. It wasn't pretty, but it always reminded her of a rambunctious family dinner with everybody talking over top of one another, competing for attention.

From the first notes of the overture, the sound enveloped her. She became so caught up in the performance, she forgot she was watching a video. That is, until Anna Netrebko, playing the poor jilted Elvira, descended into madness in Act II. The camera close-ups captured every nuance of Anna's stricken face, outdoing even the thousand-dollar seats at the Met.

In Act III, the lovers were reunited at last. As Arturo sang the famous aria "*Vieni fra queste braccia*," begging Elvira to come into his arms, Pete shifted a bit closer to Abbey.

She pretended not to notice, but every nerve ending in her body switched to red alert. He was close enough for her to smell the sweet scent of sandalwood—the same scent she first noticed when he'd wrapped his jacket around her right before their awful argument. They'd come a long way since that day. *She'd* come a long way. For once, she wasn't trying to plan ahead, to control whatever happened next. Tonight, she'd let events unfold on their own.

Arturo reached for a high note, and Pete reached over to wrap his arm around her.

"This is nice," Abbey said, snuggling into him and resting her head against his shoulder in a perfect fit.

Pete pulled her even closer and whispered, "Now we're all ready for the big finale."

The opera company launched into the final chorus of "*Ah! Voluttà*," and Pete leaned over to kiss her. A kiss even better than the first one. And this time, Abbey made no move to stop him. They kissed through the credits and kept kissing even after the house lights came up. They might have stayed the night if not for a discreet cough from the back of the mezzanine. Followed by a voice announcing, "Closing time, folks."

They giggled like two high school kids caught necking in the back row of a movie theater and ran down the stairs, hand in hand, into the chilly night.

Pete pulled Abbey close as they walked across the parking lot. "Now that's what I call a finale! Possibly my all-time favorite performance."

She laughed and pretended to pull away. "Possibly?"

"Well, the night isn't over yet."

Abbey trembled, but she wasn't cold. Or afraid.

Pete kissed her cheek as he helped her into the truck. He replaced the Roy Orbison CD with an *I Puritani* recording, and Abbey let the pure strains of Bellini carry her away again. She put her hand on Pete's thigh, feeling the taut muscle beneath the fabric, and wished she could make the ride back to Bethlehem go faster.

When they pulled up in front of her house, Pete turned to her with a questioning look.

"Beat you to the front porch," she said, letting herself out of the truck.

She got there first but fumbled with the key as he came up behind her and kissed her neck. Once inside, they took their time, kissing all along the hallway. Past the Beckel Parlor and past her office, the room that had started it all. When they reached the stairs, Pete swept her off her feet like a Hollywood hero and carried her up the steps.

"So gallant," she said, pressing her face against his chest and listening to the pounding of his heart. She only hoped she wasn't too heavy. All those beers were starting to add up.

Pete must have guessed what she was thinking because he said, "Don't worry. Handymen can carry the load."

She punched his arm, and they lurched against the wall, laughing like Saturday night drunks. Finally, he pushed open the door to her bedroom and carefully maneuvered her through the doorway. The yellow walls welcomed them, and they fell onto the bed as if this were the place they were always meant to be.

The leaves of the red maple glowed like hot embers as sunlight streamed through the double window. Abbey closed her eyes as images of the previous night rolled like a movie trailer through her mind, definitely not one approved for all audiences. For a moment, she panicked. What if it was all just a dream? Then she reached out for him, and Pete gave her all the proof she needed that this was real.

Afterward they lay entangled, arms and legs caught up in a wreckage of twisted bedding. Half of Abbey's blue toile comforter lay bunched on the floor, and her perfectly folded hospital corners had come undone hours earlier.

She kissed the compass rose tattoo on Pete's upper arm. "My father's coming to see me next month." Her eyes held his. "I'd like you to meet him."

She said the words without hesitation or doubt. A month ago, the thought of Pete and Roger Prescott in the same room would have terrified her. Now she could only hope her father would overcome his judgmental nature. If not, it would be his loss.

"Sounds great. I'm really glad he's coming to see you," Pete said, and they kissed as if sealing a pact.

Leaving the bed was no easy task, but they eventually

made their way down to the kitchen table, where they sat with two spoons and a tub of yogurt.

"We really need to make a trip to the grocery store," Pete said, forcing down another mouthful. "Maybe get some bacon and eggs? Real men need more than plain Greek yogurt for breakfast."

"And here I thought I'd be more than enough for you."

"But that's the problem." Pete reached up to play with a stray lock of her hair. "You wear me out. I'm going to need some real food to keep up!"

Abbey's cellphone rang, and she had to fish it out of her blue bag, which she'd left on the hallway floor the night before.

"I've never known you to be so untidy," Pete chided.

Abbey kissed him on the forehead. "I was in a hurry." She looked at the caller ID. "It's Adam. He keeps calling to apologize, but I'm not ready to give him the satisfaction."

Pete pulled Abbey close. "Have you decided what you're going to do with the messages?"

"I certainly won't sell them to the highest bidder. Maybe I should keep them. Put them back in the bookmark and leave them there."

"Why would you do that?"

"What happened between those two people is private. They kept their relationship a secret, and since neither one of them ever spoke about it, I'm not sure I should be the one to break their silence."

"But Liesl never destroyed the messages, did she? She

left them behind, knowing someone would eventually find them. And she may have written about Lafayette in her memoir. Didn't you tell me you thought her memoir was probably rewritten because it would have embarrassed the Moravian community?"

"You have been paying attention," Abbey said. She threw out the empty yogurt container and stared at the tea towel she'd picked up at the bookstore, green gingham with a Moravian star in the center. "I know what I'll do. I'll donate the messages to the Moravian Museum. I'm sure they'll do a tasteful display, and at least the messages will remain here in Bethlehem. I think Liesl would like that."

"Sounds like a plan, but I'm still wondering about Liesl and Lafayette. Do you think she took a tumble into Lafayette's bed that last night before he left?"

"We have no way of knowing," she said.

"I know that, but what do *you* think?"

She tried to imagine how hard it must have been for Liesl to make that fateful decision. Liesl had already suffered a major loss when the man named Matthew died. How painful it must have been to face losing Lafayette too. But somehow, Liesl had found a way forward, and now Abbey needed to do the same.

"I think if she felt about Lafayette the way I feel about you, she would have been a fool not to spend that last night with him."

Pete lifted Abbey's face to his and kissed her long and deep.

"Would you like to go for a jog?" Abbey asked when they finally broke free of each other.

"Not exactly what I had in mind, but why not? Only thing is, I left my Dior jogging suit at home."

"No problem. It doesn't matter what you wear."

The two of them jogged down the familiar streets, following Abbey's usual route. However, Pete soon slowed to a brisk walk.

"What's the matter, handyman?" Abbey taunted as she jogged in wide circles around him.

"I'm not much of a jogger," Pete said, stating the obvious.

"But you do have other talents. I'll catch up with you in a minute," she said, and ran ahead into the cemetery. "Meet me at our spot!"

A few moments later, she bent down and rested her hand on the cold, flat gravestone. "I hope you think I'm doing the right thing," she whispered.

The view from their favorite spot had changed. Now, most of the leaves had fallen, and the old trees would soon stand naked but proud. The Central Moravian Church dazzled in the afternoon sun, and yet Abbey was drawn to the older Moravian buildings, especially the Single Sisters' House. Nothing glittered there, but the resilient stone emanated warmth and comfort.

Pete took her hand, and as she interlaced her fingers with his, a delightful warmth moved up her arm and through her body until she felt as thoroughly sun-drenched as the buildings in front of her. She hoped Liesl had found solace in this place as she faced a life alone. And Abbey prayed her own life would take a different path.

"Remember the first time we met?" Abbey asked, shifting slightly away but watching him closely.

"Of course," Pete said with a quizzical expression and took hold of her other hand as if preparing to sing a duet.

"You told me you would love to restore the parlor. Would you want to tackle that project next? I know you'll be busy with the new job and may not have the time."

"I will always make time for you," Pete said, squeezing her hands.

"I have plans for some of the other rooms too. We could do a full-scale restoration. That is, if you're interested in a long-term project."

"I can do that," Pete said, his signature grin slowly gaining ground across his face. "And yes, my dear MPM, my plans are definitely for the long term."

CHAPTER 33

October 18, 1777

If you are not able to save yourself, abandon yourself, only taking care that you do not lose God. For he who has God is able to lack all other things, since he will forever possess his highest good and eternal life with God, and in God. And this, of all desires, is THE END.

—John Amos Comenius

Autumn had come at last. The day was cold but sunny with an almost perfect blue sky—a sign, Liesl believed, of the grace and compassion of the Saviour. She had risen early, anxious to read the last message Lafayette would ever leave for her.

However, she first had to endure the interminable daily worship. Since the family no longer needed to accommodate Lafayette, the ritual had returned to its usual location in the small pantry next to the kitchen. Liesl was sure her father chose this room because he preferred to keep Liesl and Mother Boeckel standing, no doubt enjoying their discomfort as he held them captive. This morning he prayed even longer than usual, and Liesl felt faint, as if the cramped whitewashed walls were closing in, suffocating her.

As soon as she and Mother Boeckel finished their chores in the kitchen, Liesl slipped out into the hallway and forced herself to slowly climb the stairs up to the sitting room, even though she longed to race to her bookmark, the one thing that would remain after Lafayette left. To the words of love that would forever convey the feelings of their hearts.

Instead of an empty room, she found her father standing in front of the fireplace with his back to her. Without turning from his view of the flames, he thrust out his left hand. "What is the meaning of this?" he demanded.

The color drained from Liesl's face as she recognized the familiar embroidery. His hand trembled so violently that the piece of white paper clumsily jammed into the open seam of the bookmark fluttered like a sail on a doomed vessel.

She raised a quivering chin. "You found the messages."

"When I came to retrieve *The History of Greenland*, your bookmark fell out, with a piece of paper protruding from the top of it. I cannot read French, but I recognize the writing in your hand and saw enough to guess at the contents."

Liesl stood in silence, her thoughts swirling like fallen leaves caught by the wind as she tried to find a way to avert disaster.

Her father turned to her and roared, "You have disgraced our Lord, our home, and me!"

His fury was terrifying to behold as his customary self-righteousness transformed into something darker, something without mercy. Cringing at the blazing fury in his eyes, she realized he no longer recognized her as his daughter. Instead, he saw only an embodiment of the evil he had sought to eradicate all his life.

"I love him, Father."

"Love?" her father thundered. "How dare you speak of love. This has nothing to do with the love of the Lord, the love of the Lamb. *This* is an abomination. To think that I have spawned such a creature. You are a pariah. No Sister will befriend you, and no Brother will ever marry you. You bring shame upon your father and your poor dead mother. I would rather see you in the congregation above!"

Too late, she realized he held the fireplace poker in his right hand. As he raised it above his head like a vengeful Old Testament prophet, she knew he had the power to take her life. She saw nothing other than the dark metal rod with its vicious hook. Heard nothing other than the roaring in her ears. And felt nothing but the thrumming of her body like the string of a lute being relentlessly plucked. Liesl knew they stood at the edge of the abyss. If only she could pull them both back from the brink.

In that moment, she found her voice, and the only words that would calm him. Her penitence was the path to safety. A true atonement and a punishment for which she had already sentenced herself.

"Please spare my life, Father, for I am prepared to do my penance," she said, forcing herself to look him in the eye.

"Penance?" the old man repeated, suddenly deflated as he lowered the poker, grazing the wooden floor with a loud scrape. "What do you mean?"

"As you said, I will never marry. I will be a nurse, nothing more."

"A nurse." He stared heavenward, seeking guidance. "At least you would be of use."

"Yes, Father, I would be most useful. I am certain Doctor Glatt would provide me with additional training, so that I might serve our Saviour and our community by devoting myself to caring for the sick and the dying."

His face, so distorted by rage just moments before, softened. And finally, she could once again recognize the father she had known all her life.

With a visible mixture of pain and sadness, he vowed, "So it shall be. As atonement, you will devote yourself to a life of service. A life of duty and discipleship, seeking no personal happiness other than the gratification of doing the work of the Saviour."

"I will do as you say, Father. And I will be grateful to you every day of my life for giving me this chance."

"We shall never speak of this again, Liesl. But we will *never* forget." Father Boeckel returned the poker to its place by the side of the fireplace, threw the bookmark into the fire, and left without uttering another word.

The instant his footsteps echoed in the hallway, Liesl lunged for the bookmark. Luckily, it had fallen short of the flames and was only slightly scorched.

Clasping the still warm treasure to her chest, she fell to her knees.

With so much to be done in preparation for his departure, Lafayette had left the house without writing a message in the bookmark. As much as he dreaded leaving Liesl, he could not deny the excitement stirring within him as he prepared for the battlefield. News had arrived from Saratoga that the British general John Burgoyne was expected to surrender any day. With this victory, Lafayette might finally be able to convince his French countrymen to enter the war on the side of the Americans.

He returned to his room at the Boeckel house, anxious to remove Liesl's bookmark from *The History of Greenland* and add one final message. But the book and bookmark were gone from their customary spot.

The sitting room door swung open, and Lafayette felt a surge of hope that Liesl might be permitted to see him one last time. But Mother Boeckel entered the room alone, as had lately become her custom. However, her demeanor was not at all typical; today, her placid face was red and her eyes were swollen.

"What is wrong, Mother Boeckel? Are you ill?"

She shook her head and said nothing.

"Will I see Liesl before I leave?" Lafayette asked, trying to control his rising panic. "I would like to thank her for the good care I have received."

"I will pass along your thanks," Mother Boeckel said, her inflamed eyes lowered to the floor. "Liesl has other patients to care for. Please sit. Doctor Glatt instructed me to remove your bandages one final time."

Lafayette took a seat in the familiar chair, and Mother Boeckel began unraveling the linen with unaccustomed briskness. His mind careened with worry and unanswered questions, but he was a soldier, and he knew how to hold his fire.

Mother Boeckel had never been as proficient or as gentle as her stepdaughter, but she practically ripped the bandages from his limb. Lafayette had just formulated what he hoped would seem an innocent inquiry, when Mother Boeckel straightened and moved toward the door. "Your leg has healed quite well, General."

"Mother Boeckel," Lafayette beseeched, but before he could continue, she cut him off.

"I must go now."

"Please, Mother Boeckel, has something happened to Liesl?"

Mother Boeckel hesitated, clearly struggling to remain indifferent. At the last moment, she whispered, "You need not worry. I promise you; she will be well."

His retinue arrived soon after, and Lafayette knew he could postpone the moment no longer. He hobbled slowly down the stairs, each step excruciating in a way that had little to do with the wound in his leg.

When he reached the front door, Mother Boeckel was staring into the distance toward the Menakasie Creek, refusing to look him in the eye. Frederick was nowhere in sight, another ominous sign. While he and Frederick disagreed on most things, Lafayette had expected to see his benefactor one more time. Lafayette knew something had happened in this household, but all he could do was trust Mother Boeckel and hold on to the belief that Liesl would be fine.

Liesl stood at the second-floor window, watching the striking figure below while still taking care to remain out of sight. She had been sorely disappointed when she looked inside the bookmark for a last message from Lafayette. But perhaps there was nothing left to be said.

She had hidden her bookmark in a safe place where Father would never find it. That bookmark would never again be placed between the pages of a story, never again mark a reader's progress. However, before hiding it, she had added a tiny bit of embroidery, something no one else would see. Something to mark a place within her heart, a secret chamber known only to herself and one other.

She could already feel the confinement that was her future taking shape around her like a prison cell being laid brick by brick. As if she were a wild, woodland creature who would soon be caged forever. Her memories were her only salvation, for no one could ever take them away.

When Lafayette mounted his horse, her hand reached out involuntarily, but she quickly pulled it back. Seeing each other would only make the leaving harder. Already her heart was heavy, and her eyes burned with unshed tears.

"*Bon courage*," she whispered, not sure whether the words were for him or for herself.

Lafayette hesitated for a moment as he searched the upper story. He thought he saw a movement at one of the windows, but it was probably only his imagination, for the house remained as inscrutable as the flushed face of Mother Boeckel.

Just a few weeks ago, he could never have imagined the pain that leaving this town would inflict upon him. But he was no longer the arrogant young man who had arrived here, fuming at his fate. Like a master blacksmith, Bethlehem had forged a better version of himself.

He closed his eyes for a moment to picture her face, the

dark blue eyes, the golden strands of silky hair. He would never look upon that dear face again, but he would never forget her. Lafayette took one last look at the second-floor window, cued his horse to walk forward, and rode off to rejoin the fight.

CHAPTER 34

The Exhibit

April 2006

Abbey and Pete stood before a narrow wooden console table flanked by windows streaming sunlight. Between the windows, the familiar visages of Lafayette, Mrs. Boeckel, and Liesl stared out at them. The very painting that had made Abbey gasp the first time she saw it.

The exhibit was as tasteful as Abbey hoped it would be. A simple glass case held a copy of the messages written between Liesl and Lafayette in their flowery French, while the original remained ensconced in the vault at the Moravian Archives, beyond the reach of even the most ambitious archivist. Behind the case, an enlarged version of Adam's English translation of the messages dominated the display. A notation at the bottom recognized Abbey for her discovery and donation and gave credit to Adam Wright for the translation.

Pete pointed to the acknowledgments. "I see Adam got his name in there."

"I guess he deserves that much," Abbey said.

Pete took her hand, rubbing the brand-new band on her left ring finger as they read another placard containing a description of Lafayette's time in the Boeckel household. The heart of the claddagh ring faced outward, but not for long. Earlier, she and Pete had pored over plans for their honeymoon trip to Egypt. Just thinking about it made her feel light-headed.

She returned her attention to the placard, curious to see what the curator had to say about Liesl. As Abbey well knew, there was little information to share, and the paragraph about Liesl was brief, ending with "Her private memoir might have told more of her story, but the only remaining memoir is an impersonal document written by others."

Lafayette, on the other hand, received a lengthy write-up detailing how this hero of the American Revolution fought alongside George Washington and played a critical role in convincing the French government to provide troops and monetary support for the American cause. According to historians, America was the making of Lafayette. The brash youth who arrived on her shores returned to France a better, wiser man.

"I never realized Lafayette came back to the United States," Pete said, reading ahead.

"Oh yes. Just as it says here, he returned in 1824 when he was sixty-six, the last living general of the Continental Army. Apparently, he received a rock-star welcome when he arrived in New York City. He spent more than a year traveling through all twenty-four states, being greeted by throngs of adoring fans. He revisited all the places he'd been during the war including Philadelphia and the site of the Battle of Brandywine."

"Look at this," Pete said. "Lafayette traveled by carriage from New York to Philadelphia with a stop in Princeton, New Jersey. That's only about sixty miles from here."

Abbey read the last paragraph out loud, "'We may never find out what really happened between the Moravian maid and the impetuous Frenchman. All we know for certain is Liesl never married, and Lafayette never set foot in Bethlehem again.'"

"Makes me feel sorry for Liesl," Pete said. "Lafayette must have been a real cad."

"I'm not so sure about that." Abbey stared at the man in the painting, the man who seemed unable to take his eyes off Liesl. "It's impossible to know what goes on between two people. Maybe Liesl and Lafayette gave each other exactly what they needed."

THANK YOU for reading *The Bookmark!* I hope you've enjoyed reading the book as much as I enjoyed writing it.

I would love to get your feedback, and a review on Amazon or your favorite bookselling website would be much appreciated!

If you'd like to learn more about the history behind the book, please visit my website at annesupsic.com

Author's Note

I first learned about Liesl Boeckel at the Moravian Museum in Bethlehem, where I've worked for many years as a volunteer docent. I knew nothing of Lafayette's time in Bethlehem, much less his involvement with a Moravian woman, until the museum added a new exhibit with a painting of Liesl, Mrs. Boeckel, and Lafayette. I could hardly believe this unlikely connection between the Moravians and my favorite Frenchman. I remember thinking someone needed to write a book about this. And then, a little voice inside me said, *Why not you?*

I began my research at the Moravian Archives, but as Abbey discovered, little is known about Liesl Boeckel and her relationship with Lafayette. Abbey's visit to the archives mirrors my own, and the historical records I describe in the book are genuine: the Boeckel family history, the transcript of the radio program describing

Lafayette's visit to Bethlehem, and even the paper receipt for Liesl's nursing services. Liesl's memoir is also housed in the archives, and the excerpts I share from it are authentic.

Another key discovery helped me to shape the relationship between Liesl and her father. The Boeckel family history contained this passage from Frederick Boeckel's memoir: "The salvation of his children was close to his heart; in a little note-book, in which he recorded the dates of their birth, he wrote at the end: 'All that are not growing up for Thee, those I would rather see soon in the congregation above than that they become entangled with this world and leave Thee, their Lord, who would so much like to have them saved.'"

Two other resources were particularly insightful for Liesl's story. *Sketches of Early Bethlehem* by Dr. Richmond E. Myers offered detailed descriptions of Moravian life, and the remarkable translations in Katherine M. Faull's *Moravian Women's Memoirs* provided invaluable, firsthand knowledge.

While information about Liesl is skimpy, the documentation concerning Lafayette is overwhelming. To understand the man behind the legend, I relied primarily on these standout resources: *Lafayette* by Harlow Giles Unger and *Lafayette in the Somewhat United States* by Sarah Vowell.

I quickly realized writing historical fiction demands a balancing act between fact and imagination and results in a constant struggle to blend authenticity with dramatic storytelling. With so little information about Liesl and her family, I needed to flesh out realistic characters and create plausible scenes within a framework of historical fact. For example, the stories of Liesl's early life are my own creation, but Moravian practices such as growing up under the Choir system and wearing a head covering called the Haube are all accurately described.

The other characters surrounding Liesl are invented but still rooted in history. Sister Adelina accurately depicts the plight of the Moravian Indians, and Dr. Matthew Oberlin provides medical treatments appropriate for the time period, including his handling of the smallpox outbreak. Every plot requires a villainess and our Labouress fills that role admirably. The Lot, which she misuses so effectively, was a common decision-making device throughout colonial America; however, I found no known cases of anyone manipulating the Lot as the Labouress does in my story.

As I crafted Lafayette's interactions and dialogue with the Boeckel family, I was able to incorporate quotes from his letters and describe actual events from his life. For example, the story of Lafayette setting out to save his village from a monstrous beast is a true retelling, and Brigadier General Kazimierz Pulaski's visit to Bethlehem is factual as well. According to legend, the Moravian Sisters, renowned for their sewing skills, later presented Pulaski with a banner to carry into battle.

Abbey and Pete and the rest of the characters in my modern storyline are fictitious, but the city of Bethlehem is very real, and it has been a privilege to write about this special place. All the sights I describe exist, and this vibrant city still hums with the spirit of the Moravians.

You may wonder why I chose a bookmark to play such an important role in my story. Much like Abbey, bookmarks are my favorite travel souvenirs, and I have collected them from all around the world. Since it is well-documented that Lafayette spent a considerable part of his convalescence reading *The History of Greenland*, a bookmark seemed like a reasonable gift. It also offered a perfect hiding place for romantic correspondence and an ideal mechanism to link our two heroines. Bookmarks are exceptional treasures, and I believe every bookmark tells a story.

Acknowledgements

Bringing a book into the world is a much bigger effort than I ever imagined. At one particularly low point, my husband found a picture on Pinterest that summed up the process well. With a heading "There's a lot more to writing a book than most people think...," the picture displayed a small boat identified as the *Reader* and the tip of an iceberg called the *Book*. Beneath the ocean, the rest of the iceberg (typically 89% of the whole) contained a long list of activities like dreaming, writing, editing, and re-editing. I would add one more to that list: being humbled by the generosity of others.

I need to begin by acknowledging two outstanding Bethlehem organizations: Historic Bethlehem Museum & Sites and the Moravian Archives. The Moravian Museum first introduced me to Liesl Boeckel, and the documents in the Archives convinced me there was a story to tell. In particular, I want to thank archivist Tom McCullough (who bears no resemblance whatsoever to my overly-ambitious Adam Wright) for translating Liesl's memoir and for reading my manuscript to finetune my historical references.

Writing is a solitary activity, but at some point, every story has to be shared, and I am forever grateful to my early readers who slogged through those terrible first chapters and motivated me to keep going: Sandy Bjerre, Laura Brown, Rachel Durs, Betty Gross, Nancy Gross, Martinn Jablonski-Cahours, Donna Jencks, Mary Lou Jones, Sue Wright, and Kathy Zoshak. In particular, I want to recognize Kathy Burger, Donna Pisarski, and Amber Whittington for their unwavering support through it all.

As I have learned, writing a book is only the beginning, and I was fortunate to have outstanding professionals help me bring this story to print. A big thank you to Erica Ferguson for a most thorough copyedit, and I will be forever grateful to book and cover designer, David Prendergast, for creating the perfect visual rendering of my story.

I am especially indebted to my stalwart editor Andrea Robinson—without her, *The Bookmark* would never have happened. Andrea shared my passion for Liesl's story right from the start and stayed with me throughout the years, guiding me through the rewriting process and helping me to take my story in directions I never would have imagined on my own. I cannot thank her enough.

Most of all, I want to thank you, the reader. I know the wealth of reading material available to you, and I am very grateful you chose to spend time in my fictional world with my dear friends, Abbey and Pete and Liesl and Lafayette.

Discussion Questions

1. Of the four main characters (Abbey, Pete, Liesl, and Lafayette), which one was your favorite and why? Which character surprised you the most?

2. How does Liesl adapt to the restraints of her circumstances? How does her spirit of independence still manage to assert itself? Discuss how you have overcome restraints in your own life.

3. How does Abbey's personal history explain her behavior? Contrast the outside restraints of Liesl's life with Abbey's self-inflicted ones. Which woman did you admire the most?

4. Lafayette is a well-known historical figure. Did the author do a good job of reimagining him? Did

anything about his portrayal in the book surprise you? How did meeting Liesl change him?

5. What have you learned about eighteenth-century Moravian Bethlehem? What Moravian qualities did you admire? What intrigued you most about the Moravian lifestyle and why?

6. Mother Boeckel represents a traditional Moravian woman; however, she occasionally steps out of that role. In what ways does she help and protect Liesl?

7. Abbey describes how she wishes she were more like her grandmother: "If only she were more like Nana. The kind of person who dove into the deep end of the pool with no hesitation. Instead, Abbey was the one hovering on the edges, studying depth measurements, gauging the distance between the pool ladders, and evaluating the expressions on the faces of the swimmers." How does Abbey's personality help or harm her? Are you more like Abbey or like Nana?

8. How are Liesl and Abbey affected by their difficult relationships with their fathers? Discuss the importance of father-daughter relationships and how Liesl and Abbey handle theirs.

9. How did you feel about the Labouress and the role she played in Liesl's life? In what ways were Liesl's personal experiences similar to those of the Labouress? How did these two women handle their circumstances differently?

10 Discuss how the memories of Michael continued to haunt Abbey. In what ways does Abbey alter those memories to protect herself? Do you think people often rewrite their own personal histories?

11. How does the bookmark establish a connection between Liesl and Abbey? What is the significance of the embroidery design Liesl created for the bookmark?

12. Abbey believes "the secret wasn't making the right choice every time but allowing herself a second chance when she needed one." Do you agree with her? Discuss how different characters throughout the book take their second chances and how their outcomes differ.

13. What were the pivotal scenes in the book? How did they change the characters and your feelings toward them?

14. How do the endings of each storyline complement one another? Did either of the endings disappoint you? Did you wish for a different outcome?

About the Author

Anne Supsic is a docent at the Moravian Museum in Bethlehem, Pennsylvania, a dedicated Francophile, and a bookmark collector. When she first learned about a possible romantic relationship between the Marquis de Lafayette and a Moravian Single Sister named Liesl Boeckel, she knew she had found the story she was meant to tell.

When she's not at home, Anne is traveling the world (seventy countries and counting), exploring other cultures, and of course, searching for bookmarks. To learn more, you can visit her online at annesupsic.com.

Made in the USA
Middletown, DE
18 November 2022